Aubrey Williams

The Knight in
Shining Armor

PUBLISH AMERICA

PublishAmerica
Baltimore

First printing

All characters in this book are fictitious, and any resemblance to real persons, living or dead, is coincidental.

At the specific preference of the author, PublishAmerica allowed this work to remain exactly as the author intended, verbatim, without editorial input.

ISBN: 1-4241-9228-5
PUBLISHED BY PUBLISHAMERICA, LLLP
www.publishamerica.com
Baltimore

Printed in the United States of America

For Friends, Family, and the occasional stranger

Acknowledgments

When writing a book, one must be focused and ready for the challenge of putting his ideas and imagination into a work of art. This is my first novel and it won't be my last. I end this thrilling adventure to thank those close to me who without them I wouldn't have had the courage, patience, hard work, dedication, or passion for my writing. It took me nearly two years to write, format, and completely finish all parts of this novel. The book started with a random idea on a hot summer's night when I couldn't sleep. Now that it is published I'd like to make a final note by thanking those close to me. I'd like to thank my advance readers Ericka Hodge, Bum Kyle, Sabrina the psycho, Joseph the overly dramatic editor, Ashley the "I'll do it" girl. All of them read my novel without hesitation and gave me helpful feedback that contributed to my overall obsession of rewriting and editing and proofreading and editing. Although I did get people to read to help me catch those random typos and my misconception of which characters were in which scenes. I want to thank Justin Wilson and Brandon Odom for being my "naggers" who always looked after me, keeping me from taking risks that I didn't have to. I really appreciate them for that. I want to thank other supporters who were thrilled to know what I was writing a book. Chick-Fil-A customer, Alberta Carten my grandma, Joseph's grandma and mom, Ms. Holland the substitute, Ms Robinson my 9th grade teacher, Ms. Ross from 10th grade and Ms. Carver from 11th and 12th, Ms. Young my geometry teacher, Tara my cousin, Tasha my aunt, my friends Tierra, Larance, Seth, Dejá, Spam, TJ my coworker, Taylor my manager, AJ, Hannah, Leah the "I don't read" girl, Caroline, Jess, Joshua Alexander, Joshua Hartley, Doug Mickey, Elisha Chambers,

Aleshia Cowser, my media specialists Linda Johnson and Aleshia Redmond, Girl Angel, Yasmine the "I want to read it" girl, All the ones who told me that my work was crap, Aneshia for telling me it was crap the first time, Ms. Bush for thinking I was cool to right a book, Melanie who couldn't wait to buy it, my aunt Taffy for showing the most excitement when I told her I was going to be published. Danielle who told me she had to read my book a little at a time, all the writers I met at school who have given up and allowed me to want to not give up, to all my friends at school that always said it was a good work and they wanted me to finish, to Gage for telling me I was awesome, Austin for being my inspiration and for giving me the greatest advice I've ever gotten (R.I.P.), to Marie for sharing a "writer's talk" with me, to Ms. Carver again for showing me the beauty of literature through her classes, to all my friends at VOX who told me I'd be the next J.K. Rowling, to Roger who said he'll want to read it, and to Meredith for helping me get into VOX, to Tasgola for helping me get published in Atlanta Journal-Constitution, to SCAD (Savannah College of Art and Design) for seeing my talents and giving me a scholarship, to google.com for allowing me to google, and too all the readers that put faith in buying my first book as a new author, to just everyone. Thanks for reading!!

Aubrey Evans Williams

The Knight in Shining Armor

CHAPTER ONE
Seeing Is Believing

The sun's heat seeped through her window, coaxing her to wake up. She sat up in bed looking out at the springtime scenery, yawning to the recollection that it was morning. The sun was shining brilliantly over the lush green grasses of the front lawn. It was another day of spring, which she dreaded. She hated it now. It no longer made her happy about life and instead gave her new inclinations of cruel things existing in the world. Those cruel things which people commit and how it so badly affects one's emotions.

Her parents had been hiding something from her and her brother. For years this secret had hung over her family and it had been so long since her parents shared any shred of honesty. She was determined to discover the true nature behind their actions. Her thoughts raced through possible reasons why these secrets were kept and why were they so important. It made no use though, they gave neither a hint as to what they hid nor as to why.

She finally got up to dress. The sunlight danced off her rich, jet black hair. She had freckles on her face. At five feet five inches, she was quite fit.

She marveled at herself, reminding herself that she could be pretty and still be saddened deep down. Life no longer brought a smile to her face. But yet in all actuality, a smile was the only thing she would let out, holding in all the burdens of her emotions.

"*Emma,*" called a woman's voice.

"I'm up mom!" Emma yelled. Her mother's voice had always been calm and serene, but now lost all calmness and gathered what could be familiarized as overwhelming stress. Emma's mom twisted the doorknob in warning.

"Ok. I'm coming!" Emma yelled back in acknowledgement.

"Don't dawdle. If you take too long, you'll be late," her mother warned calmly through the closed door. She used this method as a way to say "hurry up or I'll burst in" without using actual words.

Emma shook her head, realizing that her mother had forgotten that she was now in high school which started an hour later than elementary and middle schools. However, it was strange that she kept forgetting despite her ability to keep up with such things. Emma was fifteen, and to her fifteen was a great age to find oneself, and figure out why she was worrying so much about something that may not be anything to worry about. She hurriedly scrambled to the bathroom for her morning preparations to find the door closed.

"Who's in there?" she exclaimed, banging on the door. "Open the door!"

"*Hold on. I'll be out in a second,*" a boy called out. From his response, his voice appeared to be muffled by a thick layer of toothpaste.

"Danny, hurry up I have to comb my hair!" yelled Emma.

Daniel was Emma's twin brother. He took quite a while in the bathroom most of the time because he was overly obsessed with hygiene. He was a bit strange at times, but it didn't explain why no one talked to him. He was so isolated from life, spending a large portion of his time reading his fantasy books and never acknowledging anyone. Others thought he was simply just too weird to be accepted by most average teens. Perhaps he was destined to be excluded by his peers and people he considered to be friends. Emma gave up on trying to figure out the mystery that was her brother.

The door opened

Daniel was a bit taller than his twin. His hair was light brown, glasses hung crookedly over his nose, making him appear to be a washed-up professor. Daniel was already dressed handsomely in his denim jeans and his T-shirt that portrayed and reflected his avid addiction to the *Harry Potter* book series.

"Were you brushing your teeth?" asked Emma.

"Of course," he said flashing his strangely white teeth.

Emma blocked her eyes as if the teeth were blinding her. She hissed as well. "You know those teeth could actually be a good beacon when attracting ships to shore," she said in a matter of fact tone.

"You know what?" asked Daniel. Daniel raised his finger to his head in anger, preparing for his comeback. Acknowledging himself as defeated, he went about his business and walked off toward the kitchen.

Emma was still in her pajamas and her brother was already dressed. She was more behind than she had thought. With a deep sigh of impatience, Emma hurried into the bathroom, slamming the door behind her. Water began to run as Emma got into the shower.

Breakfast was on the table as Daniel made his way into the kitchen, catching a scent of bacon and eggs on the tip of his nose. His dad sat at the table reading his newspaper, coffee on his right side, and orange juice on the left. He sipped the coffee once while reading what could be made out as the sports section, ignoring the orange juice completely.

"Good morning," Daniel said to his father, sitting down at the table, opposite to his father.

His dad did not look up from the paper as he took another sip from his coffee cup. His mother made no attempt to pry herself away from the eggs she was preparing. They were being *different* again. Emma came into the room humming to a song on her i-pod and wearing her favorite khaki pants and shirt with her Math team, *The Math Attacks* printed on the front.

"Good morning," she said cheerfully, enjoying her preparedness. Her hair was tied back in colorful ribbons, backpack on shoulder, and lunch in hand. She was ready to tackle the day. She sat down at the table, setting her lunch down and taking the earplugs out of her ears. The music still played faintly within the otherwise silent room.

Her parents did not seem aware that either of them were there. Upon finishing her eggs, their mother looked about the table, noticing them for the first time. As if waking up from a spell, she acknowledged their presence at that time.

"Oh. I didn't see you two come in," their mother said. Their father seemed to have noticed them right at that moment as well. He lowered his paper to have a look at them.

"Oh. I guess I must have been a bit too into my paper to notice anything," their father added. "Hurry and finish so I can take you to school on my way to work."

Emma and Daniel finished eating and followed their father out the door.

During the car ride, no one talked and the music of Emma's favorite artist was the only voice heard. Dad appeared to have missed a good night's sleep again for the 5th night in a row. He didn't have just one bag under his eye, but multiple that seemed to overlap each other. What could be keeping him up so much?

Emma and Daniel did not know what their father did for a living. It was yet another mystery that they had never solved. Emma herself had become increasingly curious about her own family. Emma and Daniel rode in silence, watching the trees go by. The sign for their school ahead told them they were getting close.

Not only had they been new to Midtown High School, but to the state as well. Georgia was their new home and they liked it well enough. The people were friendly and presumably quite enjoyable. Emma was quick to adapt to the new places to which they moved because of her versatility with people. Strangely enough, they moved every single year. Her parents said that her dad was always being transferred to other branches. Emma didn't like being paranoid, but she honestly didn't believe that idea.

The car pulled into the front of the school and Emma and Daniel started to collect their things.

"Wait. Before you go. I need to talk to you about something," said their dad.

"What's wrong?" asked Emma.

"I want you to know that if anything happens to me or your mother…"

"What could happen?" asked Emma worryingly.

"Nothing," their father said blankly.

"It's nothing Emma," Daniel interrupted.

"No. It's *something*. He's keeping secrets! It's so obvious!" She exclaimed. "Lying is the not the right way dad."

"We're not keeping secrets we ."

"Look at you!" stopping her dad, as she broke into tears. "You're not happy. What's the reason? Why can't you tell us?"

"I know things have been crazy with all the moving around. Your mother and I are just tired and we have been maintaining a lot of things. They are stressful. But I assure you that nothing strange or abnormal is occurring. Emma, just listen to me when I tell you this. If anything happens to us, you'll know what to do. Now is a time in your life when you need to discover what must be told and what must be learned."

"Fine…if you say so," Emma said as she got out of the car and walked quickly towards the school building.

"You know she's right," said Daniel as he caught up with Emma. Their father was left in the car as he drove off silently.

Emma worried herself about that morning's incident throughout the day. She constantly played out several different scenarios making her appear more worried than angry as she was before. She found that this kept her from school. Throughout the day she found herself losing concentration and putting words together, somewhat like a lyrical poem A poem uprooted itself from those words:

Upon this ground I stand
For the powers which one man can withstand
For the greatest of gifts received is light
The granting of this I offer:
One half my power limited
One mind his strength combined
One hour devoted time
To which blood will endure
To defeat the greatest of all evils

Emma marveled at her creation. She had never written such an obtrusive, yet eloquent poem. She folded up the paper and placed it in her pocket.

"*Ms. Dale*, what is the answer to this equation?" her teacher asked her impatiently.

Emma gazed up in bewilderment to see her teacher's vacant expression, the entire class glaring at her like a circus freak. Emma was getting tired of losing her mind in her thoughts because of the times when she couldn't pull away from them. It was as if her mind entered a strange trance, making her unaware of her surroundings. So many ideas had run through her head and her teacher was now making her feel worse after already felling bad.

"I don't know Mrs. Baker. I don't care!" she exclaimed as she stood up. Her tone was more of anger than of not caring. She felt lost in her own world, unable to become who she really was. Her identity had been wiped clean. She was a new person.

"Ms. Dale, please sit down," her teacher demanded.

Emma said nothing and she walked swiftly out of the room, slamming the door behind her, knocking the blinds off the door. As she exited the room tears came down her face, she just wanted to be alone. She no longer loved school anymore because she now felt that the material she was learning would never mean anything to her. She was tired of having days where she couldn't think, days where she had "feelings" about something happening. She hated those feelings because they ignited headaches and strange spasms in her arms. In times of great distress she had once felt her heart beat so rapidly, as if she was having a heart attack.

Those *feelings* had appeared again today and they caused her so much pain. Some nights she wouldn't even sleep because of them. Strange dreams would follow as well, making it much more complicated than before. She was beginning to feel them again. As she ran down the hallway, she was struck by a sharp twang within her head and she fell. It was hurting so much that she just sat on the floor and cried. The pain was just unbearable. So much for being tough today.

"*Mr. Simmons*," said Daniel, raising his hand.

"Yes?" inquired the teacher. He looked up from his desk, tampering with his laptop. His teacher sat at his desk in the front while the others were working.

"May I go to the library? I'm finished with everything."

"Have you checked your answers?"

"Yes I have sir."

"Twice?"

"Yes sir."

"Go ahead."

Daniel needed to blow off steam. The rising rumors going on between him and the school were cumbersome. He needed to be away from Bert who had taken a liking to the false rumors about Daniel poisoning one of his teachers, Mrs. Katter. The reasons for that was because of Daniel's conceivable motive. The motive was more or less as a result of the horrible *tragedy* in which Daniel's book was taken and destroyed. *It was taken* from him and put through the shredder. Page by page he was forced to watch. It was a classic! He hated the fact that his maniacal teacher would do that. The teacher was now in the hospital on a respiratory apparatus. There was not enough evidence to prove that Daniel was guilty of anything.

As he got up from his desk, he recalled dreading the awkward stares from his classmates. He wanted to catch up on his reading in peace and not have to be bothered with anyone.

He finally left the room and made his way toward the library. He could now find the time to clear his mind because he would be there during lunch hour. He buried himself into the book, soaking all its goodness. Before Daniel knew it, the lunch bell rang. He couldn't help but think about how much he wanted to punch Bert for believing those stupid rumors. He knew it hadn't been him because he was a gentle-natured person and would never hurt anyone intentionally.

The thoughts scared him a little. He had obtained a strange habit of wishing bad things on someone and it happening. Strangely, poisoning the teacher was somewhat of a fantasy that just happened to occur. The anger he had built up seemed to melt away the more and more he read.

It was not all that good to him. He had no friends. Why couldn't people accept him for who he was? He accepted the fact that no one would ever like him and that he would die friendless. The media secretary had gone to lunch ten minutes ago leaving him the only one in there. Five minutes later he wounded up in the principal's office.

Daniel entered the office to see that Bert was there on the verge of explosion. He closed the door behind him and looked squarely upon the disgruntled face of the principal. It wasn't going to be a pleasant visit.

"Sit down Mr. Dale," the principal commanded.

"Sir. Why am I here?" asked Daniel as he took a seat.

"Forget to tighten your bolts?" Bert asked. "Look at me!"

Daniel took notice to the bruises at that moment. Bert had been beaten badly and seemed to have been lain to a host of various blunt attacks. Bert looked pissed.

"It seems that you attacked Mr. Byson in the bathroom a little while ago," said the principal.

"What?" Daniel retorted. "I was in the library. I didn't do...!?"

"It *was* you. You punched me in the face and the stomach....," said Bert.

"Mr. Dale I am suspending you from school for assaulting Mr. Byson and for lying about it," said the principal.

"I...," began Daniel.

"No excuses. Take this referral to your parents and I'll see you in five days," stated the principal. "And you *will* apologize to Mr. Byson as well."

"I'm sorry," Daniel said plainly as he left the room flinging his backpack onto his shoulders. He exited the room as fast as he could. This was not his day. All he needed now was more trouble.

As Daniel walked along the sidewalk on that warm spring day, he began to recount the events of the day. The school day had not been great at all. Why had he now gotten the feeling that everyone around him began to think that he was dangerous? He didn't have many friends and he found now that he was never really into making them. He was upset because he was blamed once again for something he hadn't done. He wasn't even there. He was in the library reading *Zytar*, which he was reading for the second time. He knew that his parents would be upset at yet another referral that he had received for violence towards faculty and students. He had never poisoned Mrs. Katter during lunch period. He had not been there but reading.

It was scary that every time something bad like that happened he was reading. It was like someone was out to frame him whenever he was at the library. Or maybe, every time they knew he was vulnerable, he would be easy pickings. Reading was the only time that Daniel let his guard down to vent his emotions. Was someone trying to ruin his life? Emma's life seemed to already be ruined. She wasn't talking at all. It wasn't much like Emma to be silent.

Emma was normally a spectacular student in school, but just recently she had begun doing quite poorly. Emma's downfall had ultimately become the enigma wrapped in a riddle for Daniel. He was still curious as to why such a star student could not ameliorate such a novel situation. Daniel's thoughts were abruptly interrupted as he walked straight into Emma, who had stopped right in front of him.

"What are you doing? You just stopped right in front of me!" asked Daniel.

"I want to ask you something," She took a deep breath as she turned around. "What do you think mom and dad are hiding something from us?"

"Not this again. How many times do I have to tell you to let it go? They don't care about us anymore."

"You know that's not true! I just don't understand why they won't tell us what's wrong. I feel like there is something we should know. I mean I have a really bad feeling about this."

"Is that why your grades are slipping? asked Daniel.

"It doesn't matter, let's go," Emma said as she continued walking.

They continued on, passing the neighboring houses and streets that meshed into their neighborhood. Emma and Daniel were now caught in a deep, thick fog of tension, trying to cut their way through. As usual, Daniel was the first the step up. He did this only five minutes afterwards. They were getting close to home.

"Emma. About that thing I said. I didn't mean to make you mad," he said.

Emma kept walking. She spoke a few seconds afterwards as they continued walking.

"I know you're sorry. You're always sorry for saying something mean or stupid. That's why I love you so much." she began. "But it's so hard to forgive you when all your insults are truths."

"That *is* why your grades are slipping?" asked Daniel surprisingly.

"I don't know. It could be that and the fact that I can't concentrate for two seconds. I'm scared I might change. You know the change?"

"You mean when you become someone you don't want to be?" asked Daniel.

"I stormed out of the classroom today. I couldn't take it," she said.

"I got suspended again," said Daniel

"Well. I guess we'll have to tell them again. I guess things are just crazy now."

"*You'll* bounce back," he said putting an arm on her shoulder. "You always do."

Emma stopped walking and stood face to face with Daniel. She crossed her arms.

"I don't think I will. I feel like I don't belong here. There's something else more important, but I don't know what it is."

"Now you're scaring me. Let's just get home," said Daniel as he lead the way.

As they made their way into the house, Daniel and Emma realized that no one was home. Usually their mom would be there cooking dinner, but not a peep was heard. There were no lights on in the house.

"Where are they?" Emma asked.

"That's a good question," Daniel said in agreement.

"Mom? Dad? Are you in here?" Emma called out, but received no answer.

"Maybe they've decided that two fifteen year olds can watch after themselves for a change," Daniel said with laughter.

"I don't know. I don't think that's it," Emma said concerned. She felt something from the air. There was a stench too. It was like there was a fire, but not a flame in sight.

Every room in the house had the light off. It was dark inside and Emma could hardly see. The stench she smelled was making her sick. It smelled of ashes. But she saw now signs of a fire. The strange feeling she was having was making her head throb. What was that strange feeling in her head? Emma continued to walk inside, went to her room and put her stuff down only to find a note on her bed:

Emma,

 If you are reading this then your father and I are no longer here. We are sorry to say that our mission failed and that your lives are in danger. You may not understand this now, but someone will be there to explain everything you want to know. We're sorry we never told you and your brother what was going on. It was far too dangerous. Please forgive us. You'll find out soon enough. Your father forgives you. We love you with all our hearts and our deaths will not be in vain. Wait for someone to come to escort you out of the house. We love you so much and we hope that you make it safely to where you are meant to be. May your life shine unto others. Only a knight in shining armor can bring forth justice.

 Love you always,

 Reater (mom) and Malitus (dad)

Emma reread the letter over and over. She looked for answers and found them to be nonexistent. There was no one to answer the questions either. She looked for a probable answer to those questions. Confusion was the only outcome to these millions of questions forming in her pretty little head. She heard Daniel shuffling towards her. She turned around to see him enveloped in tears.

"I can't believe they're gone," Daniel said.

"Me neither," said Emma. "But it doesn't make any sense. Dead people can't leave notes."

"Maybe it's a joke or something," Daniel started. "You know, they like to play pranks."

"I think they're really gone. I can feel it, but I don't know how," agreed Emma. "We need to figure out what's going on."

"Yeah."

There was a knock at the door

Emma and Daniel wiped their tears and stepped into the living room to decide on what to do next. They proceeded with caution.

"Should we answer it?" asked Emma.

"The letter said someone would explain what was going on," Daniel said nervously.

"I think we'd better be careful," Emma warned.

Emma and Daniel walked slowly to the door. Emma backed up and grabbed a golf club that was leaning behind the door. Daniel slowly opened the door. As the door opened a figure stood there bearing its large shadow among the two. The sunlight glistened brightly on the outskirts of its shadow.

"Hello young ones," the figure said softly. The voice was low and sensuous.

"Who are you?" Daniel asked bravely, still gawking at the spectacle.

"My name is Amethyst and I wish to come in," the figure said.

"Who sent you?" asked Daniel.

"Your parents of course," Amethyst said as he attempted to squeeze through the half-closed door.

Daniel opened the door more to allow "Amethyst" to enter. He shut the door and turned on a light to see. The figure was a man of at least six feet two inches who had stunning blue hair and blue eyes that had strange black lines extending out from the center of his pupil. They made him look really weird. Emma figured they were the weirdest designer contacts she had ever seen.

He stood with his back straight and held in his hand a small stick that looked like a short staff of some sort. He was a young man in his prime and had a very handsome face although the smirk he carried on it made him appear to be much older. He was dressed strangely as if he had come from a distant land, long robes made of blue and white silk that extended all the way down to the stub of his flat shoes. Without any delay, Amethyst continued to speak.

"It is time for you to go," said Amethyst plaintively.

"Go where exactly?" asked Emma.

"You don't know where you're going?" asked Amethyst. "I would have expected Reater and Malitus would have explained all of this to you."

"But who are you?" asked Daniel.

"Well. In short I'm your uncle."

"Hold on. You're our *uncle?*" asked Emma

"Yes I'm your uncle," said Amethyst impatiently. "I'm here to take you for mage training."

"And what is a mage exactly?" asked Emma.

"Mages are practitioners of the magical arts," Amethyst began. "They can control a multitude of magical abilities and can obtain a wide variety of power. I don't understand why you don't know. I guess Reater and Malitus have been slacking off lately. I expect they have told you of your heritage". Emma shook her head. "I guess not. Well your parents were mages of the Arcane Alliance which is the organization designed to fight the dark powers of Myred. Myred is the organization that is focused on ruling the Arcane Alliances. Oh, and Reater and Malitus weren't your real parents."

"What?!" Emma interrupted.

"They were here only to teach and keep you safe until it was time for me to come and get you. Apparently someone of Myred killed your parents and plan on tracking you down and killing you."

"And where are we going exactly? Another state or country?" Emma asked.

"Another world, Sulex. The world where magic thrives and dragons are real. A world where the strangest things are possible. We are going to my homeland, to the continent of Swiverstheee," said Amethyst.

"Swiverstheee?" Daniel asked.

"I cannot explain this at the moment," said Amethyst. "As I was saying, well…what was I saying?" continued Amethyst.

"So where are our real parents?" asked Daniel impatiently.

"They died a long time ago…," said Amethyst. "Their deaths are not in vain. They died fighting for the Arcane Alliance."

"Myred," said Daniel.

"Yes. They want you dead and I need you to come with me through the portal to reach the Alliance for your training. We don't have much time."

"How do we know you're telling the truth? I don't even believe in magic," Emma said defiantly.

"It does and I can show you," Amethyst said. "I can show you once we enter the portal before Myred attacks."

"Will you excuse us for a moment?" asked Emma.

Emma and Daniel moved away from Amethyst and walked into the kitchen.

"I don't think we can trust him," Emma said immediately.

"He does seem to be in a rush," said Daniel.

"I have a bad feeling. He just seems a bit wacko to me. I mean Mages? Come on that's preposterous!" Emma retorted.

"Pre-what?" Daniel asked.

"It's strange. I think we should….," Emma began without completing the sentence.

"We should just go, our parents, I mean Reater and Malitus are dead. What is there left here? I mean…there's nothing left for us. Would you rather rot in some home for kids with dead parents? And plus, if Myred is after us, we could end up like Reater and Malitus."

"I guess we only have one option," said Emma as she left the kitchen followed by Daniel.

"We're going with you," Daniel announced.

"Excellent," said Amethyst with a smile.

"Remember. If he is wacko we find another plan," Emma whispered to Daniel as they headed to the end of the hall where the linen closet was.

"There's nothing here," Daniel said with frustration.

Amethyst rose his hands with a strange gesture and began to speak loudly. *"Powers of Oltent I call to thee. Bring forth the portal of Swiverstheee"*. As the words finished, a portal that looked like Jell-O began to form as the gravity around it compressed. The linen closet was no longer visible and all that existed there was the silver portal. "Follow me". He then walked into the portal and vanished. Emma walked slowly toward the portal.

"Ready?" asked Daniel.

"I'm nervous, but I think I can make it," Emma said with regret.

"You have me so we can do this together," Daniel said.

"Let's go," Emma said.

Emma and Daniel walked slowly into the portal as they realized that life would never be the same. It was now that they were at a point of no return. They no longer would live in the world they called home. But now they would live in Sulex, where dragons exist.

Chapter Two
Uncle Amethyst

On the continent of Jutir lies the nation built on love and strength. Within the Castle of Olgath lies Harsie, the queen of Everstheee. Everstheee does not exist as another world, but another nation of the world of Sulex. Everstheee presides as the enemy of the greedy and power-hungry nation of Swiverstheee. Queen Harsie has summoned her mage guard to seek news of Emma and Daniel Dale from the Earth realm.

She sat on her throne, beautifully decorated with stones and symbols. Her straight face expressed her sense of calmness and serenity. In her dark blue eyes, the soul of a fearless, yet gentle mage. She stared down at the scrawny man below her, awaiting for what seemed to be the longest bow she had ever seen. She expressed her impatience with a heavy sigh, awaiting for the small mage to face her.

"Mage, what have you say of the children?" asked Harsie in a worried tone.

"They were gone when I arrived and I suspect them to be in Swiverstheee," said the mage as he stood, looking beyond the long row of ascending stairs. He was shaking uncontrollably, awaiting for an outburst from his queen.

"Swiverstheee?" Harsie retorted. "How could they have gotten there? They have no powers until they come of age."

"I believe that other forces may have brought them there."

"Arsi! Are you telling me that you believe Amethyst has something to do with this!?" Harsie objected.

"Yes your highness. How else could they have gotten there?" Arsi asked cautiously.

"How evil can he get?"

"Should I retrieve them from Swiverstheee?"

"No, I shall go myself."

"Yes, your highness."

Harsie rose from her throne immediately and placed her traveling cloak around her. She appeared to be departing but stopped at something near her chamber exit. She made a simple hand gesture and the scrying glass reacted to her command. This glass was on a stone platform that stood three feet from the floor somewhat like a pedestal. A large circular mirror lay on the platform. The device was used by mages to find someone they were looking for. *There Emma and Daniel were shown traveling through the Forest of The Dead. Amethyst was slightly ahead of them as the forest began to thicken.*

"Arsi! They are in The Forest of The Dead! Harsie yelled. "It is far worse than I feared! Daniel and Emma will be dead before I arrive. I need one of our spies to complete the mission due to my weakened state."

"I will have it arranged immediately," Arsi then ran out of the room and found his own scrying glass.

"Salari!" he called.

"*Yes?*" said Salari.

"Go to The Forest of The Dead and retrieve the children immediately by the queen's orders."

"*Not there again. I am so tired of going into that stupid forest. Day in and day out...*," Salari said sleepily.

"Hurry or you'll regret it," Arsi said with caution.

"*I'm going,*" Salari said with annoyance. The scrying glass was then disabled by the movement of Arsi's hand.

Salari got out of bed with annoyance. He had been drinking the night before and wished they didn't know his energy frequency for the scrying glass. On the other hand, he did enjoy the assignments they sent him on.

He wondered why these kids were so important to the queen. Salari knew that he had to retrieve the children. He was very satisfied that he was just miles from the forest in a nearby town called Amarion.

Amarion was a simple town with simple people. Many of the people didn't have powers to use because they were absorbed from Myred. Myred spent years trying to take over the area and succeeded by oppression and stealing of powers. Some couldn't even lift a candle with their mind anymore. A world he had once loved now made the oppression clear by his own kind. The world no longer promised peace, but there perceived to be years of unhappiness.

The war had been going on for some time now. Myred and the Arcane Alliance had been fighting for what they thought was right. Myred wanted world domination and the Alliance wanted peace for the people. Salari was lucky to have been rescued from Myred by Scion who was a very powerful mage who specialized in powers of protection. For being rescued, Salari was to swear his allegiance to the queen of Everstheee and would be called upon within Swiverstheee to spy on various occurrences within the lands.

Salari was now dressed in his robe, silver and red in color. Although it appeared to be quite plain, it contained a sufficient amount of power. He then left his room and walked down the dusty hall that smelled of beer and must. He didn't understand why he was in such a horrid place. He proceeded to the stairs and walked down them and inched his way closer to the door. Before he opened the door he forgot to do something. Then he realized.

"I'm off Gus," called Salari.

"A 'right but don' make too much of a mess out der', Myred is on the look out for people who don't pay the taxes. They may think you as one," Gus said with surprising enthusiasm. Salari always thought he was up to no good, but couldn't bring himself from turning the old man in to the Alliance.

Salari then proceeded outside the small road outside *Gus's Inn*. It was mid afternoon and the sun attempted to bring happiness to the people. People were slowly making their errands as if life left nothing but morose and Lethargic people. Even the children in the town lost all naturalizations of happiness and joyous child play. Salari started for the exit of the town to the gate that would lead him south for The Forest of The Dead. He slowly walked toward the gate and then *it* happened.

As he reached the gate, *something tickled his neck*. Salari was ready as he pulled out his staff. As soon as he whipped it out, a swarm of Mytred appeared from behind a wall and surrounded him.

"Salari Xytuxt, you are under arrest for treason against Myred," said one of the guards.

"Now why would you think that?" Salari said with a smile thinking of Gus who had most likely known about his betrayal.

"Don't move or I will be forced to attack," said the guard.

"Mytred are so stupid," Salari said to himself.

Without warning Salari jumped into the air. Several policemen began moving their arms and speaking in strange tones. Within the movements existed a clear gathering of some sort of energy. Some of those energy gatherings nearly converged onto Salari. While in midair, he summoned a strange door made up of strange ghosts that would transport him to a safe spot. The shimmering door that held its form of what seemed to be ectoplasm, forced him in and he immediately materialized five feet from his pursuers. He wished he had been farther away.

"Not again," said Salari as he sprinted off into a run as balls of fire missed him and one bounced off his robes. After turning a corner he then turned invisible with a small hand movement and quick muttering. As the policemen ran past him in invisible form he ran off into the other direction toward the forest. Mytred were so stupid sometimes. He wondered who their trainer was.

Salari was happy that he had recently learned some powers of divination from the great Seer Yambai who also swore his allegiance to the Alliance. He never thought that this branch of magic was useful. He was quite lucky to know of what was about to happen. If he hadn't he would be dead. The powers that he learned had increased over the last year or so that he knew exactly what to do. There was a cost to such great magic. Although he could foretell an event, he was not powerful enough to protect himself from detection of outside forces. The journey to the forest would not be long, but he knew that it would be hard to pry them from Amethyst who he already knew would be accompanied by them. Salari would have preferred anyone else besides Amethyst.

Amethyst, Emma, and Daniel walked along the trail in the large forest. It was autumn and leaves steadily fell from the trees above. The sun was blocked by all the trees and fog surfaced through the area. Strange noises could be heard from afar. This forest seemed really spooky to Daniel, but Emma was concentrating on something else. They had been walking for quite a while and no conversations were taking place except of the ones with the ravens in the tree tops.

"How did our parents die anyway?" asked Daniel who felt strange that this wasn't asked at first. He didn't necessarily trust Amethyst considering he had brought them to a strange land and convinced them that he was their uncle.

"Well….I hate to say it, but Myred attacked your parents along with their powerful commander and incinerated them," said Amethyst

"Was that the strange smell in the house?" asked Emma.

"It's quite possible. You wouldn't see ashes because mages don't have visible ashes."

Daniel wished he hadn't asked. He was a little sick now that he heard of the horrid way in which they died. Emma's eyes were red from tears, but she was strong and would make more sense of everything. It was her job. Daniel was not that person, because he literally went along with the way things were and nothing further.

"So what is this forest?" asked Emma.

"This is The Forest of Life," said Amethyst with a small smirk of amusement.

"Life? It doesn't seem lively to me," Daniel said.

"Well, this is where people are taken to be born," Amethyst said supporting his information. "It's a shame that this forest is so dangerous with Mytred and all."

"Dangerous?" Asked Daniel. "Mytred?"

"Mytred are the police of Myred who use magic to subdue their fugitive," Amethyst said. "I have fought them many times and you'll be safe with me."

"Are you sure about that?" asked someone from behind.

Emma and Daniel exchanged looks of horror. The Mytred were now here to kill them.

"Who is that?" Emma asked nervously.

"Just a pest of mine," Amethyst said with annoyance. "I'll take care of him, you two run for cover."

"Salari," Amethyst said.

"Amethyst," Salari began. "You should be flattered I wasted precious time to find you."

"I see you haven't changed Salari," said Amethyst. "How disappointing." He smiled crookedly, enjoying his insult.

While Salari and Amethyst were chatting, Emma and Daniel had hidden behind the bushes and were eavesdropping on their conversation. Both utilized their stealth to find out what was truly happening.

"So you have come for the children no doubt?" Amethyst asked sarcastically.

"You know I have. They don't belong to you. Especially someone of Myred," Salari said. He stood still, awaiting for his adversary's reaction.

"Well they will be of no use to me so you can have them after I have their bodies picked clean by the necromonsters. They just love taking captives and waiting for them to die to feed on." He winked at Salari. "Maybe you'll get to stick around and watch them die."

"He's going to have us killed!" Emma whispered to Daniel.

"I don't want to die so young!" Daniel whined. "I mean we're not even old enough to drive."

"We're not going to die!" Emma said reassuringly. "As long as Salari saves us."

"I'm sorry," Daniel said.

"Why?"

"I had a bad feeling about him, but I was just so caught up about what happened to our parents to say anything about it. I couldn't stay in that house any longer."

"It's ok Danny, I was scared too," Emma said. "Maybe it'll be ok after we…"

BOOM

A tree had been hit with some strange object. It had appeared to be a ball of some strange gas. Salari and Amethyst were in battle as Amethyst altered his small staff into a very large sword. It looked like it could slice a head off in two seconds. Salari looked rather stupid with just the plain old wooden staff he had. Another ball of strange gas was thrown toward Salari and he was lucky to absorb the impact of it with a gesture of his hand. The impact seemed to have weakened him. While doing that, Salari dropped his staff.

"We have to help him!" Daniel said

"How?" Emma began. "What are we going to do?"

"My Spells are too powerful for you old friend," said Amethyst.

"You will be stopped either way. Evil never wins against good."

"But Evil hasn't had me before," said Amethyst laughing.

Salari had fallen from a *spell* that hit him in the face. It seemed to have stunned his thoughts because he didn't move an inch, wavering forward and backward uncontrollably.

Amethyst began to walk up to Salari brandishing his sword in his hand looking rather pleased with his easy victory. The leaves crunched under every step he took as he slowly walked toward his kill. He reached the unmoving Salari and raised his sword. He was suddenly struck in the head by a large rock. He turned around to see Emma and Daniel throwing rocks at him. His reaction oscillated from pure joy to boiling anger.

"What are you doing!?" He asked angrily.

"We heard your little chat," Daniel said. "Some uncle you are."

"Fine if it will be that way, Uncle Amethyst will have to kill you," Amethyst said.

Amethyst dropped his sword and began working a spell. He was speaking in a strange language and moving his hands very fast. As he did that a large black sphere of energy was fabricated between his hands, gathering energy. Salari had beat him to his attempt. He sent some strange spell at Amethyst causing him to be compressed in a strong thread of energy.

"Come on!" Salari called. "That won't hold him too long!" Salari then grasped the two, beckoning them to follow him with haste and to run from the hostile force that was Amethyst. Revealed to the two was Amethyst's luring of them to *The Forest of Death*, and not the fictitious forest of life.

CHAPTER THREE
Lies and Truth

Salari had not spoken since they had left the forest. He was severely fixated on getting as far away from Amethyst as possible. As their footing increased, Emma took a glance at their rescuer. Salari was not very tall, at least five foot seven inches. He was middle aged with a graying mustache and hazel brown hair. Emma took her time and soon found a moment to question "Salari".

"Excuse me," Emma begin. "May I ask who you are?"

"Finally brave enough to speak, I see," said Salari. "I am Salari, a spy working for the Alliance. Amethyst used his lies to lure you into this world. His intentions were none other than evil."

"What about being our uncle?" asked Daniel.

"He is your uncle I'm afraid," Salari began. "He has chosen the side of evil at the most important time in Sulexian history. I was sent by my superior to retrieve the two of you. You may be the only ones left who can help us in our cause."

"What is your cause exactly?" Emma asked cleverly.

"We want to free the prisoners that are trapped and being tortured by Myred. We need them to help us defeat Myred and end their quest for world domination. They captured many of our most powerful allies from around the three continents. Our world is divided among three continents which are controlled by four of the power countries. Swiverstheee, Everstheee, Absirthee, and Mortistheee."

"What's with all the 'e's?" Daniel asked curiously.

"They are named by the founders of the continents. Swiverstheee is run by Myred who deal on world domination and chaos," continued Salari. "Among Myred are usually dark mages who practice destructive magics to build powerful armies. I have been spying and found that necromancers (mages of death magic) have been hired to raise an undead army. A most gruesome of things. Myred recently conquered Mortistheee which is composed of mainly clerics of the sort who use magics of the priest and your occasional warrior. Everstheee contains mages of various powers. Some are divine, arcane, or do many useful things with magic. Absirthee is currently neutral and does not want fighting. They are the natured race of mages who use nature as their power. They are the druids of our world."

"Why not just gang up Myred?" asked Daniel.

"Remember, we don't have the forces because they have been captured and I can see that King Vicousir of Swiverstheee plans to finish us off to gain control of the rest of the world." Salari confirmed.

"So how do we add to this??" Emma asked.

"That's for the queen to tell. I honestly don't know." Salari said. "Ah, here we are."

Emma and Daniel had not paid attention to where they were going. They had arrived at the entrance to a large city with high buildings and long streets. People filled the streets as well as buildings such as shops, inns, blacksmiths, and other resourceful places. Salari said it was Hutgir, the city between the coast of Swiverstheee and the country of Everstheee. Upon entering, the people nearest Emma and Daniel stood still, gazing upon them like strange apparitions or freaks of nature. Salari had not noticed, but it had frightened Emma to the point that she had to question it.

"We need to get a ship to get to the continent of Everstheee before anyone suspects us," Salari warned.

"The people are looking at us strangely," Emma said.

"That's because you're not mages," Salari said.

"I thought we were mages," Daniel told them as he followed the rest toward a large building.

"Not yet. You two aren't of magical age yet," Salari said.

"What do you mean not magical age?" Emma retorted.

"Mages don't retrieve their full magical abilities until the age of sixteen," Salari began. "Mage bodies have a special energy and when midnight of their birth comes, they begin to *transform.*"

"*Transform?*" asked both Emma and Daniel in sync.

"Yes. The body begins to release an energy into the blood and you inherit magical blood which allows you to weave magic with incantations and spell charging (that is moving your arms and hands to coordinate the incantation to gather energy. It also is good for aim as well.). This energy is called *mana.* The transformation is a bit tricky sometimes. Sometimes it can even kill the person from too much bottled up energy growing. There are cases where the *transformation* begins early and the mage begins to show some magical talents. Although that is very rare, I don't remember the last mage that has ever done it."

A man stood in the path of Salari. He stared back at them with suspicious eyes. He was dressed in a formal uniform, he was a policeman.

"What is the trouble officer?" Salari asked the Mytred guard.

"Why do you have youngsters with you?" the Mytred began. "Are they even of age?"

"No they are not. I am taking them to Zy to get the paperwork done," Salari said.

"Ok…but if I see them again I will have them escorted to the barracks myself," the guard said as he walked off.

"Let's go." Salari said as they all followed him passed a building that said *Zy's.*

"The Barracks?" asked Daniel.

"Underage mages are to be brought to the barracks for training before they become of age that way they will be able to produce spells of astronomical power to help in the war. That way mages can work magic without learning the art after becoming of age. They are forced to fight in the war due to Myred's control."

"That's horrible," said Emma.

"Yes I know. We need to press on," said Salari.

There before them was a small building surrounded by many people and young mages waiting in line. The street was dirt and gravel and stands were lined up selling various things from exploding daggers to plasma ball wands. Daniel could almost feel the evil of the people here and knew he had felt it before. He had felt it from Amethyst. Was it because of Daniel's pure of heart and good nature? The changes that occurred in the last few hours shocked him beyond compared. He could now believe that anything was possible be it good or bad. He wasn't sure if the transformation was good or bad, would he survive it?

Emma watched her brother and immediately knew that he was being his pessimistic self. She was pretty much the opposite of her brother. But recently, her depression had affected her grades and she wondered why she worried so much during that time. She wondered why she and her brother were so important. Why were Reater and Malitus not their real parents? So many questions and not a single answer. She knew that the death of Reater and Malitus was for the best. She knew that their purpose was sought. But what was the purpose of her and her brother's survival?

The three of them found themselves at a boat shop. The man in the shop was rather plump and stocky, his clothes smelled of sea water and it made Emma a little queasy. There were various boats hanging up within the store whose attributes varied between small and large and sinkable and unsinkable. The boat shop keeper waited patiently for Salari to request a boat of him.

"I need a boat," said Salari.

"How big ya wan' it?" asked the salesman enthusiastically.

"I have these two passengers," said Salari as he indicated Daniel and Emma.

"Where in the world are you going? You can't leave the continent!" demanded the salesman.

"I'm sorry sir, but I guess I will have to leave."

"No hard feelings, sir?" Salari continued. He then offered the man a hand shake in which the man shook. While shaking his hand, Salari then muttered a few words as an amber light encompassed the salesman. The man blinked his eyes rapidly. Salari paid the man.

"Of course you can leave. Take the boat for a trip to Everstheee. I hear it is a lovely place," said the salesman. "Here is the claim. Have a nice trip," The man handed Salari a small ticket showing proof of ownership. Salari began to walk past the salesman, and out of the front door of the building. He swiftly moved out of the salesman's view.

"What did you do to him?" asked Emma.

"It was a charm spell to make him bend to my will," said Salari. "I can't have him reporting us. This mission is too important. It's time for us to leave this dreadful place."

Emma and Daniel followed Salari to the back of the building where the small boat was. The boat looked hardly suitable to sail three people over such a large body of water. It was small. Emma didn't like the sight of the boat.

"We're going to sail across the ocean with this?" asked Emma.

"*Sail* is such a strong word. You can't sail to Everstheee. It's protected. I just needed a vessel that can carry all of us."

"What do you mean?" Daniel asked.

"We will *fly* to Everstheee to save time so that I can get you the information you are seeking and before your transformation starts at midnight in 42 hours. It will take us all night to reach Olgath Castle. I can enchant the boat with the pass spell to get through the continent's barrier."

"That's a good plan," said Daniel with enthusiasm.

"Let's go," said Salari.

Emma and Daniel followed Salari to the boat as he began to prep the boat with spells he was working. Emma had observed that Salari used a spell written in English to enchant the boat. Emma had always thought that magic was in Latin or Klingon or something strange that no one spoke. But English?

"Why are spells in English?" asked Emma

"Magic does not belong to one known language. The greatest mages of all time used English as their primary language. Of course, you also have other mages who use languages such as Greek, Latin, French, or any other languages to do spells in. The only old language still used is Latin. You'll find it to be much more efficient when you are proficient is as many languages as possible."

"Ok...." Emma said.

"Emma, are you worried about what's happening," asked Daniel.

"It's strange that just earlier we were wondering where our parents were," Emma said.

"I miss them too," he acknowledged.

"Remember when mom used to sing us to sleep?" asked Emma.

"She had such a great voice. I thought she was some kind of magic siren that calmed us to sleep."

"You knew what a siren was at age six?" asked Emma.

"Yeah. I thought everyone did," Daniel commented.

"Wow. You truly are a weird one."

"Yeah. And I loved them because they loved who I was," Daniel acknowledged.

"Me too," agreed Emma.

Emma and Daniel were now thrust backwards onto the floor of the boat. It seemed like a slow start, but it began to go extremely fast and for that purpose they were tied to the boat. Of course Salari wasn't worried and was enjoying the fast ride. The wind whistled loudly as they passed cliffs along the coast as waves smashed against the rocks. There was too much noise for conversation. Salari didn't move an inch while the wind rustled and could have easily blown Daniel and Emma into the ravenous ocean. Emma soon fell asleep, followed by Daniel as night began and the large blue moon rose to comfort their slumber.

Birds were chirping very loudly as if they were arguing about something. The sun was golden in the faces of Emma and Daniel. Daniel laid on the side of the boat as Salari un-enchanted the boat, and Emma opened her eyes. She got up and saw what seemed like the most beautiful thing she had ever seen. A beautiful emerald castle glistened in front of her. A beautiful forest could be seen in distance and a paved road made of silver lead the way to the Castle of Olgath. Everstheee was already showing its beauty as a bird flew down and landed next to her. It was unlike any bird she had seen. Its beak looked to be made of metal and its wings made of rubber. It had another set of wings under the first somewhat like a dragonfly. It chirped loudly at her.

"It wants you to touch it," Salari said.

Emma reached to touch the strange bird as its wings reflected light upon her face. It was bright but didn't blind her at all, but it felt comforting and soothed her worried mind.

"Herxes," Salari began. "These birds have magical properties that can cause a barbarian to become at peace even at a time of war. That is why these birds have never near faced extinction."

"They're fascinating," said Emma.

"There are a lot of things to be fascinated about," Salari said as he rose to get out of the boat and walk on the plush green grass that appeared to be as soft as cotton. Daniel startled awoke.

"Where are we?" Daniel asked sleepily as he yawned.

"Welcome to the country of Everstheee. It's almost the most beautiful continent in the world. Don't dally please. We need to reach the castle before…." Something in the air caught Salari's eye. It made a screaming noise that sounded like fireworks. Salari caught it as it almost streaked past them. It appeared to be a flat mirror. It awoke and a voice came from it.

"Salari! Where are you?" a voice said.

"Ah, Arsi I see you finally sent word."

"Yes I have! Where are the kids?" Arsi demanded.

"I have them right here and we are on our way up to the castle," Salari said with calmness.

"Excellent. Make your way here quickly so that we can talk," said Arsi impatiently.

"Of course." The image of Arsi's worried face vanished from the glass and Salari threw it into the sky where the glass flew back to its origin.

"Who was that?" asked Emma.

"Arsi, the mage. He's the one that sent me to come and get you. He's got no patience of any kind. Shall we get going?"

The journey ahead would bring Emma and Daniel to the answers they seek as they headed toward the castle to meet Queen Harsie of Everstheee. Perhaps the lies told by Amethyst would become truth.

CHAPTER FOUR
The Castle of Olgath

The Castle of Olgath stood high into the sky, almost touching the clouds it seemed. Emma and Daniel heaved on hoed through the field trying to make their way up to it. The wind blew softly providing what little comfort they could sustain from the strenuous walking. Although the castle appeared to be closer, it became evident that they had been walking for what seemed to be at least thirty minutes. Daniel tripped on a rock, picking himself up immediately.

"How much longer?" Daniel complained, frowning up at the sun and blocking his eyes.

"Just a bit further," Salari said.

They walked a little further and finally reached the entrance to the castle. The great big door of the castle had not been lowered yet. There was a moat separating the castle from the rest of the area. The water rushed calmly within it.

"What now?" Emma asked.

"Wait for it," Salari said.

Suddenly the door of the castle was drawn down and two men came out to greet their guests.

"Salari," said a man. "It's so nice to see you."

"Ah, Rayziel. It is a pleasure," said Salari as they shook hands.

Rayziel was a large man of about two hundred pounds with brimming muscles and a bald head. He looked as if he could take on anyone. He was dressed in a sleeveless tunic and robes.

"This is Rayziel, one of Queen Harsie's warrior clerics," said Salari.

"Cool. I'm Daniel."

"Nice to meet you Daniel, and this must be Emma. He said while turning to look at her. Rayziel was at least six feet one inch and had to bend his neck to see her.

"And this one here is Arsi," said Salari with monotone.

Arsi was slimmer than Rayziel and had a more of a wimpy look about him. His arms were scrawny, making him appear to be physically weak. He crossed his arms while Rayziel and Salari talked. His glasses laid straight upon his nose, looking quite displeased.

"Hello Salari, nice of you stop by," said Arsi.

"Shall we go in?" asked Salari.

"Of course," said Arsi.

The five of them then walked across the drawbridge and entered a very large hall that was at least twenty feet high. The walls were made of crystal and the floor was made of pure gold. There was nothing in the first hall but pathways leading to various places and a giant statue of a mage fighting a dragon. Daniel walked up to the statue and read its caption: *Olgath The Great conquered and gained this land by defeating the dragon, Oxcion in AE 78. Olgath built this castle prior to his victory and passed down the castle to each heir to the throne.* Daniel found himself alone in the hall because everyone else had left. He left to catch up with them.

As Daniel entered the throne room after searching well over ten minutes he found everyone else. They all seemed to be waiting on someone.

"What's going on?" Daniel asked Emma.

"We're waiting for the queen to come down from her room," sad Emma. "Her room is almost half a mile away. They told me it was for safety reasons?"

"That's far," said Daniel.

"Yeah, what were you looking at earlier?" asked Emma.

"Just a statue," said Daniel.

The humongous, red iron door banged open.

"All bow to the presence of Queen Harsie," announced Rayziel.

Queen Harsie was a beautiful spectacle. She had luxurious, long blond hair and walked with the posture of a soldier. She was perfect in every way. She was slim and muscular and wore royal attire as well as light leather armor concealed under her long robes. She walked up to the throne as Rayziel and Arsi took their seats to the left and right of the large throne. Everyone raised from their bow as the queen sat down.

"Welcome to Olgath Castle. I am Queen Harsie," she said brightly.

"Your highness," Salari said as he made another bow. "I have completed the mission and retrieved the children from the clutches of Amethyst."

"His evilness sickens me. We really should dispose of him one day. Now that you are here I ask that you wash up. Dinner will be served soon. You will receive the answers to your questions then."

Rayziel and Arsi got up from their seats. And came down and stopped in front of the wild haired, stinky Daniel and Emma.

"These two will lead you to the corresponding washrooms. There will be fresh clothes for you afterward," said the queen in an authoritative tone.

Emma followed Rayziel to the female washroom and Daniel followed Arsi the male washroom. They walked off in opposite directions.

As Daniel dried off himself he took notice to the clothing laid out for him. He received robes just like those of Salari and Rayziel. They were soft to the touch, made up of a mixture between silk and cotton. He put them on after drying up. He felt a buzz of excitement. Despite the material he was still cool despite the steamy bathroom. The robe was red with white vertical stripes. Daniel put on his shoes afterward, admiring his new clothing in the mirror.

There was a knock at the door.

"Come in," said Daniel.

Arsi entered the room and bowed to him.

"The queen requests your presence in the dining room."

Daniel immediately followed Arsi out the door and into the hall. It was a shorter walk than he imagined because seconds later Arsi held out his hand, muttering quickly, and made the large blue door open.

The Dining room was a sight for sore eyes. There, in the middle of the ceiling, a chandelier that held no less than one hundred separate lights. They were bright over the giant table that was at least twenty feet long. There were many chairs there as well. He finally lowered his head to see Emma, Salari, Rayziel, and the queen already seated.

"Have a seat please," said the queen. Daniel then took a seat next to Emma who was a few chairs from the end of the table where the queen sat. "Now I want to answer any questions I can," continued the queen.

"Your majesty," started Emma." Why are we so important to Everstheee?"

"Good question," started the queen. "You two were born from the two most powerful mages of the time. You are among few of the last remaining mages of youth in our clutches. Being born of a powerful family means you will be powerful in return. You were kidnapped at birth by Reater and Malitus."

"They *kidnapped* us?" asked Daniel.

"Yes," continued to queen. "They swore their allegiance to the Alliance while single handedly fooling the Myred. They pretended to be on their side, making plans to give you over to them. They began to spy for us on Myred and were going to bring you to us so we could train you and save the other young wizards captured as they have become so rare these days. Amethyst caught on to their plan and went to kill them. We knew you were in danger, but Amethyst beat us to the punch."

"So who are our real parents?" asked Emma.

"In due time," said Harsie.

"I know this may be off subject, but I was wondering where the king of Everstheee is," questioned Emma.

"Yes. I lost Siry, my husband before your birth. That was the day that Amethyst swore his allegiance to Myred, attacking Siry in anger. But Siry's power wasn't enough to defeat the anger-fueled Amethyst. It was in that battle that he disappeared, and I lost a husband. But that is a different story.

"Reater and Malitus were to keep you from Myred so that I can begin your training myself. I was once the most powerful mage of the time. The necromancer powers of Myred have left me far weaker than I have ever been. I went there to try and settle with Vicousir and stop the fighting. He had his Mytred ambush me. I barely made it back here alive and I needed to rest and didn't get to come as I had planned," said the queen with haste.

"My queen," said a guard.

"Yes…what is it?" she said impatiently.

"The *others* have arrived," said the guard.

"Thank you Wyter," said the queen.

He opened the door and two people walked through. One was a female and the other was a male. They were twins. Both of them had small freckles of the type and dark brown hair. The boy was dressed in armor and robe and had a large sword at his side. The girl had the same as him as well as an additional dagger on her boot strap. They were slightly older than Daniel and Emma.

"My darlings," said the queen.

"Hello," said the boy in a low tone. He looked rather distraught.

"How was the dragon?" the queen asked.

"Hot," the girl said as she touched her heat exhausted hair.

"I hope you've rid the peasants of it," said the queen." It has eaten several people."

"Of course," said the boy.

The two walked toward the table and sat at opposite seats across from one another.

"This is Emily and Derrick," said the queen and she then addressed them. "Emma and Daniel."

Emily and Derrick looked with eyes of shock.

"Are you sure?" asked Emily.

"One hundred percent," said the queen happily.

Emma became a little confused. Who were these two kids and why did they seem to be shocked that him and her brother were here?

"Who are they?" asked Emma curiously.

"Why your brother and sister of course."

Daniel had stopped paying attention to his stomach and more to the conversation. More questions formed.

"How could they be?" Emma asked immediately.

"Well you do have the same parents," said the queen. "Oh! that's right I didn't tell you!" said the queen happily.

"Tell us what?" asked Emma.

The whole group looked as if they already knew the answer. Why were they the only ones that didn't know? Daniel began to look angry as if this was some kind of joke.

"I'm your *mother*," said the queen calmly. "Which makes me sister to that evil little man Amethyst."

"What!" said Emma and Daniel immediately.

"I know it's a bit sudden, but you need to know," said Harsie calmly.

"You must be joking," said Daniel.

"I'm sorry, but I'm not," said Harsie. "Harsie or Queen Dale to be more precise."

Emma and Daniel looked at each other. It came with a bit of shock. They had lost two parents only to regain another. Emma began to feel strange as her blood began to pump faster. Her vision began to blur and she knew exactly what was happening. Why was it happening so soon? She looked at her hands to see them fading away as if disappearing into nothingness. Emma blacked out!

Daniel reacted very quickly and he took her from the chair and laid her on the floor as Salari got up after noticing what had happened. Daniel began to feel strange too. His hands felt as though they were on fire. He couldn't control himself and fell to the floor and his convulsions began.

The queen got up immediately and ran to the two. Why were they acting this way? She began to think of the *transformation*, but it was too soon. They were off by at least eight hours. She only wondered exactly how this was possible. Only one mage of all mages became magical before sixteen. It was highly abnormal for this because they did not grow up surrounded by magic like herself.

"What's happening to me?" asked Daniel in a weary voice.

"It'll all be over soon enough," said Harsie in a quiet voice.

Daniel lost his energy and passed out next to Emma who lost her head to some kind of invisibility. The queen immediately gestured to her guards to take the twins to the hospital wing of the castle.

CHAPTER FIVE
The Becoming

The Queen paced about the room nervously awaiting for Daniel and Emma to show signs of stability. They had been sleeping for days with no sign of ever waking up. Harsie had not understood why they were in this state. The *transformation* had never lasted more than one day. Her priest, Arte, could not find any reason as to why the two were in their strange coma.

The room was small and held four beds and two small dressers. There was one chair that sat alone between the beds in which the two lay. She spent every possible waking hour watching them as they slept and prayed to Laria, the goddess of love, to bring them back to her. Her worst nightmare had come true. She was going to lose the children she had never gotten to raise.

Derrick and Emily came in occasionally, but knew that Harsie would rather be alone with them. The fire opposite the beds was warm and provided some comfort to Harsie. She went to the sink past the fireplace to splash water on her face as Emma began to stir in her sleep. Harsie walked silently towards her bed.

"Emma," said Harsie. "Can you hear me?"

Emma opened her mouth slowly as if it were the hardest thing to accomplish.

"Mother," she said in a hushed voice.

"Emma," said Harsie. "Are you….?"

Emma began to glow as if something had emerged from inside of her. Harsie looked as if it were a miracle. Apparently a spell had manifested itself inside of Emma to revive her somewhat.

"Mother," said Emma.

"I'm here," said Harsie. Her eyes were tearing.

"Why do I feel this way?" asked Emma.

"The transformation is happening to you," said Harsie.

"I'm scared," said Emma.

"It'll be fine," said Harsie. "I'll make sure of it. Happy birthday darling."

Emma fell back asleep suddenly. Harsie kissed Emma on the forehead and looked over to Daniel who had his eyes open.

"Daniel," she said "How long have you been awake?"

"For a while," said Daniel with a smile. His face was pale somewhat in the light.

"How are you feeling?" asked Harsie.

"Different," said Daniel. "I've never felt myself before, but now I do."

"Good," said Harsie. She then noticed the strange look about his face. "What's wrong?"

"I think I already had power," said Daniel.

"What do you mean?" asked Harsie.

"At school someone I was mad at was beaten up by me. I wasn't even there though." said Daniel.

"Astral Projection is very advanced. I wouldn't expect less from you. Because you're my son. I know that power is strong among our family," said Harsie with a smile.

"Salari said this wasn't common. Being transformed before natural time," said Daniel.

"To have earned this privilege proves that you'll be far more powerful than me one day."

"Goodnight…mom…," said Daniel as he drifted off to sleep.

"Happy belated birthday son," she said as she kissed his forehead.

Harsie woke up the next morning as the sun's rays pierced through her window. Her room was extravagant with windows that reached the ceiling and painted, pixilated walls of lavender and red. She had many strong cabinets filled with many knickknacks and magical weapons and equipment. Some had varied items such as crystal balls and lances. She hurried out of her bed and slipped into her clothes to get down to the hospital wing to check on progress of Daniel and Emma. She walked to her large bronze door and opened it to leave. Before she could walk one step from her room, Daniel and Emma stood before her. They looked at her with consoling eyes. They both smiled at her brightly, running to her in a suffocating hug.

"Thank the gods for your survival," said Harsie. "I am so happy you're alright!"

"Thanks to you," said Emma. "I would have died if I didn't have anything to live for."

"Me too," agreed Daniel. "I can't believe my mother is a queen."

"Yes I am," said Harsie with a smile. "I don't want you to feel awkward around me. I am your mother and if you need me I am always there."

"That means a lot," said Emma.

"Let's get you two down to breakfast. There is training to be arranged."

Emma was so happy to have survived transformation. She almost felt like she was dead because of it. The dreams of people in cages fighting for their lives from being starved felt so real. The people within the cages were being tortured with powers of shocking electricity and fire. Mice and other vermin ate from the skin of the captives in their sleep. She wondered why she would dream something so horrible as if she were there. She hoped that that dream was only something of her imagination. She hoped Harsie would give her a way to adjust to a new life. It would be hard to adjust to a mother they never knew.

Daniel, like Emma was also thinking of the transformation. His head and hands felt on fire before. He felt so rejuvenated inside as if a new form of energy was found in his body. He had never felt like himself in all the years of his life. He felt as if he could do anything. He wondered what powers he could harness now. He had gone through his transformation before time. Maybe it was time to find himself in the magic that makes him whole. Identity was very important to him. He had always wanted to know who he was. Daniel enjoyed the aroma of the food sitting on the table as he entered behind Harsie and Emma.

"That smells great," said Daniel as he looked at the table filled with eggs, sausages, toast, pancakes and so much more; He was so hungry.

"There's plenty," said Salari as he entered from the main door. He looked as If he had a long walk.

"Great of you to join us Salari," said Harsie with a smile.

"Thank you," said Salari as he entered and took his usual seat.

Everyone took their usual seats as soon as the door on the left opened and in entered Emily and Derrick.

"Good morning all," Derrick announced in a very content tone.

"Morning Derrick," said Harsie.

"I see these two are awake," Emily said looking at the two.

"Yes they are," said Harsie with a smile.

Derrick and Emily took their seats as well. They each helped themselves to the plate of eggs on their end of the table. Emily and Derrick were very engrossed and didn't seem the slightest bit interested in getting to know their siblings.

"Emily, Derrick," said Harsie. "I want you two to take Emma and Daniel to the courtyard and get to know them better. Maybe even evaluate them on some beginner magic to get their blood pumping."

"Yes mother," said Emily and Derrick at the same time.

"Harsie," said Salari. "Can I have a word with you after breakfast?"

"Yes, I will be available," said Harsie as she finished her piece of toast.

After finishing a very quiet breakfast, Emma and Daniel followed Derrick and Emily toward the back of the castle to the courtyard. The courtyard was quite beautiful. Many different flowers were surrounding the area as well as trees of many sorts. The walls of the castle could been seen at certain angles. The sun was shining brightly in the open area.

"This is where we practice our magic," said Derrick.

"Why do you practice magic?" asked Daniel.

"The thing about Magic is that if you don't practice, your body will tire of it faster," said Emily.

"I specialize in evocation magic which is mainly used to summon spirits that complete various tasks for me." said Derrick.

"I specialize in Invocation magics which are used to summon power from the great god of power, Nexus."

"Can you do anything besides summon?" asked Emma with curiosity.

"We can do other things too, we just specialize in those fields."

"So what are we here for?" asked Daniel.

"We need to determine the power that both of you harness so that a school can be determined after training," said Emily.

"Who will be training us?" asked Emma

"We will," said Derrick. "We have already been preparing for the training of younger mages, but all the others are no longer here because of the invasion."

"Invasion?" said Daniel

"I prefer that mother tell you this," said Derrick. "I think we need to continue."

"Before we do this," said Emily. "We will give you a list of the schools in order to make your decision when the time comes." Emily handed both of them a list of the schools of magic. It also had pointers on how to choose a school(s).

Schools of Magic

1. Abjuration: This school of magic is powerful to use for protection. Magic of this type can be used to create shields or walls to stop enemies from attacking you. Other powers include the ghost door which is used to transport you away from battle. This school is used to prevent something ill from happening to the mage. It can be highly useful in times of need.

2. Conjuration: Conjuration is a powerful form of magic used to summon creatures and magical energies to the mage's aid. These spells can be dangerous if a creature you summon cannot be controlled. Caution goes to those who do not know how to harness the powers of this school. This power is also used to summon powers within the mage without looking towards other schools. Magical weapons can be harnessed by this school as well as elemental powers and powers over weather.

3.Invocation: These powers do a variety of things. Invocation is the power to summon the powers of one's god to use in combat. Strength can be offered, or speed, or any other type of power.

4.Evocation: Evocation is a school in which spirits are summoned to carry out deeds for the caster. These spirits harness powerful magics and can be used for various things. Evocation is dangerous unless you can control the spirits that are harnessed.

5. Divination: Divination is used to see the unseen. The eye is powerful to a diviner and shows what hasn't been seen. Powers of clairvoyance are the highlights of these powers as well as powerful scrying and the ability to sense evil. Empathy is also a power known to all diviners. Knowing the unknown adds to the many abilities of this school.

6. Enchantation: These powers are used to create different magical properties of an item. Enchanting creates, magical properties to an item or weapon of choice

7.Alteration: The altering of forms of matter. These powers change the form of an object.

8. Charming: The power to subdue the thoughts and actions of a being or person. Animals can also be charmed, but some can only be charmed by a druid.

9. Illusion: The powers to confuse the enemy by confusing their sight. Some spells are invisibility or multiplication.

10. Completation: This is not a school of magic. This is the complete form of all schools of magic (excluding Necromancy). This is only granted to the most powerful of mages who can harness these great powers.

11. Necromancy: This school is forbidden to all of Everstheee. Theses powers deal with death and can create undead creatures as well as cause death in an instant. These powers are evil and shall never be harnessed within the rulings of Everstheee.

Tips for Schooling

1. Learn as much of your desired school(s) as possible. If you haven't decided, learn as much as possible.

2. Learn the seven languages of magic to optimize casting time. Selecting a language is good to add a personal touch to your spells.

3. Create your own spell books to document the spells you are familiar with and practice daily.

4. Create a scrying glass to stay in contact with the Castle of Olgath and members of the Everstheee Inner Circle.

5. Begin learning magic as soon as the transformation has occurred. If you don't practice your body will begin to lose its magic and it could kill you if you don't completely harness your powers.

"The seven languages of Magic?" asked Daniel as he looked up to Emily and Derrick.

"The seven languages of Magic are English, Spanish, French, Portuguese, Russian, German, and Latin." said Derrick. "You have to be fluent in all seven to properly use magic."

"Why?" asked Daniel with confusion.

"Some mages may use one of the seven or all of the seven and you must know the language to understand what powers they want to use on you so that you can learn to counter spell them." said Derrick

"What is counter spell?" asked Emma butting in after reading the rules over again.

"Counter spells are used to stop someone from casting a spell on you," said Emily.

"I think we should start to teach you now," said Derrick with a smile. He was amused by their curiosity and knew they were his siblings. He too was once a curious young boy trying to understand magic in its entirety.

"We are about to show you a simple spell to upstart a fire," began

Emily. "I use this spell in Spanish because that's my preferred language, but English will do for now." She held up her hand and closed her eyes. "Nexus I call to thee. Bring forth the flames I call to thee!" a large flame ignited a nearby bush.

"Whoa," said Daniel with amazement. "That was great."

"Yes it was," said Emily.

"Do it in Spanish!" said Emma enthusiastically.

"Nexo, le llamo. Traiga adelante las llamas ardientes que llamo de usted." Soon after that a flame started on another bush.

"It doesn't matter what language you use except for some spells that are known only in Latin," said Derrick

"How do you use magic?" asked Emma.

"Magic is not difficult to use, but you must get the words to your spell right and have your spell charging coordinated with the spell. If you don't, your spell will be off target and may do something other than the task you asked it. And you *have* to concentrate. Spells take a lot of concentration so you need to learn to concentrate in the most agile of situations."

"What did these notes mean about using magic?" asked Daniel.

"Magic must be used often in order to keep your body ready for it," began Emily. "If you do not use magic often, mana will dissipate and the next time you do magic, it will consume more energy than before. Some people have died from not using their magic and using advanced magic that drained the life out of them."

"What about the spell books?" asked Emma.

"Spell books are used to keep track of spells you know by heart. It is good to have one while traveling if you need your memory refreshed. You can learn many spells and have them memorized from your spell book," said Derrick.

"When do we get to practice magic?" asked Daniel excitedly.

"After you've become fluent in the seven languages of magic," said Emily with a smirk.

"Let's get to work," said Derrick with a similar smirk.

The day went on trying to learn seven languages at once. French and German were difficult for Daniel because he couldn't get the conjugations right. He was wondering how long it would take him to be fluent in seven languages. Why did he have to wait so long to have to use magic? He just wanted to at least try something like that fire spell. The classroom was nothing more than the hospital wing with desks instead of beds.

They had been working for hours, learning and translating various spells into English and their desired language; Some were written in various languages. Daniel was happy, after a few hours, that they had been given spell books to put various spells in. He had selected a lot of spells from Evocation, Conjuration, and some from Enchantation. He was fascinated by the spell used to make a man freeze in time while the rest of the world moves. They had been told to select a language to use for all of the spells not including spells written in ancient Latin. Daniel was leaning towards Portuguese because it was easier for him to pronounce.

Emma enjoyed this quite well. Her spell book had many of the spells from abjuration including ghost door and sphere of light that protected her from some spells(both of which she had memorized in German). Illusionist powers intrigued her and she entered some of those spells into her book. Divination sparked her as well. She had a feeling that she would use these powers because of her *sixth sense* to know when something bad was about to happen. Emma decided her language would be German because she loved the sound of it; it made her sound fearsome because of how harsh German words sounded. Emma spent most of her time studying and preparing her spell books.

She wondered where Harsie was at that moment. She had not seen her since after breakfast that morning and it was nearly night time. It was strange how fast she was adjusting to her new life. She never really looked at it until now. This was her family. Perhaps this was a good thing. Emma started to get tired.

"Yes?" said Emily as Emma approached.

"What is mother like?" asked Emma.

Emily looked at her for a second and then opened her mouth. "Mother is a powerful mage who loves us. She's depressed lately because of father's absence. He's been gone since I was two. I never really knew him."

"Do you think he's still out there somewhere?" asked Emma.

"If mother is this strong, our father must be even stronger," said Emily confidently.

Derrick came up to Emily. "I think we should call it a night," he said as he turned to look at Daniel sleeping at the desk with drool coming out of his mouth. "I'll show him to his room."

"I'll take Emma," said Emily as they walked out of the door.

Derrick walked up to the desk to wake up Daniel. He pushed Daniel off the desk and he woke up after plummeting to the floor.

"Why did you do that?" asked Daniel sleepily

"Time to go to sleep little brother," said Derrick with a laugh. "Get your things and I can show you to your room." Daniel followed Derrick out of the room and into the castle corridors. He soon walked into a room followed by Derrick. Daniel couldn't believe his eyes. The room was huge with high, maroon colored walls and marble floor. Bookcases caressed the walls opposite his bed. They looked to have been freshly placed there. The bed looked quite comfortable and it was inviting him. He hurried and jumped to the bed. He landed on it instantly and fell asleep. The bed was so comfortable and fluffy. Daniel was soon fully asleep.

Emma couldn't sleep. She was still thinking about those people and if they were real. She had been practicing her spell charging from the books that lined the bookcases to the right of her bed. It gave her various tips and strategies to use when charging a spell. She had found out that most spells have specific spell charges for successful completion. It worried her because some of them were so similar to each other she wondered if she could do one. She had memorized many of the spell charges for the spells in her spell book.

She was ready to turn the page when her neck began to prickle as if something was crawling inside it. She couldn't move. She was deep in thought again. It was like the trance she witnessed at school. Her thoughts meshed together giving her the impression of danger. She tried to break away. It was minutes later she finally broke way from her thoughts. The spasms of her neck told her to get off the bed.

She got on her feet just before a bolt of lightning stuck through her window at the exact spot where she had been seconds before. A large, black spot smoked up from where she was previously residing. Another bolt came and barely missed her head. She ran to the door as it opened and bumped into Daniel.

"Let's get to the entrance hall!" he said. "We need to find the others."

Emma nodded as another bolt hit the side of the door. She followed Daniel down the halls and into the entrance hall. There they found Arsi, Rayziel, Harsie, Derrick, Emily, Salari and another person they did not recognize.

"What's happening?" asked Emma.

Salari spoke first and hurriedly. "Amethyst has come with Mytred to take the castle!"

"They broke through the barrier as I predicted," said the man. He was a few inches shorter that Salari and he wore a gleaming robe of white cloth and held a small club in his hands. His dark skin made him very distinguished.

"Who are you?" asked Daniel.

"I am Yambai," he said. "And I summoned Salari and Harsie to give them the information of this occurrence. I saw it in a vision."

"There's no time to chat," said Harsie as a group of Mytred entered through the broken windows. All of them were equipped with weapons from sticks to axes.

"We have to escape my queen," said Rayziel.

"No. I will NOT lose my castle to that idiot brother of mine!" she said as one of the Mytred came running towards her. She spoke quickly in Latin, stopping the Mytred guard dead in his tracks and falling flat on his face. "Let's go!" she said as twenty more came through various entrances. The Mytred were dressed in black and red robe-like uniforms. Their insignia of a black shield and lance with a strong red background was on the backs of their uniforms.

Daniel and Emma were standing in awe as they watched them fight, but they felt so helpless at the moment. Spells were being flung in all directions. Some were entwining the Mytred in a very powerful magic thread. Yambai seemed to not be fighting but rather meditating. Harsie was fighting four at once with her Staff. Derrick and Emily were working spells that blocked the Mytred from coming in through the windows.

Rayziel and Arsi seemed to have conjured weapons made of magic to their aid and were forcing many of them to give up.

"I'm going in," said Daniel.

"No...you can't," said Emma.

"We have to help them," he said as he ran toward the center of the hall where the others were fighting. As he reached the center a force field pushed him back.

He looked back at Emma and screamed. "Look Out!"

Emma turned instantly to see the approaching Amethyst with his large sword in its hilt. He looked rather pleased with himself. He seemed to be happy to see Emma.

"Emma, how is my favorite niece," said Amethyst with a sly grin.

"What are you doing here?" she asked with anger.

"I'm here to take what is rightfully mine," said Amethyst.

"You won't get it," said Emma.

"And who's going to stop me?" asked Amethyst.

"*I am,*" said a voice. Emma turned around to see Harsie standing behind her. Harsie had come from the battle immediately to stop her advancing brother. She seemed slightly flustered from her battle with the four Mytred. They were now lying unconscious in a pile.

"I see," said Amethyst "The battle has only just begun."

CHAPTER SIX
The Battle for Olgath Castle

Emma realized that this was the battle for Olgath Castle. Amethyst had come to claim it as his own in efforts to complete his plans of diabolical domination. Emma's neck prickled uncontrollably, warning here of danger. Amethyst was too powerful to be defeated easily. Emma ran from the scene to hide behind the statue of Olgath. Emma watched them as they fought while the others kept the Mytred from entering the castle any further.

"It comes down to this doesn't it?" asked Harsie.

"I am afraid so…you see I want this castle and I will have it any way possible," said Amethyst darkly.

"This castle will stand strong against your efforts," said Harsie as each of them were circling, ready for battle.

"Then I guess I have no choice but to take you down," said Amethyst as he stopped in his sentence and began to charge a spell. As his hands moved in the motion he yelled with a horrid voice. *"Esta pessoa é incomodam-me. Faça este sono de pessoa durante algumas horas!"* he said loudly as a ball of crimson energy shot at Harsie. As the ball descended upon her she charged a spell faster than Emma had ever seen. The spell created a barrier made of pure light that absorbed the spell instantaneously.

"Knocking me out is not an easy task," said Harsie behind her shield.

"Foolish sister….that barrier won't last you," said Amethyst with a smirk as he charged another spell. This spelled shot out a stream of energy that seemed to drain the power of Harsie's barrier. The barrier slowly disappeared.

"Tsk. Tsk. Tsk. What a weak spell Harsie, you of all people should know my powers are greater than yours."

Harsie didn't speak as she whispered something under her breath and with a slight movement of her hand a fireball ejected from her hand. Amethyst quickly moved to dodge it.

"You think a fireball could stop me?" asked Amethyst.

"Who said that was a fireball?" asked Harsie.

The so called fireball rebounded like a boomerang and hit Amethyst in the back creating a cylinder surrounding him. It was light yellow and contained Amethyst within. Amethyst looked pleased.

"How pathetic," he said as he moved his hand in one motion and the cylinder cracked and broke. The pieces fell to the floor as if glass, disappearing into the floors. "Just like mother and father."

"What are you talking about?" asked Harsie in confusion.

Emma watched them as they argued. Harsie and Amethyst were now on to hand to hand combat as the battle became even more intense.

Daniel was worried. The Mytred had broken their defenses and were gradually advancing into their midst. He felt so useless as he watched them struggle to keep them away. More and more poured in by groups of two to six. Arsi and the others were stunning them or caging them as they appeared; they were getting restless. Daniel had surprisingly gotten into the barrier after it took a spell...he was safe from the Mytred, but he could almost feel the barrier deteriorating as everyone began to lose their power over it.

He wondered how Emma was and wished he was there with her. He was so afraid. He shouldn't have left her, but it was to help the others. He didn't know any spells and wondered for what purpose was he here. Why had he run here if he knew nothing of how to fight or defend himself? The question wasn't answered by him, but by another.

"Daniel," said Yambai.

Daniel looked back to see Yambai looking over to him.

"I am in need of you," he said calmly.

"To look stupid and stand still?" asked Daniel with sarcasm.

"You have a lot of power and I need you to use it," said Yambai.

"What do you mean?" asked Daniel.

"You are your father's son and I know that you have the powers he can use with ease," said Yambai.

"What do you want me to do?" asked Daniel under the distant yells and spells weakening the barrier.

"I want you to strengthen the barrier," said Yambai.

"What?" said Daniel. "How am I supposed to pull that off?"

"With a simple spell," said Yambai.

"What do you want me to do?"

Emma watched the horrific battle as Amethyst reflected every spell created by Harsie. It seemed that Amethyst had known every trick before Harsie pulled it. She wondered if she could pull something off to distract him. It was too dangerous because Amethyst was almost twice as powerful as Harsie. There were too many risks involved. Her spells probably wouldn't do much to him.

They had abandoned a childlike quarrel to fight in melee. Amethyst and Harsie fought strongly, but Harsie did not have what it took to fight her brother. She was struck by his sword on the leg and fell to the floor.

As Harsie fell to the ground something inside Emma awakened and she felt energy pulsing through her. Her hands began to burn intensely. She was not in control yet again. She walked up to the scene as Amethyst prepared a final spell to annihilate Harsie. Before Emma realized what she was doing, she was speaking in an unfamiliar tone. Her words were the words of magic.

"Hören Sie diese Beschwörungsformel jetzt auf! Machen Sie es nicht mehr verwendbar!" she said loudly as a strand of ember light emitted from her hands and immediately stopped the flow of energy building on Amethyst's spell.

"Retched Girl," he said with anger. "You are getting more annoying by the second."

"I'm a quick learner," she said with a slick smile.

"You'll pay for this," said Amethyst as he quickly began another spell.

Emma didn't understand it, but she had to act fast. She did the only spell that came to mind.

"Blockieren Sie diese Beschwörungsformel! Schützen Sie mich vor seinen Wirkungen!" She screamed as the spell came. The spell didn't cause any affects to her and was blocked completely, but Emma was drained from it and she collapsed from exhaustion. Amethyst walked closer to her.

"Stop," said a voice from behind.

Amethyst turned around to see no one. He knew it had to be some trick as to draw his attention away, but then a spell was shot towards him and knocked him off his feet. A figure began to blur into vision. Harsie stood facing Amethyst.

"So I see you have come to," said Amethyst as he got up.

"Can't keep a good mage down as I always say," said Harsie.

"Well you have lost. The castle is mine," said Amethyst.

"You won't have it," said Harsie.

"Oh. It doesn't matter if *this* castle still stands, but the grounds on which it stands. This will be a nice new location to take over Everstheee," said Amethyst.

"How do you expect to get them then?" asked Harsie.

"Simple," said Amethyst. "Like this," he continued as he rose his hands and he began to speak in his usual tone as black strands of magic emitted from his hands and touched the walls of the castle. The walls began to deteriorate as the strands made contact with the wall. More and more, strands emitted from him, touching different parts of the walls. Harsie looked confused at the site of this spell.

"What magic is this?" asked Harsie.

"Forbidden magic!" said Amethyst as the walls began to crumble and pieces of castle began to fall. "Time has aged this castle hasn't it sister?" said Amethyst.

Harsie knew nothing of this magic and knew there was nothing to do. She desperately ran and scooped up unconscious Emma and ran towards the barrier. She ran for a while and finally reached it. She was allowed entrance into it and took Emma to the cleric Rayziel.

"Can you watch over her while I help strengthen the barrier?" she asked.

"The barrier has been strengthen from the help of the young one," said Rayziel.

"What can we do?" asked Harsie as her eyes gleamed with a speck of hope.

"We must abandon the castle," said Arsi as he approached.

"There's no time," said Harsie as castle shards fell onto the barrier.

"A portal would help," said Yambai.

"We don't have the power for that," said Salari.

"A ghost door would work, but we won't go very far," said Rayziel.

"Fine," said Harsie.

The preparations for the ghost door were more difficult because of the amount of people being transported within it.

Amethyst's spell began to slacken from the continued usage. His power was draining, but it would only be for a while. Harsie had informed them that Amethyst knew well enough how to preserve his power. He wasn't done just yet.

Daniel had helped to strengthen the barrier making him nearly faint in the process. He was in charge of watching Emma while the others prepared the door. As he leaned over her, he wished that she could reassure him that everything would work out. He was angry now because he had failed to help Harsie or Emma in a time of need. As Amethyst watched from behind the shield, he knew that he had won. It was almost time for him to leave the castle in its ruins.

It was obvious that Amethyst wanted Harsie to feel the pain of failure. She had already lost her husband and now the place she once called home was falling apart. Daniel wanted to make it up to her one day. She was his mother and he felt that she among all people deserved justice for what Amethyst did. Daniel vowed to take revenge for what he's done to his newly discovered family.

Harsie was having more trouble than she had expected. Her powers had been drained from her fight with Amethyst. She was doubting that it was possible even though she was the most powerful to conjure such a powerful object to her disposal. Emily and Derrick were not familiar with her magics of abjuration as Salari was, therefore she had to teach them how to do it; time was running out.

"Are you ready?" Harsie asked Emily and Derrick.

"I think so," said Derrick with exhaustion.

"Try to concentrate," said Harsie.

Salari, who stood next to Harsie, was next to Daniel followed by unconscious Emma as they tried to form the door on the back wall where the barrier ended. The Mytred had retreated when Amethyst had begun his spell acknowledging their victory. Amethyst's spell had unexpectedly grown stronger as he found more energy in him to utilize. The walls came down faster as the spell grew stronger. A vital part of the castle was hit and the rest of the walls began to crack and crumble.

Satisfied, Amethyst stopped using his spell and summoned up a door similar to the ghost door, but it looked to be made up of souls. He winked at Harsie and walked into the door and disappeared. Harsie and the others worked frantically with their spells with total concentration despite the walls coming down onto the barrier. As they began the spell the barrier began to weaken. After minutes of total concentration, the door opened up.

"Let's go!" she said as she grabbed Emma and gestured Daniel to follow.

Already the door was starting to shrink, created on a small amount of magic. Everyone ran toward the barrier and stopped to wait for Harsie who was carrying Emma. When she arrived Harsie immediately went through the door followed by the others. As soon as everyone went into the door, the barrier broke and the walls caved in. The castle fell upon itself. There was nothing left of the castle except for the rubble. That was the last of Olgath Castle and that which belonged to the great mage, Harsie of Everstheee.

CHAPTER SEVEN
The Forest of Knowledge

Harsie paced back and forth. She had lost everything to Amethyst. She wanted to do something in her power to get it back, but it would only endanger everyone else. The ghost door had brought them to the Forest of Knowledge. She and the others would be safe from Amethyst trying to find them. She needed a plan.

Amethyst had destroyed the castle and Emma and Daniel got their first taste of magic. Emma was slowly recovering from the spell she had cast. The forest was quiet in the night and she awaited the others to return with some form of food. Before they did, Emma woke.

She opened her eyes to see nothing but stars. She didn't know where she was. She sat up and looked over to the right and saw Harsie standing there.

"What happened?" asked Emma.

"You basically saved my life from Amethyst," began Harsie. "That spell would have killed me had you not counter-spelled it. He didn't see it coming and that is why you were able to complete it. And then he assaulted you and it was too much and you collapsed."

"Are you alright?" Emma asked.

"You almost die and you ask me if I'm alright?" asked Harsie curiously.

"Yes," said Emma. "You're my mother. I want to know how you are."

"I'm worried on what needs to be done. I have no castle, but I know what we must do. It's a risk that we have to take."

"Ok," said Emma.

There was rustling in the bushes as Emily, Derrick, Daniel, Arsi, Salari, Rayziel, and Wyter emerged from them carrying berries of some sort. Harsie gestured them to place the food on the ground near the fire.

"What are we to do now that the castle is gone mother?" asked Emily.

"I want us to go the Alliance Headquarters," said Harsie.

"The headquarters?" asked Arsi.

"Yes. Not many people know of its location, but I do," said Harsie.

"Isn't that dangerous your highness?" asked Rayziel.

"Yes it is. We will have to pass the Forest of Knowledge onto the plains of Tyut and across the Mountains of Nexus."

"The Nexus Mountains?" asked Salari. "I didn't know they existed."

"Very much so," said Harsie. "It will take us several days to reach our destination."

"We're going to need supplies," said Wyter.

"We can stop and visit an old friend on the way," said Harsie.

"I sense that this destination will be dangerous," said Yambai.

"That it will," said Harsie.

"What about the children?" asked Arsi.

"They will be trained more everyday. They show high potential," she said with a smile.

"I will train Emma extra everyday," said Emily.

"Do as you must," said Harsie.

"What about our stuff?" asked Emma.

"Spell books never leave the caster," said Derrick.

Emma looked in her bag that she got with her spell book to find it in there. She happened to glance at a page to see a new spell in there she showed it to Derrick. "I don't remember entering this spell into my book." she said.

"New spells that you use without knowing it will appear in your book. You used the *To block an unfriendly spell*, spell. It seems that you learned it on your own."

"Cool," said Emma.

"Let's eat," said Harsie.

Emma was still awake. She had saved Harsie's life and it felt good. She didn't know what came over her that time. She didn't even mean to use the magic she had used. It seemed to her that another lived in her and told her what to do. That was not the main chunk of her restlessness.

Daniel had been very distant during dinner. She knew he was angry at her. She could practically feel it in him. She looked back at the times in which he got angry at her. It seemed that he got angry when she got praised for something and he didn't. Daniel's insecurity made him feel that he will never amount to anything. She didn't want her brother to be like that. She had full confidence in him, but he didn't have confidence in himself. He always second guessed himself and made simple things complex. She needed to tell him a few things.

The stars were beautiful that night. Despite their beauty they didn't help Daniel sleep. He was so angry. Emma had found another way to steal his thunder. He tried his best with the barrier and Emma goes and saves Harsie's life. He hated the fact that she was so much better than him. She always surpassed him in everything from school to sports. He had no inert talents to do anything special. He kept into his books to escape the reality that he was excruciatingly average.

Dinner was basically a discussion about the events of that day. Emma received a lot of praise while he was shunned and had none of the attention he wanted. He disliked the fact that she never said anything about it. Did she know how angry he was? It seemed like everyone, once again, rewarded Emma and left Daniel in the gutter. Harsie was so happy and proud. It almost made him sick. He just wanted to be recognized for his accomplishments as well. Why did she always do that to him? There were footsteps and someone sat down next to him.

"I'm sorry," said Emma.

"For what?" asked Daniel as he sat up.

"For being a big shot and making you feel bad."

"I don't feel bad."

"Yes you do! I know you Daniel, you're mad at me."

"Yeah I'm mad! You have made me feel less important for the thousandth time."

"It doesn't matter what I did," began Emma. "You're the one that protected the barrier…we could have died if you hadn't."

"Well…now that you put it that way."

"You're such a downer sometimes!"

"What do you mean?"

"You do good things, but you think that you're not worth it."

"I don't feel that way."

"I know you! You always feel that way."

"I guess I do. It's just hard to follow *your* act."

"You are a good mage."

"Really?"

"You had the power to strengthen the barrier to keep us safe," stated Emma. "I'm happy for you."

"I want to be powerful like you."

"You can with more practice and study. How about I help you with more practice?"

"Yeah…that'd be great thanks."

"I promise we'll work at it together," said Emma with a small smile.

"Yeah," said Daniel said with a smirk.

Daniel awoke at the sound of a bird chirping. He sat up and saw various birds talking among the tree tops. He wanted to eat something while everyone was still asleep. He didn't eat much because he was so upset that night. Finally he had done something right, but not recognized for it. He felt differently now that Emma realized what she had done. He felt better even. It didn't matter anymore now, because he was really hungry. There was a lot of rustling going on, but it seemed normal. He noticed a tree on the far right. It had a multitude of berries on it so he decided to get one. He inched slowly forward when he noticed he couldn't move his legs.

"The berries on the trees are dangerous," said a voice.

"Who are you?"

"I should ask you the same question," said the voice.

"What do you mean?"

"I should know everyone who comes into *my* forest."

"*Your* forest?"

"Daniel!…who are you talking…?" asked Harsie as she entered the scene. "*Seri* is that you?"

"Yes it is," Seri said.

"You two know each other?" asked Daniel.

"Do you mind releasing my son please?" she asked.

"Oh of course!" said Seri.

The roots that entwined Daniel's legs left the surface and went back under ground. Daniel turned around. The figure known as Seri had leaves as ears and skin made up of a greenish plant. He looked like *Jolly Green Giant*. He looked strong and strapping for a nymph.

"Who is this?" asked Daniel.

"Seri the nymph. He protects this forest," said Harsie.

The nymph walked up to Daniel and held out his leafy hand to Daniel. Daniel shook the hand that felt like the leaves off a money tree.

"What brings you to the forest madam?" asked Seri.

"The castle has been destroyed," said Harsie.

"That's terrible news!!" said Seri consolingly.

"Yes. We will be leaving shortly." said Harsie.

"I see." said Seri

"Daniel come along. We need to wake the others," said Harsie.

Daniel turned to follow Harsie back towards the camp.

"How do you know that nymph?" asked Daniel.

"Old friend," said Harsie dully.

Daniel and Harsie emerged from the trees to the camp area to find that everyone had awoken.

"Time to move out!" said Harsie

Everyone got their things together and were on the way leading out of the forest. Harsie was the lead and everyone followed her. Derrick was teaching Daniel some magics he needed to know.

"Now try this spell, but in your language" Derrick said as he began to work the spell. "*Les feux de Connexion viennent en avant!*" Fireballs emitted from his hands and hit a nearby tree. "Now you try."

"*Os fogos da Conexão vêm adiante!*" he said as a small fireball ignited and hit Salari on the head. Salari's head caught a small flame. Salari put the small fire out with his hands.

"You're going to have to practice the spell charges and put more concentration in. If you don't, you could make some grave mistakes.

Everyone seemed to be bored with the forest. Nothing exciting had happened and it seemed that nothing was important to this forest. Emma was the first to break the dull silence.

"So why is this called the Forest of Knowledge?" asked Emma.

"No person has ever documented evidence about the forest," said Harsie

"Why is that?" asked Emma.

"The nymphs prevent those who want to document the information from leaving the forest," said Harsie

"I see," said Emma.

"The plants here are like animals, they can protect themselves," stated Harsie. "Don't touch any of the plant life here, some can use magic and others have incredible strength."

"Is that why the nymph didn't want me to touch the tree?" asked Daniel.

"Pretty much," said Harsie.

"Opening ahead," Salari announced.

The forest opened up to show the outside plains. Everyone was happy to see the opening to rid themselves of the forest. It was mid-day and everyone was ready to move on to another area. Daniel and Emma had stayed in the back of the line to help Daniel with his magic. With her help, he was able to make a fireball hit a tree to the left of them. Daniel thought Emma helped more than Derrick, who was straightforward and a little condescending.

"After we leave the forest we will walk ten miles to Aryit that is close by. We will rest at an inn in town and we will awaken to go towards the mountains," said Harsie.

A snapping twig alerted her to something.

"What was that?" Emma asked.

"We have visitors," said Yambai.

Mytred appeared out from behind trees surrounding them.

"Queen Harsie, we have come to retrieve you for King Vicousir," said one of the guards.

"I think not," she said.

"If you don't come. We have to take you by force." said the guard.

"You have taken my castle from me already. Now you want *me*?" asked Harsie. "You're foolish if you believe I would come peacefully. Send Amethyst my regards."

"Be it that way!" said the guard as the rest began to converge onto them.

"Os fogos da Conexão vêm adiante!" yelled Daniel. A small fleck of fire came out and the guards began to laugh at him.

"Stupid child, you can't do anything to us," laughed the guard.

"What are you doing?" asked Emma.

"Giving them a taste of my power," said Daniel angrily.

"But…." started Emma

"Os fogos da Conexão vêm adiante!" Daniel screamed again. For a second nothing happened and then three fireballs emitted from his hands and hit one of the Mytred square in the face.

"You'll pay for that child!" the guard said as he began to charge a spell. With great speed and accuracy Emily began a spell.

"¡Le llamo la barrera de la luz! ¡Protéjanos!" she yelled as the familiar barrier of light surrounded the area protecting them from the spell.

"Leave us and all will remain unhurt," announced Harsie.

"I'm afraid not!" said the guard.

"So be it!!" said Harsie. She began to charge a very fast spell. *"Insomna!! Apportez à mes ennemis à un sommeil profond!"* She yelled. There was a very large flash of light which blinded everyone. The searing light was white and covered over all of the guards at once. When they opened their eyes, all the Mytred had been knocked out instantly. Harsie fainted from it. Salari ran to break her fall.

"We have to get going while we have the chance," He said.

"Let's go everyone!" said Salari.

Everyone followed Salari out of the forest to the plains where they would meet their next destination. Harsie had harmed herself to protect the others. Now it was time to leave and find what lies ahead.

CHAPTER EIGHT
Next Stop, Aryit

The plains welcomed them strongly. Salari, carrying Harsie, was leading the way. They had been walking for several hours to evade the enemies behind. Daniel had felt bad about the incident. Had he not been brave and provoked the Mytred, Harsie would not have had to cast the spell in the first place.

Daniel wanted to make sure she wasn't harmed from it. He then thought about the "invasion" that Derrick mentioned on his first training day. Was that the day that her subjects were taken away? There were more questions and Daniel didn't know if they'd be answered. Even though he was upset about Harsie, he did find that his spell was an accomplishment. He couldn't wait until he reached a town to rest.

The heat was starting to get to Emma. They had been walking for hours without stopping. The bare plains gave little enjoyment as there was neither animal life nor people in the area. The plains were like deserts to some degree in her thoughts. It was hot and tiring, but there was plant life. She figured that the sun was not hot enough to form deserts. Mountains could be seen from afar. Her hair was starting to fry under the sun and it made her frown. They hadn't eaten or gotten anything to drink in a long time. She felt like it was time for a rest.

"Can't we rest a little?" asked Emma whiningly.

"No time for rest, Emma…we need to get to Aryit before nightfall," said Salari.

"But we've been walking for hours!" stammered Emma.

"We will be there soon enough. We will rest when we reach it there," said Salari.

"Ok," said Emma defeated.

Daniel was just as tired as Emma. He knew that Emma was only being her whiny self. He, on the other hand didn't want to appear weak in front of the others. He had a new confidence in his magic. His lessons on the voyage toward Aryit seemed to be improved as he mastered the ability to freeze an object in time as well as summon a fireball. He was improving at a very fast pace. It surprised even himself. He was "growing in power each day" the others would say. He felt very accomplished at his new ability to harness magic. A little confidence goes a long way.

He felt a little guilty for mother being hurt. He told himself that it would have come to that no matter what he did. He looked up to his mother now and didn't accept her at first because he didn't know her. Now, he realized that she was very powerful and dependable. He wanted to be as powerful as the "Queen" of Everstheee. It occurred to him that learning about his family helped him in his thoughts.

Him and Derrick had formed a brother-brother bond. Derrick was cool and funny. Daniel had learned a lot from Derrick such as being confident and being brave. Derrick had done a lot in his nineteen years of life. He became a "knight" among the townspeople. A knight was a powerful hero of the people rich and poor. The "knight" showed courage among his people as well as strength against animosity.

Not much was known about Emily from Daniel or Emma. Emily was quiet and didn't speak often. She was very brave and nice, but she normally kept to herself. Daniel and Emma had no special bond with her. She acted as if talking to family was not on her schedule. She was strict and forthright with her words. Emma and Daniel started to get used to her stoic behaviors. Emily was not much of a talker, but her actions told all. Her power was strong and her faith was even more immense than her power. Nexus was the god of power and strength. He granted power to his followers that believed in him. Nexus had a close connection with

Emily. Emily was very powerful in invocation spells. Emily, for the first time since the spell in the forest spoke.

"We have arrived at Aryit," she said.

"I don't see it," said Daniel.

"Look harder," said Salari.

Daniel squinted and still saw nothing.

"I don't see it," Daniel repeated.

"I see it," said Emma.

"Where?" Daniel demanded.

Emma pointed straight ahead. Daniel didn't see anything at first, but after a few seconds later he saw a town. He could see younger kids playing outside in the plains.

"Oh…I see it now," said Daniel.

"Let's Go," said Salari.

Seeing the town refreshed everyone's mood. They would finally be able to rest and find out the next steps. The sun was now setting. Emma was hungry, dirty, tired, and thirsty. She had never felt so bad before. She wanted to take a bath and eat and sleep in a bed. Her mind was beginning to tire as well. She was starting to forget what she was going to say before she would say it. It felt like her need of energy affected her mind and body. It didn't occur to her, but it had something to do with mana. They had at least one hundred yards until they reached the town.

"You are tired young one?" asked Yambai.

"Very," said Emma with exhaustion.

"Do you know why?" asked Yambai.

"Because we haven't rested since we left the forest."

"No."

"What?"

"Mages do not tire quickly. The magic in their bodies keep them going."

"So I'm tired because I'm running out of mana?" asked Emma.

"Exactly."

"I see."

"Of course you do. You have the inner eye."

"What do you mean?"

"The Inner Eye is the eye that helps you seek the future as well as the present."

"I don't know about that," said Emma.

"Have you been having strange dreams lately?"

"How did you know that?"

"I have the Inner Eye…I know things that I don't even know I know," said Yambai. His dark skin gleamed in the sunlight.

"Well I've been having these dreams about people being tortured."

"So have I."

"You have?"

"They are the prisoners from the invasion."

Daniel had been listening on their conversation since they started talking.

"What about the invasion?" whispered Daniel. He didn't want the others to hear him from behind asking about an event each of them refused to repeat.

"The invasion happened just a few months ago," said Yambai.

"What happened?" asked Emma.

"Amethyst brought the Mytred to enter the castle and capture our colleagues who were either finished or trying to finish training," said Yambai.

"So Amethyst took them back to Swiverstheee as his own troops?" asked Daniel.

"Exactly," said Yambai.

"Why were you training so many people?" asked Emma.

"We knew of the growing threat within Swiverstheee. We were trying to prepare for a war," said Yambai.

"How do we rescue the others?" asked Daniel.

"We would need help from the alliance as well as travel to Swiverstheee and get them that way," said Yambai.

"We're here," said Salari interrupting their secret conversation.

Daniel saw the town up close. It had high buildings and winding roadways. The people were cheery and joyful. As they walked ahead, Salari stopped as if struck by something. He had Harsie on his back. She was still in her unconscious state. Salari stood there gazing at something.

Daniel looked around and saw a man somewhat taller than Salari. The man had brown skin and he seemed to have had a rough time. He held a staff on his side and stood there gazing at Salari. He dropped his staff and walked up to Salari. The mysterious man walked up the approaching group.

"Long time no see old friend," said Salari.

"Indeed it has been," said the man.

"I see you have friends," said the man.

"Yes…you know everyone except for Emma and Daniel," said Salari.

"Emma….Daniel," said the man. He walked up to Daniel slowly and stuck out his hand.

"Scion Cray," said the man.

"Daniel," said Daniel as he shook his hand.

"You look just like your mother," he said.

"Thanks," said Daniel.

He repeated the step with Emma and then beckoned Salari to follow him.

Emma didn't know who this man was. He seemed a little too friendly for her taste. He seemed to have taken a liking to her for a reason unknown. He walked about as if the years had been difficult. Her suspicions were only to be cautious. After Amethyst's betrayal, Emma became very critical of new people. She followed closely down the bend towards a house that looked to be in need of fixing. It was not very large and had a few cracked windows. To her insinuations, she figured Scion to be poor.

"Here we are," said Scion as he helped bring Harsie in and lay her on the dingy bed.

"So how do you know Salari?" asked Emma.

"I'll answer that," said Salari. "This man saved me from Myred."

"Really?" asked Emma.

"I was about to be brought in for negligence and have my powers drained, but he appeared out of nowhere and saved me from them."

"You must be really powerful then," said Daniel as he took a seat in the chair next to the bed.

"Oh I don't know about that," said Scion.

"Don't be modest!" said Salari. "You showed those Mytred who's boss."

"I guess I did," said Scion laughing.

"How are you Scion?" asked Yambai.

"Yambai. It is a pleasure to see you," said Scion.

"The pleasure is mine," said Yambai.

"Scion!" said Derrick as he walked in the door followed by Emma.

"Derrick old boy how goes it?" asked Scion.

"Wonderful that you're here!" said Derrick.

"Thanks," said Scion.

"Scion. It is an honor to see you after all these years," said Emily.

"Is that you Emily?" asked Scion.

"Yes," she said with a smile.

"You've grown so much," said Scion.

"Thank you," said Emily.

Daniel had never seen such an expression on Emily. She seemed to be delighted in the presence of Scion. He had a feeling she had somewhat of a crush on him. Yambai and the others began to converse about the "old days". Daniel started to wonder about Harsie. Why hadn't she woken up yet? He started to wonder if she was more ill than he thought. He was going to ask when his thoughts were interrupted by Salari's talking.

"I am going to the store for supplies. Use whatever you need here and rest. We leave at sunrise." said Salari as he left out the door.

"Is she going to be alright?" asked Emma pointing to Harsie.

"She may wake up by tomorrow. Her mana has been terribly stressed," said Rayziel.

Rayziel seemed to be the type to keep his opinions to himself. He didn't talk much, but when he did, he said something of importance. Rayziel was a good priest. He had shown his talent at the battle for Olgath Castle. He was dark like Yambai and carried himself as someone who was not prideful, but put his faith in others. His faith in others seemed most efficient. It had been him to recommend Daniel for the barrier. Rayziel was a priest and couldn't harness any powers of Arcanian descent. He, like other priests, served their purposes with their magically divine powers. Rayziel seemed more confident to speak after the battle. It seemed he was coming out after being closed in for so long.

"She did a great deal of magic in a short time. Another night of rest will ease her," said Rayziel.

"I hope so," said Daniel.

"Don't worry so much son. She'll be fine," said Wyter

Wyter was the optimist. He always looked on the bright side of things. His power was not much to be impressed by, but he always knew what to say to cheer someone up. Wyter was another priest. He was known to bless those in battle. A blessing granted strength and courage. He loved to talk about the beauty of life and how wonderful it is to live. He was a bit younger than Rayziel and "fresh" off the press. He had only been a guard for a few weeks before the battle at the castle. Wyter was somewhat mysterious as well. He seemed to be holding back his fears and replacing them with optimism. Emma had noticed this from the day they met. Her powers were even strong enough to see a poser.

Emma took a while to discover something. She had no idea why everyone was risking their lives on this voyage? Was it because of the Harsie or Everstheee? But she came to realize each and every person was loyal to her. It would be only the commitment to their queen and their kingdom to be by her side. She felt the same way as well. With all the motivation present, Harsie and Everstheee would prosper.

"*Shining armor.*"

"Who said that?" asked Arsi.

"I don't know," said Derrick.

"*Knight*"

"Harsie? Is that you?" asked Yambai.

Everyone watched as Harsie began to speak again.

"The knight in shining armor," said Harsie with her body still and her face pale.

"What are you talking about?" asked Yambai.

"The *knight,*" said Harsie.

"What's she talking about?" asked Emily.

"I don't know," said Yambai. He addressed Harsie once more. "What knight? Speak to me!"

"The knight...," she said as she drifted back off to sleep.

"I wonder what she meant by 'the knight in shining armor," said Emma curiously.

"Sounds like a fairy tale to me," said Daniel.

"We can't worry about it now. Salari will take care of this," said Yambai.

He told everyone to go to the public baths and bathe and return for rest.

Salari had returned by nightfall tired and irritated. He had bought a lot of supplies such as books, maps, food, water and other items. He had also bought horses for the journey to the mountains. Emily and Derrick were to wait for him while the others rested.

"Mother spoke earlier," Emily announced.

"What did she say?" asked Salari as he brought in the stuff.

"She didn't necessarily wake, but she was muttering in her sleep."

"What did she say?" Salari repeated.

"Well...she was muttering about a knight in shining armor."

"Hmm...."

"What is it?" asked Derrick

"The knight in shining armor is a very power being. He can only be summoned by the greatest of mages."

"Has anyone ever summoned it?" asked Emily.

"The spell to summon it has never been found. It is said that this *knight* will bring justice to the lands and promise peace. It is also rumored that Olgath himself has seen the knight."

"This could be what we've been hoping for!" said Emily.

"Yes it could. It could give us the key to defeating Amethyst," said Salari

"But why would she bring this up now?" asked Derrick.

"I don't know," said Salari.

"Maybe she knows something about it," said Derrick.

"Right now it is not important. We must rest for tomorrow is a big day," said Salari.

Derrick, Emily, and Salari each left for their sleeping dwellings to rest for the journey to the Nexus mountains.

CHAPTER NINE
The Nexus Mountains

Emma tossed and turned in her sleep. She repeatedly heard Harsie's voice muttering about the knight. In her sleep she recalled something. It was the day that her parents died. It didn't occur to her until then that Reater and Malitus had in fact mentioned the knight in their letter. It was a clue. A clue to a mystery yet to be solved. She was struck by something.

Emma woke with a start. The sun was shining through the window of the room. The dream she had was so vivid that it had frightened her. Someone woke that morning to leave without the others. She didn't know how she knew this, but she had to see for sure. She threw the sheets off her and hurried down the stairs. She went into the room in which Harsie lay and saw nothing but a made up bed. She walked up the bed and a letter appeared in a flurry of static sparks from the top of her and landed squarely on the bed. Harsie wondered if Reatus and Malitus had done the same with their letters. Emma picked it up and began to read:

> *My place is not on this voyage, but another. I have left to complete the quest that is destined for me. Continue on to the Sky Mountains. The path of light will lead you to the Nexus Mountains. Follow the Nexus Mountains to the Alliance. Be safe and I shall see you again.*
> *Love,*
> *Harsie*

Emma clutched the letter in her hand. How could she leave them? After all that had happened. What is this "quest" she had to go on? She ran up the stairs to alert the others.

"I was not aware of the quest," said Arsi.

"Neither were any of us Arsi, she has made a choice and she has followed it," said Salari.

"What will we do now?" asked Rayziel.

"We will do as she asked," said Salari.

"Do you think her quest has anything to do with the knight?" asked Derrick.

"I don't know," said Salari.

"How did that letter appear when I got down there to her room?" asked Emma.

"That was a conditional document. Mages use it to leave messages when they can't deliver them themselves," said Derrick.

"We should leave now while it's still early," said Arsi.

"So be it. Let's go," said Salari.

Everyone packed their belongings to leave. Harsie had left without telling anyone of her voyage. It started to make Daniel on edge. Why did she leave after being in an almost two day coma? She always seemed mysterious at times and he wondered what she was truly doing. How were they going to reach the Nexus Mountains without her?

It occurred to him that her quest must be more important. The "knight" intrigued her. Had she gone in search of it or has she gone to fight Amethyst? They left the town waving at the courteous people in the village and Scion as they made their way outside the gate. The addition of horses helped a lot. They were on their way to the Nexus Mountains. After ten minutes of riding Daniel spoke to Emma.

"So why do you think she left?" whispered Daniel.

"I don't know. I *felt* her need to leave. She had something important to do," said Emma

"Do you think it's the knight?"

"The knight is an urban legend. It's not real."

"I don't think our mother is crazy."

"I didn't say that! It's just that she was dreaming."

"Dreams unlock many things within the mind, Emma."

"I don't think it's important. She may have gone back to fight Amethyst."

"She's too weak to fight Amethyst."

"She's the most powerful mage of Everstheee!"

"Not anymore now that Amethyst is here."

"What are you two talking about?" asked Derrick interrupting their secret conversation.

"Nothing," said Daniel quickly.

"Arsi?" asked Emma as she converged on him while they rode.

"What is it Emma?" he asked.

"Do you know where mother could have gone?" asked Emma.

"I know nothing."

Emma didn't have much of a liking to Arsi. He seemed to always be agitated by something. He happened to be one of the best mages protecting the queen. There were times when she thought he was lying about something. He was really good at hiding his emotions. He wasn't much on talking either, but more on actions. Emma felt he had jealousy toward Salari. Arsi had been acting in a way that gave Emma the impression he wanted to be in charge. She felt that they may not be on good terms with each other. Salari interrupted her thoughts when he began to speak. She rode to his side.

"Emma," he said.

"Yes?" asked Emma

"What is troubling you?"

Emma wondered how he knew she was troubled.

"I just wish I knew where mother went."

"I'm pretty sure it's important."

"Did she go to find the knight?" whispered Emma.

"The queen does not give me all her information," said Salari.

"You knew she was leaving?" asked Emma. It seemed strange the way he said it as if he knew she was leaving, but to where he did not know.

"Of course…so did you and Yambai," he whispered

"I guess that's another piece of divination."

"Yep."

"Why didn't you tell Arsi you knew?"

"It was best he did not know. His knowing would threaten the success of our journey."

"I guess so."

They had been riding for hours and Emma was starting to get hungry. They stopped for a short break to eat a few sandwiches. It would be another hour's ride until they reached the Sky Mountains. It was starting to get dark, but Salari insisted they continued.

Daniel and Emma got to know Emily better. She had become more sociable throughout the ride. She admitted to not liking the idea of new brother and sister, but they were cool now. Daniel and Emma had a short lesson in magic. Daniel learned the spell for Magic repelling shield and Emma learned the spell to gain a truth. Daniel was coming along well. He had gotten better at his aim and controlling his mana (to use only the amount needed and not too much to cause a quicker exhaustion). Yambai, Rayziel, and Arsi began to practice their magic "just in case" as they said. Salari looked over the map and was still dumbfounded about how to get to the Nexus Mountains. Everything seemed to go well until they got some more visitors.

"Salari!" Emily yelled.

"What is it?" he asked as he ran to her.

Salari saw that Mytred were unmistakably following them. He realized they shouldn't have stayed longer than they needed. He came up with only on idea.

"Get your stuff and get on your horse! Time to go!" he said as everyone began hustling to get their things and get on their horses. Before Salari made it to his horse, a ball of green energy hurtled toward him and missed him only by inches. He hopped on his horse and lead the others away.

They had made it away from the Mytred, but they were steadily behind them. They were riding fast and it was almost dusk. Something caught Salari's eye and he halted his horse. Everyone else stopped completely oblivious to his thoughts.

"Why did you stop?" asked Arsi.

"*The path of light will lead you in the right direction,*" Salari muttered to himself.

"What are you talking….?" Arsi began. He had seen it too. In front of them lie a path shimmered in light. It seemed to be beckoning to them. It held some doorway that seemed to be cutting into the mountain. Salari spoke to reassure everyone.

"The path of light is here. Let's move on." He told the others. The Mytred were getting closer. Salari was leading everyone to the path of light. It began pulling them in. It's brightness blinded everyone and no one could see clearly. As they got closer the light began to fade and it seemed like the light was gone. Salari began to halt, but he was absorbed into the mountain. The rest followed and all was dark, but somehow the moon could be seen clearly from below. There was little noise but water dripping onto the hard ground as well as the noises of unfamiliar animal life.

"What happened?" asked Emma.

"It would seem we were absorbed into the mountain," said Yambai.

"What now Salari?" asked Emily.

"We keep moving," said Salari.

"I don't see anywhere we can go," said Arsi defiantly.

"These are the Nexus Mountains," said Yambai as he pointed up. Everyone followed his finger. The moon and sky could be seen clearly from below. But they were inside a mountain. It didn't take long for someone to notice the other feature within.

"There are mountains inside this mountain!" exclaimed Daniel. He was correct. Mountains towered extremely high above them.

"Precisely," said Yambai. "The Sky Mountains are only here to camouflage that of the Nexus Mountains. The Sky Mountains are quite hollow it seems."

"So the Sky Mountains don't exist?" asked Emma.

"Pretty much," said Derrick.

"We need to move on before the Mytred realize we're in here," said Salari.

The night sky provided light and comfort as they pressed on. It was nice and calm inside the Sky Mountains. The ground was distinctly rock and it seemed a path had been lain out to follow for anyone who made it inside. Everyone was too tired to talk and too tired to care about not talking. Wyter, Rayziel, and Arsi had been silent for quite some time. Yambai could be heard praying in his gentle voice. Salari seemed to be angry, but he focused it on the journey. Although everyone else wasn't talking, the Dales were.

"I wish Arsi would chill out sometimes," said Daniel.

"He's always like this. You'll get used to it," said Emily.

"I hope so," said Emma. The path began to sink and they began to descend down it.

"I guess we're getting closer," said Derrick.

"I suggest we use a little magic for our own goods," said Emily.

"Ok. Are we going to have another lesson?" asked Derrick asked excitedly.

"Nope. I have something else in mind," said Emily.

Emily had convinced Emma and Daniel to spar on each other. It took a while for Emma to agree. Daniel was eager to try anything at that moment. After everyone stopped for the first rest, Emma and Daniel ate and met up in an open area surrounded by three tall peaks.

"The rules are," began Derrick. "There are no rules! Begin."

Daniel reacted quickly because he wanted to surprise Emma. He was charging his spell and speaking his incantation. *"Os fogos da Conexão vêm adiante!"* he yelled

Emma was already ready for that as she used her protection spell to absorb Daniel's fireball. She knew what he was going to do because she knew him so well. She began charging her spell while circling around him. *"Ich verlange Hilfe. Erlauben Sie mir, unwirklich zu sein!"* she yelled. At this her body broke apart and formed at least six different Emmas around Daniel. He looked really confused. He had something up his sleeve.

"Conexão! Chamo-o! Pare este objeto a tempo!" He screamed using the spell on every duplicate. Soon someone yelled. Emma had been hit by the freeze time spell, but it was from her neck down.

"That was genius," she said.

"Thanks," said Daniel.

"Can you release me?

"I wish I knew how," he said with a sly smile.

"Good job Daniel!" said Emily who was smiling at the situation.

"That was great. I didn't know you had it in you!" said Derrick as he ran up behind Emily.

"Thanks," said Daniel proudly. He enjoyed beating his sister with his small amount of knowledge.

"Hello! A little help here!" said Emma.

"*¡Pare este conjuro! ¡Hágalo vaciar!*" said Emily.

"Thanks," said Emma as the spell was dispelled and she was free to move. She was a bit numb though.

"Great job Daniel," said Emma.

"Thanks. You too," said Daniel.

There was a shrieking scream

"What was that?" asked Emma.

"I don't know. But we need to find out," said Derrick.

"Someone may be in trouble," said Emily.

"Let's go!" said Derrick.

There was another scream. They were getting close to the screams of the woman who was in trouble. Emma ran into the back of Derrick and realized what he was looking at. A young female mage had been cornered in the back of a mountainous wall by a strange looking beast. It had horns on its head, scales on its back and it was large and red. It looked sort of like a giant bird with scales. It was trying to eat the girl. She frantically tried to stun it, but nothing seemed to work. Derrick hurriedly ran to her to try and help, but the beast took a swing at him with its tail and he flew twenty feet into the air. Emily ran to see if he was ok. He had a bump on his head.

"He's ok!" she yelled back at Emma and Daniel who were staring at the spectral before them. The beast drew nearer to the girl and began to rapidly inch toward her and a giant spark of energy flew into to the beast knocking it backwards onto the hard ground. The tremors could be felt from the fall of the beast. The girl left her frightened stage onto confusion.

"What happened?" asked Daniel. He too was confused. "Where did that come from?"

"*I did it,*" said a man who walked up into the midst of Emma and Daniel. The man was tall and strongly built. He was dark-skinned with long hair and held a club in his hands. He did not look like any other person that Emma or Daniel had ever seen.

"Who are you and why are you here?" he asked impatiently.

"Uh….," started Daniel.

"They're here because of me," said the girl from behind.

"What are you talking about Cecil?" asked the man.

"The beast tried to kill me and they tried to help."

"They don't look from around here. You! How did you get here?" he asked Emily who was now next to Emma.

"*The Path of light,*" she said.

"How did you obtain this information?" asked the man.

"Queen Harsie of Everstheee," said Emily.

"And how do you know her?" asked the man.

"She's my mother," said Emily.

"Good answer," he said.

"What happened?" asked Derrick and he got up rubbing his head.

"This man is giving us trouble," she said.

"No. No trouble at all. I have been expecting you," he said.

"Who are you?" asked Emma.

"I am Chaos Aires. I am an energy wielder for the alliance," said Chaos.

"We need to get to the alliance," said Emily.

"So be it. Follow me," he said as he began to walk off.

"There are more of us," said Emily. "*You* follow me."

"So be it, Cecil…meet me at the alliance. I have some work to do," said Chaos.

"Yes Sir," she said obediently as she ran off in another direction thanking them in the process.

"Shall we continue?" asked Chaos.

"Let's go," said Emily.

Chapter Ten
The Arcane Alliance

Emily had led Chaos to the camp where the others were. They had stopped there and gotten the others to come along to the Alliance which the voyage was lead by Chaos. Salari was skeptical of this until he saw something on him. A symbol of some sorts. After that he immediately rallied the others to follow Chaos to the Alliance. On the way, Chaos explained that he was only skeptical of their presence. Not many were worthy enough to pass through the path of light. Only those with the purest of hearts were allowed through. Chaos explained many aspects of the path as well as the Arcane Alliance.

"So there's a big giant underground mountain dwelling as a base for the alliance?" asked Emma.

"Precisely. It is used to hide from those who threaten us," said Chaos.

"So who threatens you exactly?" asked Daniel.

"Myred, Swiverstheee, and large alliances of dark mages," said Chaos.

"Do you know where Harsie has gone?" asked Arsi butting in.

"No. I am sorry I do not know her whereabouts," said Chaos quietly.

"Why are you so wrapped on the whereabouts of Harsie?" asked Salari.

"I feel it my duty to know the whereabouts of our queen!" said Arsi in a vile tone.

"I think she can do what she wants. Stop bringing it up. It's bad enough she's already gone!" said Emma immediately. She felt so uncomfortable around Arsi. His interest in the queen's whereabouts gave her the feeling that is was more than what he was letting on. It was something he was hiding and she knew she would have to find out soon. Her powers were growing and as the hours went by she began to *feel* Arsi's thoughts, but they were not of anger, but of fear. Emma had been inadvertently staring at him when he spoke to her.

"Why are you gawking at me girl?" asked Arsi.

Emma was startled when he suddenly spoke to her. She was going to be honest and confess that she knows how he feels.

"Why are you afraid"? asked Emma

Arsi looked suspicious. "What nonsense is this?"

"I know what you're feeling….you're afraid because Harsie isn't here…why?" asked Emma

Arsi looked redder than a tomato at this question, but he soon mellowed down as he lowered his tone as to not attract the others.

"I just don't want to die. My powers are nothing compared to Harsie," he said nervously.

Emma realized that Arsi's anger was only to distract the constant fear in him. The fear in his eyes showed a desperate dependence on Harsie. There was something more.

"That's not all," Emma said

"Yes it is," said Arsi quickly

"NO….there is something you're not telling me…," said Emma

"Don't flatter yourself girl. I'd never tell you," he said.

"Well then. I'll get it my own way." she began. *"Geben Sie es, daß ich wünsche. Geben Sie es Wahrheiten Ihrer Lügen!."* Arsi was encumbered by a light. A strong urge to tell the truth came over him.

"She was supposed to keep her promise," he said.

"What promise?" asked Emma.

"I serve her, she protects me."

"Protect you from what?" asked Emma.

"Them," he said.

"Who are them?" asked Emma.

"Sorry Girl. Your spell is running out," he said.

"One more question. Where is Harsie?" she asked quickly.

"On that half-asked goose chase for the knight. She is so foolish." he said

"So she is searching for the *knight in shining armor*. Well….thanks for the info," said Emma.

"Don't tell a soul. It was not my intention to tell you this information," said Arsi.

"Fine. But I will find out this secret of yours if magic is necessary again," said Emma. Divination is an ancient magic used to find secrets, she was proud that once she rested she could probably eliminate the mystery in Arsi. But Arsi could wait because she became more concerned about Chaos who was leading them down the dark path that seemed to be getting more narrow. Daniel noticed it too.

"How much further?" he asked as they were walking down the path. His feet were hurting from walking so long on the hard rock ground. It was very rugged and he almost tripped over himself.

"Just a short distance," said Chaos.

"I'm getting tired of hearing this," said Emma.

"Well….I say what I can to keep you going. This time I really mean it. Here it comes now," said Chaos.

Everyone noticed that the darkness was starting to diminish and light overshadowed it. As they drew closer it became brighter as the light source became obvious to everyone. There was a lot of commotion going on as if approaching a bustling city filled with many people and tall buildings and people selling things on the streets. It was obvious that that was what they were heading towards. But no one expected what came next.

As they drew nearer, the light became immensely illuminate to where it made everyone squint to not take in too much of it. It appeared to be some form of matter. As if light was a corporeal entity, it formed a solid door made of photon-light energy. The immense light did not go dull for a second and then Chaos spoke.

"If you are worthy, the door will not hurt you," he said calmly.

"How could a wall of light hurt me," asked Daniel sarcastically.

"Well…it could make your heart explode," said Chaos humorously.

"Oh…thanks for the info, now I won't be nervous," said Daniel.

"We need to enter. Who goes first?" asked Salari impatiently.

"I'll go!" said Emily as she came from behind him and headed toward Chaos.

"Just walk through…if you aren't worthy, you will die a very painful death," said Chaos.

"Gotcha," said Emily as she walked up the wall and put her hand through. She yelped in pain as the door burned her hand.

"What's happening to her?" asked Emma immediately.

"The wall is made of light! It's going to be hot. If she makes it to the other side she'll be healed of any injuries immediately," said Chaos.

Emily continued and walked through the wall. "Whoa!!!" she said immediately from the other side.

"I'll go next!" Daniel said enthusiastically.

Daniel was ready to take on the next challenge as he walked past the others to come closer to the wall. He held his hands up to block the searing light and walked slowly to the wall. It got hotter as he hoped he wouldn't have a heat stroke before reaching it. After two long minutes of approaching the wall ever so slowly, Daniel finally touched the wall. He yelped instantly as the agonizing heat burned into his skin. He hated the feeling, but he knew he had to get in so he kept going inching into the wall that scolded him as he entered, he felt his hand reach the other side of the wall as he got most of his right arm in. On the outside he could feel a colder, more comfortable temperature that completely relinquished his pain in his hand. Something touched him. The hand suddenly forced him through the wall!! He felt so hot as the heat went cleanly through him and he finally reached the other side.

What Daniel saw next was beauty and amazement. He was standing on a cliff that overcast a vast land with lush green grasses and great large waterfalls that emptied into the river below. People were moving about and making commotion below as they went through their activities. A large building lie straight ahead from the path that lead from the cliff to large massive stairs to the temple made of pure white marble. He couldn't keep his mouth closed. He had never seen such a powerful sight. He was interrupted in his thoughts when someone spoke to him.

"You took way too long," said Emily furiously.

"Sorry….it was a little hot in there," said Daniel immediately.

"Well if you would have gone faster you wouldn't have been hot…I wasn't hot at all." said Emily.

"Whatever," said Daniel.

Emily and Daniel waited patiently for at least an hour for Arsi, Salari, Emma, Derrick, Wyter, Yambai, Rayziel, and Chaos to enter through the wall. They all did what Daniel did and take their time to embarrass themselves with pain that shouldn't occur if you rush.

"There are too many of us," said Chaos in an exhausted voice.

"I agree. That took way too long," said Derrick.

"Patience is a virtue," said Yambai.

"Not when you're ready to eat and rest," said Salari who had apparently lost his will to "carry on" without cause. He too was getting restless and appeared to show a sign of fatigue for the first time.

"Since when are you up for resting and eating?" asked Emily.

"I just want to rest so that we can sort everything out," said Salari.

"Sort what out?" asked Derrick.

"Now is not the time. Let us go to capital and speak with Nefarine on the matter at hand," said Salari as he walked off toward the cliffs to follow the paths to the capital. His life was to serve Harsie and she was gone. Had he grown a dependence on her as well as Arsi? There was more to say as soon as Nefarine, the head of the Alliance, would reveal to them the matter at hand.

CHAPTER ELEVEN
The Matter at Hand

It had been a long day and no one was in the mood to talk. The walls of the temple were made of hard marble and black slate as the floor. As they entered the temple, a figure from afar began to move toward them. He looked to be an old man with short, gray hair and a small mustache. He waved from afar. Suddenly he disappeared out of thin air and reappeared in front of Emma who bumped into him. Emma looked up to see the man and of course she asked a question.

"Hello…umm…who are you?" asked Emma.

"Emma! Do not speak so…," Salari started.

"It's alright," said the old man. He had bulging muscles most old men didn't have and he wore a festive robe with the sleeves off and sandals. "I am Nefarine Terit, head of the Arcane Alliance," he said properly.

"Excuse me sir. I am Emma Dale," she said.

"Queen Harsie's daughter no doubt. And this must be Daniel," said Nefarine looking at him.

"Yes sir," Daniel said shaking his hand.

"Nefarine," said Salari.

"Ah Salari. It has been years," he shook Salari's hand wholeheartedly. "I hope everything is going well. Where is old Harsie anyway?"

"She has left us to join another venture oblivious of our knowledge."

"I see," he frowned slightly. "Well. I guess you are all tired and we can discuss later," he said as he vanished in thin air.

"Where did he go?" asked Daniel

"I believe he went to his room," said Salari dully.

"He's a very powerful mage," Emma pointed out.

"Yes he is," said Salari.

"How do you know him if you've never been to the alliance?" asked Daniel.

"I met him long ago when I was a child. But that's for another day," said Salari.

"I think it's time to get some rest for tomorrow," said Yambai solemnly.

"I will meet you at the inn later for a little chat. I think you'll be fairly interested in what I have to say," said Chaos.

"Fine come by later and we can see what you have for us," said Salari who had forgotten that Chaos was even there as well as the other members of the fairly large party.

After meeting the strangely powerful mage, Nefarine, the group found themselves guided through the vast fields of the Arcane Alliance to an odd looking cottage that was meant to be an inn. The air was dense as if under great pressure, but it didn't bother anyone. Children played near the inn entrance and a little boy slowly approaches. Somehow he knew who they were.

"You're Emma and Daniel Dale right?" asked a little boy.

"How do you know that?" asked Emma curiously.

"Well…everyone knows about you two!" said the little boy cheerfully as he ran off.

"That was strange," said Daniel.

"He only knows because he has inner eye," said Yambai.

"Really?" asked Emma

"The Alliance holds connections with the most powerful of people be them old or young. Training is offered here and I highly suspect you will signed up."

"Don't worry…it'll be fun!" said Emily.

"She's lying you know? It'll be extremely difficult, but it will prepare you," said Derrick as they entered the inn.

Inside was a large circular room that held chairs of the sort, books, and other knickknacks that were spread across the walls. Salari walked up to the desk in the center of the room to speak to the counterman.

"How much are the rooms?" asked Salari.

"Oh…they are free to fellow mages of the Alliance," said the clerk. The clerk was bald and tall with a slick smile. Some of his teeth were missing as he smiled confidently.

"Thank you. You'll need to accommodate all of us. Our party is quite large," said Salari.

"Of course," said the clerk. He soon began a spell out of the blue. *"Envoyez ces mages à leurs pièces par la porte que je crée!"* Soon a door materialized out of thin air.

"Through this door," said the man.

Everyone walked through the door to find their room on the other side. It was a large room with eight bunk beds (too many for their count), a kitchen, a dining room, and windows that clearly showed they were inside one of the mountains surrounding the Alliance Courtyard. Salari began to tell them about such things as the name of the village, Cyr. Cyr was the village in which loyalties of the Alliance lived and thrived.

"So Cyr is this village?" asked Emma.

"It's pretty nice actually. I hear they have an excellent training program for young mages," Salari responded.

"Yes we hear," said Daniel. "I bet you signed us up too."

"You bet your boots. It starts tomorrow at around seven and I want you to attend it while the rest of us go to see Nefarine and find out what we need to do next. I want you to be careful here. These kids may seem innocent, but they know their magic. Don't challenge anyone…"

"Ok," said Emma and Daniel at the same time. A gust of air alerted them to Chaos who had come through the door into their room. He looked nervous.

"Sorry I took so long, traffic was beastly….literally," said Chaos.

"What exactly do you need from us?" asked Arsi rudely.

"A mission. I need a few of you," said Chaos hurriedly.

"What kind of mission?" asked Salari.

"There has been rumor that a great mage has been seen in the outskirts of Absirthee," he said breathing hard.

"Which mage?" asked Salari.

"A mage by the name of Siry Dale," said Chaos.

"Father?" asked Emily.

"What could this mean?" asked Derrick.

"He was seen there just a few days ago. We think he is hiding from Swiverstheee," said Chaos.

"We have to go on this mission Salari. We have to find him," said Emily.

"I will allow this only because we can't afford to lose him. Wyter, Emily, Rayziel, and Derrick will accompany you to Absirthee. Daniel, Emma, Yambai, Arsi, and myself will remain here until ordered otherwise," instructed Salari.

"We leave at dawn. I will come for you then," Chaos said as he left the room.

"Father," said Daniel.

"Yes our father. We will find him no matter what," said Emily with dedication.

"I think it's best that we go and find him. Maybe mother is doing the same thing," said Derrick.

"Caution is recommended. Absirthee may be a peaceful place, but many dangers exist," said Yambai.

Daniel was once again plagued with lack of sleep. His thoughts kept him from sleep. It was kind of strange to hear of his father whom he knew nothing about. His mother had left and now his father was found. It was a change for him. Now he was left just with Emma. Yet again, it was just him and Emma. Not that he didn't like Emma, it was just that after all that had happened, he knew he would still be just with Emma and no one else. He didn't like the fact that Emily and Derrick were going, but they had to. They were powerful enough to make it and would give him a chance to learn from his own mistakes.

From the start, his father had been a mystery to him, and now he had the chance to get to know him. It was time for him to learn of his roots so that he can become the person he had always wanted to be. He wanted to be brave, kind, passionate, smart, and agile as a person. Some of those things were hard for him to deal with, but now was the time for him to become a better person deep down.

The night was diminished as the sun rose above the Sky Mountains. Daniel was the first to awake. He didn't get much sleep, but it was worth the thoughts present in his head. A lot of things were going on. Today they would go to their first class about magic. He hoped he would make friends and learn more about the mysteries of magic. He guessed there wasn't much left to magic but more spells. Emma and Daniel ate breakfast while Emily, Derrick, Rayziel, and Wyter prepared to leave. Derrick approached Daniel as they began to exit the inn.

"Daniel," said Derrick."I want you to watch yourself and Emma."

"I should protect her at any costs," Daniel said acknowledging.

"Also because she's the key to finding mother. Her powers are closely tied to people. I don't know if she knows that just yet."

"Ok. I got you."

"Be careful. I'll come back with dad by any cost," said Derrick boldly.

"I hope you do too."

Derrick then placed his equipment on his back and followed the others outside of the inn. Daniel watched them as they made their way back through the path of light. He figured as much that it would be easier leaving than coming. Now it was time to leave for class. He packed his spell book, paper, and writing utensils. He was ready for any challenge.

"Welcome to class. I am your teacher Mr. Qatu," said the teacher. "It is my job to train you all for an immense amount of magic and first I want to see what you can do."

He then ordered them to form a line ten feet in front of his desk. Lucky for him he was using the Mausoleum as a classroom. His plan was to launch a fireball at each student and grade their reaction time, spell usage, and aim. Many of the students were frightened, but it didn't seem that bad once they got in line.

"What are you going to do when the ball comes?" asked a kid behind Daniel.

"Uh. I don't know. I guess it depends on what I think then," said Daniel.

"My name is Alexander, how about you?" said the bright kid.

"I'm Daniel, nice to meet you," he replied. He had never been that prone to meeting new people. This kid was a little younger, blonde, and he had an odd crooked smile. Daniel wondered how long he would go on before Mr. Qatu was ready.

"What kind of mage are you?" asked Alex.

"I don't really know yet, I just do different things. What about you?" he replied.

"I'm an alterist mage. I can change the form of things. It's really hard to do," he said.

"Cool," said Daniel. He wondered exactly when they would begin, but it came shortly afterward.

Mr. Qatu stood in front of his desk with a clipboard and began to speak.

"I will call you one by one from my clipboard. I will fire a single fireball. If you can block it, I will be pleased. Now the first name on my list…*Daniel Dale.*

Daniel hadn't even had time to think about what he wanted to do. But he guessed it wouldn't be too bad. He slowly walked up the "X" marked in the spot in front of Mr. Qatu. Several seconds after Daniel arrived at the spot, Qatu began his spell.

"Les feux de Connexion viennent en avant!" he yelled.

The fireball came so fast that Daniel did the only spell that came to mind. One of which he knew from memory.

"Conexão! Chamo-o! Pare este objeto a tempo," yelled Daniel.

The fireball instantly stopped in midair.

"How impressive."

"Thank you sir," said Daniel feeling accomplished.

"I think you have talent Daniel, thank you for showing everyone that. I will give you extra points."

"Thank you sir."

"Emma Dale."

Emma approached the "X". She was ready for the fireball. It would be so easy to block it. She was having trouble figuring out which spell to use. There were a lot in her head and she naturally knew them. She was pleased with Daniel, he did quite well for his first time using that spell under pressure. He was developing at almost as fast a rate as her, but it just seemed more like Daniel became more enthralled in learning the craft and became somewhat dedicated to learn it. She knew what spell she was going use now. She finally made it to the scene.

"Are you ready Ms. Dale?" Qatu asked.

"Yes Sir."

There was not a waste of time as Mr. Qatu put his clipboard down and began his spell.

"Les feux de Connexion viennent en avant!" he said

Emma just stood there as if nothing happened. The ball made it quite close to her until she placed a spell upon herself.

"Ich verlange Hilfe. Erlauben Sie mir, unwirklich zu sein!" she yelled.

Emma's appearance was blurred and the fireball went through the false Emma clone made by her spell.

"Interesting. Although that was a little unwise don't you think?" Qatu commented.

"What do you mean?" she asked as she scratched her head.

"Well. Who's to say that the real you wouldn't be in the same spot as the target?"

"I don't know," she said with confusion.

"I won't accept this. This was clearly not a true effort. I will only give you half credit." he said bluntly

Emma had never been given half credit for anything. She felt so upset. It wasn't fair that he was so critical of her magic. But maybe he was right. It didn't seem like her to be so stupid about something so simple. She was doing it again. She was being too prideful. In school she was the most popular nerd, but people didn't truly like her because she was too arrogant about her grades. It taught her again that she had to refuse to be that person she left behind. It was time to start new.

"Thank you Ms. Dale. You may sit down," Mr. Qatu continued.

The next few hours went by quickly as other mages did their method of defying the fireball Qatu created. To Daniel's surprise, Alex had turned

Qatu's fireball into a dove. His magic was very powerful. Qatu thought it was very creative. Erianna, who had just met Emma earlier, used her powers to call upon a spirit to save her from the fireball. She was a shaman mage. She held powers over the spirit world and dreams. Qatu was pleased to have a shaman to train. Soría, another friend used her powers of the mind to make Qatu confused and aim his spell at the wall. It took a lot of her power, but she stood her ground. Other mages also went up, and Qatu recognized their powers. Qatu was really pleased with his students.

"I am so happy to have you all," he began. "I have never had such a variety of mages in my group. You all have powerful standards and I will be glad to teach. Right now I will give you all textbooks to learn more about other types of mages. As you all see, everyone is different."

Qatu then passed out books to the students, *Mages of All Kinds,* everyone immediately opened the book.

"I want you all to write about your type as a mage and give a presentation. Tomorrow night we will have our weekly practice and spell hall. I hope you all have a great afternoon!"

Class had ended mid-afternoon. Daniel and Emma were wondering exactly where Salari was, they had the impression he would retrieve them from the class.

"I thought he was going to come get us," said Daniel.

"Maybe he went to speak to Nefarine."

"Let's go."

Emma and Daniel walked the thirty minute walk back to the inn to find Salari, who had not come to see them once. He may have been busy talking to Nefarine because he was there when they arrived.

"Ah…you have returned!" said Nefarine as he greeted them.

"I thought you were coming!" Daniel interjected to Salari.

"Well…something came up," he replied.

"What happened exactly?" asked Daniel in somewhat of a rude tone.

Salari didn't speak anymore. He walked immediately through to the door, opened it and went through. He seemed really upset.

"What happened?" asked Emma

Nefarine looked at Emma consolingly and mimicked Salari. He went through the door and disappeared into the room. Daniel and Emma looked at each other and followed through. When they entered, Salari was bending over one of the beds and a young mage was resting. He was sweating profusely. Emma and Daniel approached and Nefarine spoke to them.

"His name is Kero," he began. "He was found just inside the barrier, exhausted, sweating. We know his name because it's on his cloaks. And the fact that Salari knows him. He was captured by Myred during the Invasion of Olgath Castle. He was a dear friend and quite a useful mage."

"What kind of powers does he have?" asked Daniel.

"Electro kinesis-the power to manipulate electricity," said Nefarine.

Salari had wetted a wash cloth to cool Kero's sweltering head. He got up after laying the rag on his head and walked toward Daniel and Emma.

"This is why I was late," he said as he walked out of the room through the door.

"Where is he going?" asked Daniel.

"To get a medic to see what's wrong with him," said Nefarine.

Emma didn't say anything. In fact she was stunned beyond belief. She had already been acquainted with Kero in a vision she had had. He was a mage that had been trapped under the clutches of Myred. He rebelled against them and was constantly punished, testing them with his life. Her silence was not oblivious in the senses of the others. For Nefarine questioned her.

"I know him from a vision."

"What do you mean?"

"He was tortured. I know why he is sick like this."

Daniel was covertly listening in on their conversation. To have visions like that was a burden and he knew he himself could not carry it as his sister did. Daniel was curious as to what else she saw in these strange visions. Now wasn't the time to bring it up because Salari had returned with the medic. The medic wore a uniform that was made of silk and white and a belt around it that was used to hold herbs and such. He quickly approached the ill and spoke to Salari who stood opposite of him.

"It looks as if he has been poisoned," said the healer.

"I don't know. I've seen poisoned and this is not it." said Salari.

"What do you think?"

"This is no ordinary poison sir, like *Tainted Extract*."

"You know your medicine, but I say it's *Serum of Inability*."

"It's neither," said a voice. The two looked up from their conversation at Emma who stood behind them in a determined stance. It was this outburst that lead Salari to a place of uncertainty and unexplained phenomena. Salari said nothing at first, allowing the healer to beat him to the first plausible interrogative.

"What do you mean child?" asked the healer.

"I know everything to what poisoned him and who did it," she said.

"And can you explain how you've obtained this information?" asked Salari astonished.

"In my vision," she began. "He was poisoned by Amethyst himself. He was being tortured for being rebellious, trying to escape over and over again. He was given a toxin. I remember the label on the bottle. It said *Serum of Tainted Souls*. Amethyst expected immediate results, but Kero was too strong. One night he was able to slip past a guard. His powers had been drained, but he made it all the way here. I saw him coming every night since mother's departure. He's sick like this because of the symptoms."

"Of course. Young child. This explains everything," the healer said as he beamed down at her.

"Emma. I want you to tell me all your visions. When the time comes they will be an asset to us all," said Salari firmly.

Emma didn't feel up to that. There were so many things she had seen. She didn't want her visions revealed. But now her opinion didn't matter. She wanted to help Kero. And it would be her vision and insight to fuel the quest to saving his life.

"This is a grave matter though." began the healer. "This is the most difficult of poisons to cure. The power of this serum is stronger than anything I've seen and there is not a very good chance that he'll live. The only thing we can do is make him comfortable unless his body fights it off. He may be able to help himself. His power could nullify the effects of it. But he'd have to be awake to do it."

"What about reflexes?" asked Daniel. He had slowly made his way back into the conversation.

"Hmm. I don't know. I can't think of anything that would make him use his power subconsciously. Unless we tell him to, but how are we to tell him if he is in a deep sleep?"

Something struck Emma in the head. As if a light bulb appeared over her head, she spoke confidently.

"I know someone who might be able to," she said.

Emma's plan was to get her friend, Erianna. She didn't know if she could literally dream hop as a small percentage of mages could do, but it was worth a shot.

Salari was not open fully to the idea because he didn't want to endanger anyone, but a little reassurance and persuasion swayed him to the other side. Erianna was summoned and came quickly to hear of her task. This shocked her.

"What do you mean?" she asked.

"We need you to go into his head and try to get him to use his power. Challenge him to a duel or something," said Salari.

"I know that," she began. "It's just that I have never done it, only my mom. But she's not here anymore. I only know how people get in, but I don't know if I can."

"Erianna. You can do this. I know you can. Just concentrate and try. If you want I'll go with you," Emma said.

"Are you sure? I don't want to mess it up," Erianna said twiddling her thumbs. She was such a nervous girl. "Fine I'll do it, but I can't guarantee anything."

"Thanks!" said Emma. "Let's go!"

CHAPTER TWELVE
Inside a Troubled Mind

Erianna requested that a few items be gathered before they could go into Razor's subconscious. They would need candles for serenity and water for purity as to create a calm and serene environment to prevent any mental breaks or uncontrollable convulsions. Erianna was soon ready to begin as she stood in front of him with Emma beside her. As protection for her spell, a circle was formed of a compost of salt and rosemary to promote balance and prevent influence of malevolent spirits. Kero would also have one around him as well for the same reasons and necessities.

"I must warn you," Erianna began. "This may endanger you. I don't want anything wrong to happen."

"Why would you say that?" Emma asked with frustration. Such pessimism did not go over well for her.

"I have never done this before. I don't really know what I'm doing. I just don't want you to think that I know what I'm doing when I don't."

"I'll be fine," she reassured her.

Erianna left the circle (that had no physical barriers) to get her spell book. The book had an odd vibe about it. Its strange markings seemed to be moving, unless it was just the lighting. The markings etched the front of the book formed a large circle with star-like figures within the circle. It had been clearly handed down. Erianna grabbed the book from its pedestal behind them and returned with it flat across her hands. Its pages were old and antique. They ruffled from the breeze that had found its way inside the room.

"Ready?" she asked.

"The book wouldn't be a good idea if you plan on saying a spell," said Emma informatively. "It'll block your aim."

"Shaman mages don't really need as much spell charging. I don't need aim. All I need is concentration and I can have a perfect spell. It's quite an advantage for me at least on spells like this."

"Sorry about that. I guess I need to start reading that book Mr. Qatu assigned. It might keep me from making stupid mistakes."

"It's ok. Don't worry about it."

Erianna started to read from her book. It emitted strange lights as she began to say the spell. Her voice echoed throughout the room. Daniel and the others were watching silently.

"*¡Sómsis! Tómenos a la mente de nuestro amigo. ¡¡Permita que nosotros lo limpiemos del mal!!*"

The star-like shapes on the book's cover seemed to remove themselves from the cover of the book and encompass Emma and Erianna. They began to move faster and faster and energy began to grow. It was a few seconds after Erianna said the spell that Emma started to feel dizzy and in no time, she blacked out. Her body felt like dead weight now that she had collapsed, but she had felt something stretch. It was as if her body was being stretched, but in a sense it was her essence of being. For she felt the pull as she tumbled into the mind of Kero. It wasn't what she expected at all.

Emma touched the wall, but it was strange because the walls were hollow. It had appeared that this castle wasn't even real. She looked up to see that the there was no ceiling but clear blackness. She explored more by walking on toward a fountain near her. It was a beautiful fountain of a mage fighting a strange figured creature. The fountain was beckoning her to have a sweet drink of its waters. She was attracted to it fully by its luminescence. She attempted to back away but found herself walking forward regardless and being called out by an invisible person. She scooped her hand down to get a drink.

"*I wouldn't do that if I were you,*" said a voice.

Emma turned around to see Erianna looking squarely at her.

"Drinking from that fountain will only make you a part of this castle, fake, nothing. Don't be tempted. If you were to drink, you could become attached to this castle. I don't think that's a good idea."

"I don't know what happened. One minute I was looking and the next…"

"Don't worry about it. Let's go."

"Which way do we go?" Emma asked looking around. There were so many hallways and wrap a rounds. It was going be hard to determine which way to go and if that way would be valid.

Erianna pulled out a strange circlet. It was a miniature dream catcher. Dream catchers had been popular when Emma was younger. Little kids would use it to protect themselves from nightmares. It always helped her sleep. It had been made into a chain that could be worn, melded in metal. Emma took it as some sort of amulet. It glowed in Erianna's hand and she took it out and put it around her neck.

"The *Amulet of Conya*" she said. "It will help us find the source of his subconscious. It will direct us in the right way and protect us from any being that has no solid form.

"Ok. What is this place exactly?" asked Emma.

"I'd say it's the most important place he's ever been. I'd say it's somewhere where he either thrived or struggled."

"So. Which way?"

"Left would work. I feel a strengthening in that area. Let's go down this corridor to see what we can find."

The corridor was lit dimly by torches split two feet apart from each other and sprang to life to emit fire as they drew nearer. The corridor grew wider after minutes of walking into an opening that was indistinctly identified as the dining room. There were large tables that extended from the front end of the room to intersect a long table. It was similar to the largest table where people of authority would eat. Over the table there was an insignia present of a black shield and lance in a strong red background. Emma thought it looked familiar. There were other insignias there as well. There were also different carvings on the floor.

Emma and Erianna walked further into the room looking for a clue of some sort. As they walked farther, a large shadow consumed theirs, bulging over their tiny shadows. They rebounded to see the shadow rise from the floor and take corporeal form. It was now a solid shadow.

"Why are you here?" asked the shadow. It had now become the form of a man's shadow with its voice incoherent and sounding as if under water.

"What are you?" asked Emma.

"That is not for you to know. Answer my Question!" spoke the being.

"We're here to save a friend! Where is he?" Erianna spoke furiously.

"You won't find him!" he said. He spoke in a very intense tone. *"Your fate ends here and my reign will soon begin."*

Erianna started panting hard. She was looking at the being now with fearful eyes. She started to sweat quickly as if sickened to be in the presence of the being.

"What's wrong?" asked Emma.

"What I've always feared. It's a morphus (an evil shape shifter that corrupts dreams and the subconscious). He is the only thing that my amulet cannot protect us from because he has a solid form. We have to fight it!"

"How?"

"Like we would fight anyone else. We can use magic to weaken it. Destroying it is a mystery. When he becomes weakened, the Morphus's evil energy won't block my good energy. Therefore, when we weaken him, my amulet can guide us directly to Kero."

"Fighting me will be futile!! You are weak mages," the man said. The being had now become a strapping young man clothed in battle gear. He had formed skin, hair, and clothing all in a matter of seconds. "Shall we begin?"

"Of course," said Erianna. She had become unusually confident at this moment. "You'll back me up?" she asked Emma.

Emma didn't say anything. She didn't know how to answer this question. She had never fought something so foul before. She just felt better observing until Erianna needed help.

Erianna reached into the pocket of her robe and pulled out a small circular object. Once again, it was a small dream catcher. She closed her eyes and touched it with her thumb. It grew from the size of a quarter the size of a chakra. About the size of a dinner plate. She clutched it in her hand, ready for battle. It's sharp edges made it a formidable weapon.

"Humph. I'll fight yet," he said. Out of the air a large sword formed. He caught it in mid-air. Although a sword appeared, he clutched a dagger behind his back and swiftly threw it at Erianna's head. Erianna, with lightning-fast reflexes, hurled the chakra to intercept the dagger. She reached into her pocket once more and made another one. She had a massive amount of those chakras. She retaliated by hurling the chakra at him. It narrowly missed him and rebounded from interception of the wall and was caught by Erianna.

Emma just watched. It just felt as if this wasn't her fight. Erianna was so determined to fight. This had to be of some significance to her. It seemed that she couldn't help. Fighting a creature was something she was not experienced in. She felt prideful for Erianna. She was such an agile and brilliant fighter. She kept hurling her chakra one by one, but she couldn't get a good hit. The battle seemed to be effortless.

"Why won't you get hit? Who sent you?" Erianna asked the man agitated.

"I cannot reveal that my dear. It would ruin my business. You see. Power is to be gained when I complete this job. More power will make me stronger," he snickered.

"Fine. I guess we'll have to play hard ball," Erianna remarked as she put her chakra behind her on a holder on her back. She put up her hands and closed her eyes. She was starting a spell. *"¡Tysir le convoco! ¡Venga a mi ayuda!."* At the completion of this spell nothing happened.

"Ha. I see nothing from that spell!" he laughed.

As if he had just jinxed himself, a strong gust of wind emerged. It steadily attempted to draw him backwards. It was like being in a strong blizzard struggling to fight against it. Erianna used this as an advantage to get him to talk.

"Who sent you?" she repeated. Tysir the spirit of wind was transparent within the gale. It whistled excitedly, making Erianna speak loudly against the noise.

"An evil man with deep blue eyes!" the man yelled against the wind.

He was struggling to keep his footing. The wind was strong and close to knocking him off his feet.

It took Emma half a second to realize who he was talking about. She knew exactly who had sent this creature to torture Kero's mind. Emma now understood that the battle had something to do with her after all. She now knew how to weaken him. It was another trance of thoughts that told her the spell in her head. Her spell echoed loudly through the wind.

"Entzünden Sie sich! Ertränken Sie diese Finsternis. Schwächen Sie ihn mit Ihrer Sauberkeit und Charme!"

A strong burst of light emitted from Emma. Rays of light gathered around the being, smothering him. He screamed in agony. He fell from exhaustion. Tysir became corporeal. Erianna nodded and the spirit vanished.

"That's a cool power," Emma remarked.

"Thanks." said Erianna. "We need to find Kero! My amulet will lead us the way!" Erianna hastily took off her amulet, placing it on the floor.

"¡Dirija nosotros al perturbado!" she told it. Immediately, the amulet sprang to life rising from the ground and levitating in mid air. "Let's follow it" said Erianna.

Erianna and Emma ran after the amulet, following it during every twist and turn throughout the various corridors.

Exhaustion was soon getting the best of them after ten minutes of running. They were panting hard and their legs were starting to hurt. They kept up with the amulet until it sped up at an incredible speed. In the distance there was a loud thump. Emma and Erianna made it to a door. This door had the amulet attached to it. It was lured to whatever was on the other side. Erianna pried the amulet from the door and replaced it around her neck.

"Ready?" she asked.

"Just give me a few seconds to catch my breath," she said panting. After a few seconds she spoke once more, not panting this time. "Ok. More ready then I was fighting that morphus."

She opened wide the door. As they entered torches blew a lit. The lighting was dim throughout the room. In it, were various things such as a bed, dressers, maps, and a variety of other things. One thing that stood out was the exhausted Kero chained to the wall. He had been there for quite some time it seemed. He looked fatigued and meek. He looked up in surprise to see them.

"Why are you here? Who are you?"

"We're here to save you," said Erianna. She walked up to the chains attempting to remove them.

"I *can't* leave," he said slowly.

"Why not?" asked Emma

"He won't let me. The serum won't let me leave this place."

"He who?" Erianna asked slowly. She looked into his deep brown eyes. Contemplating his thoughts.

"Amethyst," he began. "This serum leaves me trapped inside this castle to die. His servant won't let me leave. His morphus."

"We've weakened the morphus," Erianna stated. "This castle must be your mental image of the Castle of Oltent. You can only leave if the serum is destroyed. Your power can release you. All you have to do is use your power on yourself."

"I'm not strong enough. There's no way I can do it."

"Yes there is," Emma said determined. "Duel me. If you want to get out of here. I want to see how strong you say you aren't."

"No," he said. He looked up to her and was lost in her eyes. He couldn't escape her emerald eyes. They gave him the courage to fight when he admitted weakness. They comforted him in a way that only a loved one could, someone devoted to him and determined to preserve his life.

"We don't have all day! You need to decide before that morphus comes! He won't stay down for long," interrupted Erianna.

"Fine. I'll do it," he said impatiently.

"Befreien Sie meinen. Freund von seinen Ketten"

Kero's chains were shattered from Emma's spell and he now stood on his feet, placing his battle gear on, preparing for a fight.

"Emma will spar with you now. I'm not going to watch I'll stay here. I will be concentrating on where the morphus is at all times. We can't fight here. This room is too small. Let's find another one."

Kero walked toward another door. His delicate red robes ruffled as he walked. His boots clashed on the floor. He wore an artillery tunic over his red robe. His black, long hair came down to his shoulder oscillating on his back. Kero opened the door. What he led Emma to was a great main hall; Quite suitable for battle.

"Ready to fight?" Emma asked.

"Yes," He said as he picked up a sword from the nearest wall. He positioned himself opposite of Emma. He put the sword in an empty hilt on his hip.

"I suggest you get a weapon," he told her.

Emma had never even touched a weapon of any kind to let alone use one. She only knew magic. It now occurred to her the importance of melee combat. Combining the two was a great benefit especially if you were too tired for magic. She had no other choice. She picked up a set of a strange looking weapon. She remembered it being in her World History book, the Japanese sai. It was similar to daggers.

"Ready?" he asked.

"Yeah. Of course."

Kero made the first move. He combined his hands through his fingers and closed his eyes. He spoke one single word.

"Kosten!"

After this, his body began to make static noises. Electricity streamed through his body, his eyes. He was ready for battle. He focused his eyes towards his opponent, determined and ready. In the blink of an eye he ran towards her with incredible speed.

"Blitzfaust!" he screamed as he took a strike at her. Emma wasn't ready, but her intuition told her to lean to the right, causing Kero to miss her by several inches. His lightning fist dissipated after the failed strike. He looked up at her stunned. How could he have narrowly missed?

Emma too was surprised, but she realized it was the natural thing of her. To see something before it happened and be aware of the only way to predict it. Divination was a powerful branch of magic. It was so that she knew exactly how to defeat him. Only time would be a factor in her victory.

"How did you do that?" he asked.

"My little secret," she winked at him.

Kero made another attempt. This time he would try something new. He extended his hand out.

"Blitzschock!" he yelled.

Emma was ready. She rolled out of the way causing his strike to hit the wall behind her.

"Blitzschock!" he repeated.

This time she wasn't ready. She was struck on the leg. The searing pain burned her skin, luckily she was wearing thick clothing. She had to be careful next time. Her powers were working on and off because she was already drained from weakening the Morphus. She couldn't make the same mistake. She got up and whispered a spell to herself. So that Kero could not hear.

"Geben Sie mir Kenntnis von meiner Waffe. Geben Sie mir die Fähigkeit, um zu kämpfen," she whispered to herself. A spell that would allow her to fight with her weapons. A new spell made up; It was derived from divination. She didn't know how long it would last, but made it worth while. She took her sai and charged toward Kero swiftly. At that time, Kero removed his sword from its hilt and blocked the colliding Emma. They met between their weapons.

"You're strong," he told her. "How do you fight like this?"

"You'd like to know," she said slyly. She was starting to feel weak now. Her strength was not equal to his. He was forcing her down to the ground. Emma was looking through her mind for another way out.

"Hemmen Sie den Angriff meines Feinds!" she said with difficulty. *"Zwingen Sie ihn weg"*. Kero was immediately flung twenty feet away through the air. He was hurt after plummeting against the hard castle floor. He was trying to get up, but his leg hurt. After a few attempts he got up, angry. Erianna came bursting through the door.

"It's coming!" she exclaimed. "We need to get out!"

"Wait," said Emma. "Something is about to happen. I think I'm about to win.

"Blitzbach!" he exclaimed from behind. Emma turned around to see a strong stream of electrical energy heading towards them. It was aimed at Erianna.

"Look out!" Emma screamed as she pushed her out of the way,

making herself the new target. *"Reflektieren Sie die Kraft von meinem Feind. Machen Sie es berechnet zu viel seinen Körper."* The stream of electricity was absorbed completely, and as it did so, it emitted back to him. It was overcharging his body with electricity, more than his body could take. He now had sparks flying from his body. The castle was starting to fade.

"It's working!" exclaimed Erianna. "We need to leave before he wakes up. *Vuélvanos a nuestras propias cuerpos. Seperate de éste.*

In a flash of hot light, Emma and Erianna were propelled back to their bodies. It was over now, Kero would live and the morphus inside Kero's mind would be punished for his failure by his master, Amethyst.

Emma opened her eyes. She was once again in the darkened room. The air was strangely scented with the distant fragrance of the incense from earlier. Emma sat up and looked next to her, looking for Erianna. She must have gotten up, because she wasn't there.

"BOO!!"

Emma jumped.

"Erianna don't do that!" yelled Emma.

"I couldn't resist! Just wanted to scare you," she explained.

"Why are you so happy?" she asked in surprise. Erianna was rarely one to show her emotions so vividly.

"Look," she said pointing to Kero's empty bed.

"Where is he?" Emma asked.

"He went to see Nefarine with the others," she began. "He said he had valuable information for us. He knows something about Swiverstheee. They told us to meet them as soon as you woke up. Come on."

It was not too far a walk. They arrived in minutes. Their feet echoed throughout the hall as they entered. From the distance, Emma made out the others from afar. They were standing near a platform from which Nefarine stood, full of energy. As they approached Emma heard Kero talking to the others. He spoke with great confidence. He stopped talking and walked straight up to Emma.

"Emma," he cleared his throat in nervousness. "I want to thank you and Erianna personally for helping me fight for my life, literally. Your fighting is really good, he winked at Emma.

"Thanks for helping me help you. I was more than willing to save you." Emma looked rather flattered under the bright sunlight. He eyes glimmered in its rays. She stared at Kero for a while until Nefarine interjected.

"Kero," he said. "What is this information you were so justly going to reveal?"

"I apologize. I just wanted to thank my heroes."

"Of course. My apologies, but we do need to get to the information."

"You're not going to like it," he said honestly.

"Try me," said Nefarine.

Kero led the others to the room adjacent to the hall entrance. It was Nefarine's office. It was composed of a library and study. There were various books, scrolls, maps, and other such things. Everyone entered behind Kero. Daniel closed the door after them.

"Why lead us here?" Arsi asked.

"This news should not be spread, it will cause a panic," said Kero.

"Out with it! Tell us your news!" exclaimed Nefarine. He was quite impatient at this point.

Kero sighed. "Amethyst, Vicousir's knight, now controls all of Swiverstheee, and becoming the new leader of Myred."

"What is this you speak of?" asked Nefarine concerned.

"Vicousir was killed by Amethyst the night I escaped," he said.

"You lie child!" erupted Nefarine.

"I don't lie!" he spoke out. "I'll tell you what happened, and then you'll believe me."

"He's telling the truth!"

"What do you mean Emma?" asked Daniel.

"I saw it too. It's like I was connected with him or something. I saw everything."

"You knew and you didn't tell us!?" asked Salari. "Why?"

"I was told not to. I took my gut and agreed to keep quiet about it. I didn't want to let that person down."

"Tell us now then girl. Tell us everything. It is fairly prudent that we know, said Nefarine.

"I think Kero could tell it better," she said.

"Fine. Tell us then boy, what happened?" said Salari.

"Well. After the invasion I and others were brought to Oltent Castle. For reasons I don't know. They took me to these cells where I had to stay. Terrible cells were vermin and disgusting lifestyles thrived and then one day *I was just about to wake up. It all started when I got there that day....*

CHAPTER THIRTEEN
Kero's Struggle

Water dripped from the ceiling. It fell slowly onto the hard floor. It had rained that night. The battle had been fierce, and they lost valiantly. The Castle of Olgath had been invaded and many were either killed or captured. Kero was in a corner of a cell, staring at the wall hoping it was all just a dream. The walls were made of brick, old and molded. He looked over every aspect he could find of the place. He didn't know exactly why they took him as well as others or the how long they would hold him. His queen would surely save him from this terror. She treated him like her own. She would surely come and save him. His stomach churned at the thought of being stuck here for even a few days. The foul stenches, the dripping water, the desolated walls all made it seem twice as worst possible.

He looked around the cell. There wasn't much to it but bars, a window (with bars on it), the floor, and three walls. There was no bed or place to dispose waste. It wasn't meant to be of any comfort, but to torture. That was the way of Myred. They were built on torturing their victims to gain something from them. Kero wouldn't be mistaken if Myred would use any of them for some sort of gain. Hopefully Harsie would come to their rescue or at least find some way to communicate with him. He heard a door open. Guards were stepping in, checking the guests. They were lead by Amethyst himself.

"Welcome to your home!" he said enthusiastically. "I hope you are all doing well?" No one answered him. Some gave him hatred looks, closed their eyes, or pretended he wasn't there. He had always been a well feared man in Everstheee. The guards snickered behind him.

"Not speaking huh?" he announced loudly. He looked among the cells making eye contact with some of them. The people in the other cells did not react well to this. It was said that his eyes could stun a man from several feet away. Kero didn't want to appear like anything similar to them. He looked on wondering what they wanted. His curiosity was singled out by Amethyst who acknowledged him.

"You!" he called out, pointing at him. "What is your name?"

"Why does it matter? Does the killer need to know the name of his victim?"

"Don't be smart with me boy! Answer me!" the ground rumbled from his anger.

"Kero. Kero Erin," Kero answered.

"Good. You'll be the first to be interrogated," he said. The cell bars rose with a wave of Amethyst's hand. He went in and grabbed Kero by the collar of his tunic. He resisted hurting him and dropped him to the ground.

"What do you want with me?" Kero interjected.

"No more questions. You'll find out soon enough." He went out and lowered the bars, now addressing the guards. "Come. Let's get back to Vicousir," Amethyst had addressed the guards to follow him back to Vicousir, king of Swiverstheee.

"I'll deal with you later," he said pointing to him.

"How do you speak to an evil man like him without fear?" someone asked. His cell was right across from his. A man. He was older and gray. He looked at Kero with curious eyes.

"Fear is something that my mind lacks. It is a waste of time to have that feeling. It is a sign of weakness to express fear."

"Quite an interesting philosophy. My dear boy, Kero, was it?"

"Yeah. Did you also come from the invasion?"

"No. I was attempting to help the locals with my power of telekinesis, but I was silenced by the Mytred."

"A noble cause I suppose. It's great to know not everyone is too afraid to fight back."

"I would like to get out of here and go to Everstheee. I hear it's nice this time of year." He expressed it as a dream of his. Something for him to escape to.

"That is where I come from. I will help you get you there," he promised.

"How? The security is strict. There aren't many ways to get out."

"All we need is a distraction. Just have to wait for the right time."

"How long?"

"Just be patient. Only a matter of time."

"My name is Vyshu by the way. It was nice to meet such a nice young man. I hope you're right about this."

"I'm more sure than I've ever been. Just wait. It will happen."

"Goodnight son, nice chat we've had."

"You the same."

Kero awoke to the footsteps of guards. They were marching in and talking loudly. They came in and pointed out that Kero would be taken today. They demanded that Kero get up. Of course Kero would be cautious once more.

"What do you want with me?" he asked as they gathered him from the cells.

"I guess what I heard was right. You ask too many questions," the guard remarked. "It'll be at our discretion to reveal what we want with you." The guard placed clamps on his wrists. The other guard grabbed him and they headed out. Before they went any farther the other guard holding him stopped.

"*Oslepite yego glaza,*" said the guard. A spell in Russian.

Kero's eyes were instantly blinded. His vision was gone completely. He stumbled for a bit having the sense of sight removed from him. They continued on through something. Kero suspected it was a method so that he can not be familiar with the castle if he had the opportunity to escape. Every time he tripped, they would kick him in the stomach and exclaimed he was wasting their time. It was ten minutes later that his vision started to revert back. He now could see that he was in some sort of chamber.

The chamber was definitely a sight for sore eyes. It was some sort of torture chamber. The chamber was host to an odd variety of devices. Kero had never even seen some of them before. One ancient machine that he saw was in fact an enflaming machine. It was a devastating contraption used in the old days to punish wrongdoers of the law. It was no longer considered to be owned by civilized people. A person would lie flat on the platform of this contraption and would be witnessed to small fire balls that would etch into their skin from the severe heat, despite their small size. Deformities would develop from this as well.

Not only did that machine exist there, but many others. The guards brought him to the center of the room and threw him to the floor. An older man with a black mustache, long brooding robes, and strong muscles started walking toward him. He walked with great confidence. His eyes expressed how evil he was. His eyes were a deep black, the color of his soul no doubt. His violet robes signified his royalty. And his mesh like armor reflected his wealthy nature.

"Good morning young mage," he said politely to Kero.

"Vicousir?" Kero asked.

"Yes. I am so happy that you can recognize a man such as I. I had no idea that I was so popular in Everstheee. How did you know who I was young mage?"

"Just a lucky guess," said Kero emotionlessly. "What do you want with me?"

"My dear boy. Don't you know of the information you hold toward us. Tell me where it is. How to get to it."

"What are you talking about?"

"Don't play games boy. According to my sources, you were as close to Harsie as her own children. Unfortunately, we couldn't get them, so we got the closest thing."

"Even if I did know, I wouldn't tell you anyway," Kero mustered out.

"I could kill you if you don't know. It would be a waste for you to live longer." He pulled his sword from his right hilt. He raised his sword, ready to strike.

"Vicousir!"

"What are you doing here?"

"There are other ways to kill a mage. Some of them can be used to avoid blood all over the castle floors. I have a little treat for him," said Amethyst. He was now walking up to Vicousir. He reached into his robe pocket and took out a small bottle. The *Serum of Tainted Blood*.

"Ah. That will do nicely. Good work Amethyst," Vicousir announced triumphantly.

"Will I be allowed a short prayer."

"I don't see why not," said Amethyst looking him over.

"Kosten!" he screamed. Kero had charged his power, No longer did his cell keep him from using his power. He had an advantage because his power was not bound by spell charging. He quickly broke his shackles by using his lightning shock. Kero low-kicked the guard to his left and uppercut the other guard. After this, Kero ran for the exist of the chamber.

"Stop him!" announced Vicousir. Amethyst took the initiative to charge a spell. To Kero's luck, the strange ray of energy narrowly missed him and gave him the chance to dart down the next corridor. He didn't take the time to take notice to the lavish paintings in the corridors, but he did use this time to memorize his routes. Guards spotted him up ahead.

"Blitzbach!" Kero used his lightning stream to fuel the guards with a powerful electrical air. The collapsed as they were struck. Just as the guards fell, Kero was nearly hit by a fireball. He turned around and ran right into Amethyst. Kero made a dangerous mistake by looking into his eyes. He couldn't move at all.

"Gotcha," he started. "I think it's time for you to die now. I can see you don't have the news we are seeking." He looked up at Vicousir who was behind Kero and nodded." I think it is time Callus. I will give him the serum."

"Fine. I guess this it," Kero acknowledged.

"Yes it is. Be still." Amethyst grabbed him roughly and opened the bottom of the serum. Kero could feel it rushing down, searing his esophagus. After a few seconds Vicousir intervened.

"Why isn't he dead yet?" he asked.

"He is stronger than I anticipated. He will die soon. The symptoms will come sooner or later. Let's lock him back up."

Before Kero knew what was going on he was thrown back into the cell where he started from. He didn't understand the significance of this serum, but he wanted to be gone before he symptoms would start. He leaned against the wall, sobbing. He had never felt so overwhelmed before. There was no hope of escaping from this prison. His doom was inevitable.

"Why do you cry my dear?"

Kero looked up to see a transparent apparition of Harsie.

"Harsie?" he asked

"Yes. I come to bring you news," she began. *"Yambai has come to the castle to reveal to me that you will be out of that castle soon. Have patience. We will recover more mages, a boy and a girl, they will be trained. Yambai says to wait for the right moment."* She paused for a moment so that Kero would understand completely. *"Be careful."*

"What have they put in me? Why are they asking these questions?" he asked in sadness. Talking to her like this was painful. It was not like talking in person the least bit, it just brought back memories.

"In due time. I want you to be careful. Go to the Alliance once you escape. My daughter Emma, and son Daniel will help. I will soon leave them to get to the bottom of this. Goodbye."

"Wait." He called out. It was too late. She had already disappeared. He didn't understand how she would know these things, but Yambai was a reliable source. He would wait for that moment she mentioned.

It would be a month's wait until that day finally came. A disturbance hit the Castle of Oltent and created reliable means for Kero's escape. It was a powerful fight that had become the perfect distraction. The only thing that would help this would be the Battle of Oltent Castle. This brought about a battle for power and greed.

CHAPTER FOURTEEN
A Mage's Return

Two months had followed since Kero had revealed the facts he had laid waste upon the group. Amethyst did fight Vicousir as Kero said. However, Kero explained that he didn't necessarily know what they were fighting about nor did he see them. He did recall guards running to that area and a collapsing roof that broke the bonds of his cell. He was able to get out easily once he had access to his power once more. Kero's evidence of Vicousir's death was the mark upon the sky, one used for the death of a king. Kero had no doubt in his mind that Vicousir fell to Amethyst's power.

He had run for weeks trying to get to the Alliance. It had been hard for him because his symptoms had started and he was weighed down with chronic fatigue and the occasional convulsion. The chronic fatigue that had plagued him caused him to act rationally and even attack people. He had then realized he was unstable and needed attention, so he made haste with his travel. Harsie's apparition assisted him emotionally and mentally to help Kero reach his goal. Her motivation had helped him to survive. This information helped the group, but hurt Emma.

Emma had known all along the events that had taken place and chose to keep it a secret at the discretion of herself, Kero, and Queen Harsie. Yambai was not upset or worried, but Nefarine and Salari were condescending towards her judgment. Emma was now expected to tell them every time Harsie or anyone of importance revealed themselves to her. She felt like a machine that was just being used to simply spit back information. Not only was she affected, but the entire group was.

Yambai, Nefarine, Arsi, and Salari worked diligently to find out exactly what Amethyst killed Vicousir over. Kero didn't know the events of the battle so it made it much more difficult. They worked day in and day out as Kero, Emma, and Daniel attended the school to brush up on their magic.

They were two days off from graduation of *Basic Magic Mastery in Preferred Skills*. They had come a long way through the weeks of learning from harsh training drills and abstract tests. They had met good people and worked on all sorts of magical follies while learning. They were happy now and had accomplished something for once since they came to this world. Life was not simple on the other side.

"Emma," Daniel said as they all walked from class.

"Yeah?" she asked.

"Well. I'm just so happy now. I'm glad we're here."

"Yeah me too. I just wish everyone wasn't so stressed."

"Sorry about that," interjected Kero.

"No. They needed to know. I'm glad you told them," said Emma smiling.

"You two need to get a room," said Daniel.

"Ha. Ha. Ha. Very funny Daniel," said Emma with sarcasm.

"What's funny?" asked Kero.

"Nothing," said Daniel.

They continued on their walk to meet the others at the inn. The day had gone quite well in fact. Emma had learned a new spell, Kero mastered a technique, and Daniel had a crush.

No one knew of this but Emma. She had somewhat mastered going into people's minds, seeing emotions, and feeling feelings that were not her own. Soría had shown her the process, instructing her in the ways of an empath and mind reader.

Daniel had a crush on Soría, the mentalist mage. It wasn't anything real major, but Emma just thought is was neat that he even had the courage to have a crush. It was never like him to have one, especially considering his stagnant social skills.

Kero, Emma, and Daniel arrived at the inn shortly with books in their bags preparing them for finals. School was important to each of them because it distracted them from the stress of the others who were very concerned about Kero's evidence. It wasn't that they didn't care, but they just needed that time to not stress over anything. To have a sense of identity in this world. What they saw at the end made their heart drop

"Hi," said Chaos smiling brightly. "King Herbus of Absirthee has been overthrown by Amethyst. The others have been captured."

"What?" asked Emma.

"Yep. We're going to have to save the people of Absirthee in order to save the others. But we don't have the people do it."

"Yes we do," interrupted Daniel. "All of us students are about to graduate in two days. That gives you mages to help form a suitable party."

"That's a great idea" said Yambai coming in behind them. He was flustered. "Nefarine wants to see all of us immediately."

Emma woke up with a start, sweat beading down her forehead. She had just experienced the most vivid dream she had ever had.

It was all just a dream. Emma woke up the morning of finals ready to take on a challenge. The strange dream was so real, and she didn't take it as a good sign. Every aspect of it was real, especially Chaos who was dressed in his normal attire, but with a new fatigue added to him. The question now was when would he return. Was the news he gave be true? Emma accepted this. Chaos spoke to her through a dream. He gave her information that was important, but was Chaos capable of revealing it himself?

Emma got up ready to leave and went to the table with her book for quick study and breakfast. Daniel and Kero joined her shortly with their books, They noticed the disgruntled look about her face. She appeared to have had something heavy on her mind.

"What's wrong with you?" Daniel asked her.

"Nothing's wrong. I'm just tired," she lied.

"Fine. Don't tell me. I know you had a vision," he said.

"How do you know that?" she asked him.

"Don't you remember who I am?" he asked her. "I notice everything about everyone. Qatu said that after having a vision the person becomes avoiding and oblivious to anything else. And besides I'm your brother. I know you better than anyone," he said smiling.

"It doesn't matter. I don't think it was a real vision anyway," she interjected.

"Why don't we all just eat," said Kero intervening.

"Fine," said Emma.

Emma, Daniel, and Kero ate in silence. Emma had forgotten who Daniel was. He was the observing type, but lately his inquisitive nature felt more like prying than actually being concerned about the situation. He could tell anyone if they were angry, sad, mad, or glad. He was inertly empathic with people. He was always in touch with people's emotions. He was right. Emma had had a vision. It was an important one too. She just hoped that it was just a dream and that Chaos would just return and tell them that her vision was purely her imagination.

But Chaos didn't. Another week went by and final grades would be posted soon. She realized she had one thing left to do. She was going to tell Salari about the vision she had. She hoped that maybe it wasn't real. The possibility of that was not great considering all of her dreams were visions in some form or fashion. The only real proof would be the name of the king of Absirthee. If his name was real, then they were in for a lot more stress.

Emma got off the top bunk she was laying on and put her shoes on. She then made her way out of the inn and into the temple where Nefarine and the others were. When she arrived they were talking loudly and arguing about something.

"The *Paradox of Xeri* is not real. Amethyst would not need it," said Nefarine.

"Of course he would," said Arsi. "This thing has as much power as *Pandora's Box*..."

"Excuse me," interrupted Emma.

"I highly doubt Amethyst would need it," said Salari. "Unless he would want his people to be really sad. Plus the fact that..."

"Excuse me!!!" Emma yelled. Everyone stopped talking and looked at Emma whose face was red hot.

"What is it girl?" asked Arsi. "You are interrupting us."

"I think I had a vision," she said.

"What was this vision about? What happened?" asked Salari.

"Well. Daniel, Kero, and I were leaving class and made it back to the inn to find Chaos there," she began.

"Why was he there?" Nefarine asked.

"Well. He revealed to us some information," she started. "He said that Herbus of Absirthee had been overthrown by Amethyst and that the others had been captured."

"Herbus. I hope this isn't true." said Nefarine.

"It is true. If Herbus is the name of this king. That is your real proof," she began. "I think that he is dying as well."

"Why do you say that?" asked Salari.

"In the vision, he was really calm and peaceful. He seemed a little too relieved."

"You may be right girl," said Arsi.

"*What else did he say?*" asked Yambai who was approaching her from behind.

"He said we had to save them. Use mages to save the people. Daniel, in my vision, said something about the mages here graduating and that he'd have his forces."

"How long ago was this vision," asked Salari.

"Umm…about that. It was a week ago," she said awaiting a brash of furious faces.

"A *week?*" asked Nefarine angrily. "Dear girl. We will send mages to Everstheee following graduation. I suggest you find some. You'll be leading this voyage," he said quickly. "Try harder to tell us these things, I'm too old to be angry at anyone, especially someone of your esteem."

"I understand sir," said Emma softly. "But I don't understand why I should be the one to lead a voyage to a place I've never been with mages who don't travel. Why can't one of you do it?"

"You are old enough to go out on your own. You know the arts. You will lead a band of mages like yourself into Absirthee and help save the king while the rest of us…travel back to the Castle of Olgath.

"I don't understand," she said.

"It is what it is," he said. "You are dismissed. We have work to do."

Emma left the room silently. She had never thought that they would make such a dangerous call. She had never experienced the world without an adult before. She would have never expected to be placed to lead a voyage to Absirthee or called to do a job. She now had to think who to take. She also had to decide what supplies to take, what powers she needed of those people going. There was a lot to think about. She made her way back to the inn where she laid down on her bed and came up with a plan.

She narrowed it down to eight people including herself on this voyage. She chose Daniel, Soría, Erianna, Chris {Conjuration mage}, Kero, Aurora {Anti-Necrosic Cleric}, and Alexander. She had figured up the list of mages by who was in her class and how their talents would be useful in battle and during the voyage. She figured up the supplies by the real necessities: ammunition, weapons, food, clothing, everyone's separate spell books and many other things. She spent hours on her plan. She didn't look up from what she was doing until Kero, Daniel, and Soría appeared at the inn.

"Hey Emma!" said Soría. "What are you doing?"

"Oh. Well I was just…"

"Final grades came today. I brought yours for you. I didn't open them," said Kero.

"Thanks Kero," she said as she reached down to get the paper. She had forgotten that finals would be out today. She opened the envelope hastily and looked at the paper.

Emma Dale

Proficiency: Your proficiency is beyond many students. I am proud to say that you are a very proficient and powerful mage. Very good work Ms. Dale. I award your proficiency an eleven out of ten.

Power: You are a very powerful mage no doubt. There are other powers you have but you may not know it. Look into yourself and find what you're not looking at. I compliment you on your power. I give you a ten out of ten.

Usefulness: You are a very useful mage. I give you ten out of ten for usefulness.

Knowledge: Your knowledge of the arts is very good. I can see there are things you know that other students have never even touched. I give you a nine of ten. There are simple things you need to be aware of.

Spell Usage: Your spell usage needs improving. Make sure that you think out your spell reaction and use the right spells that will be more beneficial and not dangerous or risky. I award you a nine of ten for your clever, but dangerous use of spells.

Weapon Certified: You have been certified by myself and the Arcane Alliance in the Weapon of Japanese Sai.

School Classifications Certified: You are now certified by myself and the Arcane Alliance in the fields of Divination, Abjuration, and Illusion magic.

Total Score: You have been awarded **49** over **50**. Congratulations new mage of The Arcane Alliance!

Emma looked up over her paper. She was quite proud of herself. Mr. Qatu gave her really good advise as to why he gave her the scores he did. She was certified in all the things she sought to be. She had forgotten that Kero, Daniel, and Soría were beaming up at her.

"Oh. Umm. I got a 49 out of 50," she said.

"Great job Emma," said Kero.

"Thanks," she said,

"So. What are you working on?" Daniel asked.

"Well….," she began.

Emma explained the voyage to Absirthee and who was going and what supplies were to be taken and all of the other information. It didn't take long for the others to realize that it was the first time they would be out in the world without the guidance of an adult. It was going to be very difficult on their own. Emma explained everything that had happened and told them to tell the others. She asked that if they see the other mages to tell them to meet with her. She was nervous on the inside. She looked calm and ready, but she wasn't.

Emma spent the next few hours looking over her plans when it happened again. She was falling into another trance. This time she received really bad news. It was strange that she had these strange trances. It was as if someone was giving her information again. She got up from her bed and left for the temple again. She ran into the temple, hearing them arguing again. They stopped again.

"What is this time?" Arsi asked.

"Chaos is dead," she said.

"What?" asked Nefarine.

"I don't know how I know. I just felt it."

"What do we do now?" asked Salari.

"The same things we were going to do," said Nefarine.

"I'll leave you guys alone for a while. I'm about to meet with some mages," she said.

"Good then girl, make us proud," said Nefarine smiling back at her.

The expressions on their faces were devastating. It would seem that Chaos was not just merely an errand boy, but someone everyone loved. Chaos was dead now. The others presumably think that Chaos would not want to be held in regards for his death. They were to continue what was important and what Chaos died trying to do. Emma returned to the inn and she revealed to Kero and the others what had happened.

"Chaos is dead. He died trying to save these people. We are now going to do what he couldn't finish. We are going to be proud of what he did and we are going into Absirthee to save those people. I have called you all here to tell you that I have been selected as the leader of this voyage. I have been given the power to choose who is to accompany myself and my brother on this voyage. If you are scared, don't worry, because I am too. If you have any questions or comments tell me now. We leave tomorrow at sunrise for Absirthee. If you're going, you'd better be there with your respective supplies."

Emma went to the kitchen table to sit and see if anyone wanted to ask questions. She had prepared sheets of the supplies, people going, and other things. She wondered exactly how she was going to do something so important. It seemed that everyone was eager for questions because everyone followed her straight to the table.

"Hey. Umm. Why are we doing this again?" asked Chris. He seemed completely lost.

"We have to save Absirthee. Don't you want to help them?" Emma said.

"I guess so. I mean I haven't been out there much. But I'll try," he said.

"Do we have to go if you invited us?" asked Aurora. "I mean. Do we have a choice?"

"Well. If you don't want to go. Don't show up." Emma answered. "That's the end of questions. Please leave."

Everyone left after that last question. It didn't occur to her that a lot of people wouldn't take such a big risk to go to a distant land and fight a battle. She sat at the table thinking that most of them may not show up the next morning to go. She was afraid of the possibility of them refusing attendance. She didn't want them to feel forced, but she was desperate. They had little time to travel and even a smaller amount of time to save everyone.

"It'll be alright Emma," said Kero. He was always there to consol her.

"You're such a good person Kero, thank you," she said.

"Oh. Anything for a pretty girl that's down," he said smiling.

"Thanks for being a good friend," she said. She got up from the table and kissed Kero on the cheek. Kero blushed at this.

Emma didn't know what she had just did. Did she just kiss Kero? She hadn't realized it until she got in bed. Her thoughts took over again. She had wanted to do it for quite some time now. She fought her urges to hug him. He was the type of person she was looking for. He was sincere and honest. Kero spent a lot of time trying to cheer up

Emma when she was down. She just went to sleep. Maybe Kero didn't take it seriously.

The next morning Emma woke up early to make sure the supplies from the local store had arrived. Daniel and Kero woke up shortly afterwards to pack up their belongings. It was going to be a long journey. The estimated time to get to Absirthee would be at least one week total travel time.

Emma had received the scrying glass she had ordered to keep in contact with the alliance. She spent most of her morning making sure everything was perfect. She took the extra time to say goodbye to Salari and the others at the temple. They hadn't slept the night before so their arguing was on hold. They gave her a good farewell and told her to keep in touch. Emma returned to the inn to wait until sunrise came.

After waiting several minutes, the sun poked its head from behind a mountain. The only problem was that no one was there besides Kero and Daniel. Emma suspected that the others had chickened out and decided not to come. Emma gestured for Kero and Daniel to follow her to get out of the alliance.

"Wait!" someone yelled.

Emma turned around to see Alexander lugging his belongings with him. Alex made his way up the hill to join them.

"I couldn't bear to think you guys were going by yourself. So I'm coming. Oh and that crowd back there."

Emma looked back and smiled. The entire group she invited was ready to go. Emma was very pleased with this. She started walking. Everyone followed her as they made their way through the barrier and out back into Everstheee. They were on a new journey to save the druids of Absirthee. It would take a while to get there, but her mission was much more important.

CHAPTER FIFTEEN
Destiny's Bane

The woman paced quietly about the cave. Her heels clashed with the stone floors beneath her. Her luxurious blonde hair appeared almost yellow in the darkness of the cave. She whispered silently to herself, creating a sphere of pure light shrouding the darkness surrounding her. Revealed before her, were the remains of ancient hieroglyphics created by the civilization that had once dwelled within the cave. She stopped to observe her findings when she heard distant footsteps. And as she did, she whipped around.

"Oh. It's you," she said dully. She held no surprise by her guest's presence.

What she saw was a young man with a fresh face, pudgy and crooked, yet almost attractive. He had long blonde hair and hazel eyes; despite his youthful face he looked rather exhausted for his age. He looked at her disappointedly as he crossed his arms with impatience.

"You are far from home, sister," he began. "I have been looking for you for days. You need to return home."

"I will go where I please. I'll be queen soon, so I must take advantage of my free time." She sat down on a rock, placing her in her hands. "Besides, I need the air. Being cooped up in that castle is purely dreadful." She ran her fingers through her hair as she talked.

"I know. I know, but you are so late with child, you could go into labor any moment."

"I just wanted to get out and explore. I don't have much time to do research on these walls."

"Research about what? All I see are pictures of a knight. It looks like some kid drew it." he said amusingly.

"That painting depicts the *knight in shining armor.*"

"It doesn't exist."

"Yes it does," she said defensively. "I have seen it, felt it, and I know it exists in this world as a pure entity of power."

"Power? I thought the knight was just a person."

"No. It is a person fused with the power of the knight, protected by the essence of the armor. The knight can perform miracles, destroy entities of evil, absorb energies, and many other things that can be used on both sides," she confirmed by pointing at the correspond paintings, depicting the knight's power.

"I see," said the mage calmly. "That's some power."

"And if it falls into the wrong hands——"

"Pure catastrophe!" he said. "I understand now. We have to find it."

"No. It's too dangerous now, not with Vicousir coming to power in Swiverstheee."

"I understand sister," he complied.

The woman fell silent. It was as if she felt something about the mage standing before her. She no longer looked at him, but down to her bulging stomach. She rubbed it softly, feeling the movement of her children. It was strange to her again she would birth twins. She looked back up to her brother who stared at her consolingly.

"I wish you didn't have so many burdens," he told her.

"Sorus. My burdens of queen are almost here. The council is ready to give the thrown to me."

"Never use my old name again. I am Amethyst now," he said in a firm tone. "Come. Let us get back to Siry. He is worried."

Harsie walked slowly out of the cave and back outside. She screamed in agony. Her image began to blur in obscuring white smoke, the image was gone.

Emma and Daniel looked up at each other. Emma had used her powers of empathy and divination to look down upon the past. The druids revealed to her the origins of her power, where they came from and what they meant. She was connected to people in a way that she can channel their minds, their emotions, their memories to gain insight on them. It allowed her to peer into the soul and travel its vastness.

They had traveled for seven days in the deep dark forests of Absirthee, while facing issues along the way. The first day of traveling had been a treacherous and adventurous time. Emma now looked down back into the smoke as she looked on the past to gain power over their future. Emma now knew the answers to the questions she asked. She knew what the knight was, that Harsie knew it existed, and that her destiny would not be fulfilled until the life of another is reborn and the power of the knight would take shape. She gazed back into the fog, remembering how their journey had brought them to where they now took refuge.

"Emma!" yelled Aurora excitedly. They had been traveling only a few hours.

"Whah?" asked Emma. She was not concentrating on where she was going, oblivious to the hole in the ground. She lost her footing as her foot dropped into a small hole, catching her by surprise. Emma tripped and all of her belongings now scattered the ground. She was lying face first, weighed down by her overly cumbersome backpack. She couldn't get up.

"Here you go," said Kero as he lifted her up.

"Thanks. I kinda couldn't get up," she said smiling. Daniel emerged from behind, completely undetected.

"Watch where you're going please. And don't go so fast, we have to follow you," he said. He looked back directing Emma to where the rest of the party was.

Emma didn't say anything as she just watched her brother walk back toward the group. Daniel had been crabby all day, but Emma couldn't figure out why. Even his voice carried a harsher tone, rasp even to the point that Emma questioned if he was coming down with something.

The party continued to walk. This time it was different because Emma was not ahead, but parallel to Chris, Aurora, and Daniel with Soría, Erianna, Alexander, and Kero coming up the rear.

"How long is this trip again?" asked Chris.

"We'll be walking for another six days." Emma answered.

"And how do you not know this?" Aurora began. "You should know how long you'll be. What did you tell your mom?"

Chris let out a short laugh. "I don't know. I just told her I'd be back after I finish the mission. She said 'ok' and that was it."

"You're insane," Aurora said shaking her head.

Emma found Aurora and Chris entertaining; their bickering was childish, yet surprisingly humorous. Chris was the complete opposite. He was fun-loving, excited, and youthful in his behavior, yet very mature in some cases. When he laughed, everyone else laughed with him. Emma was accustomed to his drama and his acting out by acknowledging arbitrary occurrences.

Aurora, on the other hand, was much more stoic and hardened. She never seemed to stress out or have fun at all (when it wasn't necessary). She was a very critical person as well and Chris wasn't too concerned about it, or at least most of the time he wasn't. Chris took her seriousness lightly, which made her all the more angry.

They had been walking for several hours and the sun now began to set. Emma noticed this and signaled everyone to camp in an area enveloped by trees. The growing number of woods showed them that Absirthee was not too far away. As they made camp, Emma took time to herself to think about things that were bothering her. She watched Kero attempt to put his tent up, he was making a clumsy preparation of it. Inside, Emma laughed at him.

Emma looked down at him with passionate eyes. It wasn't often that she felt that way about a person and didn't know why, because that day Emma discovered something about herself that she didn't know was possible. She was in love with Kero, stranger than anything she had ever felt in her life. She saw him for what he truly was, a mage who cared deeply for her, but was always too shy to admit. She had felt love. It felt like the morning sun or the wind in the trees. Who could love such a selfish, rude girl? Emma took her time to discover the true reasons why she felt that way.

Mind reading was not her profession, but after careful consideration she tried to pry and see how Kero really felt. What she received from his thoughts were deep feelings of caring, regret, love, apprehension. Those feelings mirrored how Emma was feeling about the "surprise" kiss she gave him. She had never truly understood what was happening to her and why at that moment did she do the most unsuspected thing. She had never even kissed a boy before, but for some reason it all made sense. She had recalled an ancient power called empathy to which the person can read the feelings of another and in some cases act on it. Her final conclusion was that she was an empath, a reader of feelings, she knew how he felt, but could she make him feel what she felt?

As Emma thought about such things, she was awakened from the screams of another person. They had settled down to rest before continuing on, and now something was happening. Emma hurriedly departed from the campfire in her cloak and ran towards the sound of the disturbance. Her mind ran over many different possibilities. She could hear Kero's footsteps behind her. As They ran through a barrage of trees ahead of them, dodging to make their way through. What they saw next was a shock.

Daniel was now charging a spell, not at an enemy, but at Soría." *Queime-se em chamas e podridão na cinza!*" he screamed. A giant ball of fire emitted from his charged spell and converged onto her. She creamed.

"Izmenite ogon' v pticu!" someone screamed. In that instant, the ball of fire developed feathers, a wing, a head, a tail, instantaneously. Before anyone could notice, the bird flew away. Alexander emerged from a nearby tree, exhausted and flustered with anger.

"Why are you trying to hurt her!?" he yelled.

Daniel stood there, trying to control his own movements. He then began to walk forward, then back, then forward again, and giving up by resting on the ground.

"What's going on?" asked Emma, looking over at Soría who had been speechless the entire time.

"I-I don't know what happened," Soría began. "He was acting normal, and then he went psycho on me. He almost hit me with a spell. I was trying to stop him, and that's when I screamed."

"Why did you scream?" asked Kero.

"I felt a presence in him when I tried to enter his mind. Something else is there, fighting to control him."

At that moment, Chris, Erianna, and Aurora entered the scene. They had been sent to fetch water earlier on. Now they were returning to find a struggle.

"Why is everyone so quiet?" asked Chris.

"Daniel attacked Soría," said Alexander.

Everyone looked over at Daniel who silently sat on the floor, not moving at all and giving everyone else a blank stare.

"Soría, I need you to reach into his mind and find out what's wrong," Emma commanded.

Soría acknowledged the order and walked over to Daniel who was now laying flat on his back. Daniel didn't move, but looked straight up to the sky. He was breathing very slowly and appeared to not have noticed Soría when she walked up to him. She placed her hand on his head and closed her eyes.

Emma watched as Soría concentrated on Daniel. She breathed heavily trying to calm herself. Soría returned in a matter of minutes and put her light leather gloves back on her hands and she walked over to Emma.

"He's fighting himself," she said simply.

"Himself?" asked Emma.

"He has this alter ego that apparently has power over him, but Daniel will be ok as long as he releases the ego every so often. It's actually a good thing he has this problem."

"What do you mean?" asked Kero who had walked closer to hear the conversation.

"Well. He basically has this power called telepathic projection. He will have the ability to project his mind into another and control it, anyone familiar to him will be seen as Daniel, and others will see the poor soul being controlled."

"How can you get him back to regular state? I mean look at him!" said Emma defiantly. She pointed at her pitiful brother who had lost all instinct and now lie motionless on the ground.

"A simple spell I can perform will work, just give me a few minutes," Soría said. Everyone followed her back to Daniel as she performed her spell on him. She spoke softly. "*Ego that binds this mind, be released on command, and no longer control the friend for him we stand.*" Soon after saying the spell the fog reappeared.

Emma and Daniel looked up at each other from the bubbling pot. Emma made a wink to her brother indicating something sneaky. They both got up off the hard rocky floor of the cave they were in. Emma and Daniel preceded to the wall where the cave paintings of the infamous *knight in shining armor* were. The paintings made more sense to them now.

"That's it," Emma pointed out to a strange depiction. "The painting clearly depicts a great summoner. That must mean that to use the power of the *knight* means to find this summoner."

"How do you think we'll find this summoner?" Daniel asked her.

"I don't know. But I think that if we can find this summoner it can stop Amethyst before this world is torn apart."

"Maybe Razor can help?" Daniel asked her.

"I don't know. He can barely control his metamorphosis powers. He won't be able to help us go that far."

"*Why do you doubt me so?*" a voice asked.

Emma and Daniel turned around to spot their new friend, Razor. Razor was a bushed haired, tall, and lightly tanned druid they met at the border of Absirthee and Everstheee. By the look on his face, he wasn't happy by her comment. He stared at her, searching for an apology.

"I only said that because you can barely control your powers. How do you expect to be of any value?" Emma asked bluntly.

"I am a druid. And I can easily get you to the Castle of Sular to save Herbus. You need to leave this idiotic cave and return to everyone else. It's a waste of time to look into that fictitious fantasy. There's nothing there."

"This cave can very well save all of Sulex. I think that your complaints are stupid. But we should get back. Let's go," Emma said.

The Castle of Sular was two miles from the ancient cave. Razor revealed to them the coming of Lucras, Amethyst's new inducted second in command. Amethyst has once had him as second in command while following Vicousir, now Amethyst was the king and Lucras was the second in command. Lucras was a very powerful necromancer who was following specific orders from Amethyst himself. Lucras's talent was to use his necromantic powers to summon legions of undead to overthrow Herbus's power.

Razor's gifts alone were not in close proximity to Lucras's. Razor was a druid and that meant that his powers were connected to nature itself and explained that druidic powers don't work on the undead and provide no support, but for distracting them. His other ability, to alter his physical form into a wolf, was bonus. This power also did not prove useful because Razor could not control it well as he almost killed Emma in wolf form. Emma never forgave him for his incompetence.

Emma and Daniel were now one mind, thinking and planning alike. They combined their thoughts into a plan of action to stop Lucras and rescue the other druids. Emma and Daniel slowly walked out of the cave, but before reaching the exit, Emma stopped. She reached down her cloak and obtained the vibrating scrying glass from her pocket. She had yet again received another message from Salari and the others. Salari's haggard and scarred face represented the message, He was rather tired, exhausted to a point of collapse. His eyes were weary.

"Emma," he breathed out deeply. *"I'm sorry that we sent you there, but there isn't much time. You need to make haste with the current mission of rescuing the druids and defeating Lucras. Once completing this, bring Herbus along on the journey to Olgath, you wouldn't believe me if I told you."*

"But—," Emma retorted. It was no use, the message was a recording of some sort. Salari's message had ended and now Emma stood there, contemplating the next move, unaware of what fate lies in Olgath. The city of Olgath was simply the city closest to Olgath Castle, named after it as well. Daniel approached her now, wondering what exactly made Emma react in such a way.

"What happened?" he asked her. He looked at her face, she was more or less looking into empty space, at something that wasn't there. It took her seconds to compute Daniel's presence.

"I've been told I don't have much time to save Herbus, because the others need us." She looked down at the ground, thinking of exactly what to say next. Her head was spinning in many directions, she was once again mentally distracted as she had been before. Her subconscious made her only aware of what she was thinking, not of what she was seeing with her own eyes. Emma's clumsiness, her disorientation, her confusion, had all been because of the state of mind. She looked up finally. She was determined now, focused on the mission.

"It's time to go save Absirthee," she began. "We're going to have to plan this out. Go get everyone, we'll make a plan right now."

Daniel followed orders quickly and rallied the others who were resting nearby. The others were now in the area south of the cave, facing the back entrance of the castle. Chris opened up one of the cases to show the map of the area and to help Emma strategize exactly what was going to happen and how. Emma was now with them to pick each and every individual for a task.

"Alright," she began. "We're going in at dawn tomorrow. We're going to infiltrate the perimeter. It'll just be like school, except this is real. I need to assign tasks. Chris. I have one for you."

"What is it?" he asked her.

"I need you to be our archer. I need you to use your magic arrows and missile weapons to provide back up in case we have surprises. I need you to use light arrows. How long will it take you to conjure them?"

"A few hours at least. I have to start now." Chris said. He then got up from the fire they had made and went off in his own direction.

"Soría and Erianna. Your jobs are to infiltrate the northern tower of the castle and rescue Derrick and Emily. After they are released we can make it."

"Ok. How are they going to make it inside?" asked Razor.

"Well. Simple. Just a mind spell here and a sleep spell there. I don't think it's that complicated," said Emma.

"Daniel, Alex, Razor, Kero, and I will fight off the guards heading towards the entrances. We all will rendezvous inside to fight off Lucras.

"Is that all your highness?" asked Razor.

"That's all I can say for now. I have to talk to Daniel and Soría privately as well. That's all for now. Thanks guys. Get some rest."

Daniel and Soría followed Emma into another area.

"What is it?" asked Soría.

"I have a plan for you two."

Chapter Sixteen
Phase One

The plan was commenced and it was now time to save the citizens of Absirthee, those captured by Lucras, and the king of Absirthee himself. After a night's rest, the gang woke and geared up, ready for what lie ahead. Emma had revealed to Daniel and Soría a plan that would of course defeat Lucras himself. Everyone gathered in the circle around the now ashen fire. They looked into each others eyes, some nervous, some sad, and others unidentifiable.

"May all of you be blessed on this mission, safe and sound. May the gods protect you," Aurora announced. Her blessing from the gods was the closest thing to a lucky rabbit's foot. She spoke softly with confidence in her voice and determination in her eyes.

Everyone left the circle in silence as Chris headed off into the woods ahead of everyone to place his mark on his ranged skills along with Aurora at his side. Kero, Daniel, Emma, and Alex all followed by taking a different path into the deep forest. Soría and Erianna closely followed behind everyone, to await the moment they would infiltrate the northern tower. Everyone was now separate and different stories would be heard, if they made it out alive.

Chris walked hastily through the forest, trying not to make much noise from the thick layers of leaves on the ground. The forest was dense. It almost appeared to be dusk in response to the heavy amount of trees blocking the sun from above. Chris had spent several hours summoning light arrows as a conjurer mage the night before. He was a conjurer mage of arsenal, and weak level animals. Light arrows were the only arrows that took time because they were far more powerful than any other arrow in his arsenal. Chris's long hair wavered in the light wind as he walked, cloak on back, quiver around his mid section. He listened closely to the words of Mr. Qatu who instructed him in the ways of stealth. He was also trained to master the art of bow.

He stopped. There was a distant sound he could hear, rumbling of some sort. He took his bow off his shoulder, awaiting for the predator's next move. Another tremor alerted Chris.

"Arrow of Fire!" he whispered to himself. His hand was now occupied by a long arrow, made of strong wood and embellished with intricate symbols indicating its power. He nock his bow, ready to aim. At that moment, a silhouette of a strange creature sprang up. He released the arrow and it flew quickly to its target, encompassed by a large flame. The creature was hit, instantly it fell to the ground. He ran to it quickly, identifying the creature.

"Grotus," he said. "I had a feeling it'd be one of you." The creature was filthy with a thick layer of dirt careening its body. It was the size of a small man with claw-like feet and hands. Its nose was pudgy, flat even with a small mouth and smooth head.

Chris heard more rumbling from under the ground. He quickly hopped onto a tree, climbing as fast as he possibly could. The others would have a better chance at fighting them off. He supported himself onto a branch and rested. It was time to make his way safer between the tree tops.

"I was wondering what happened to you," Chris said looking up at his guest.

"Well. I figured it'd be safer up here. I see you have found me," said Aurora.

Aurora was on a thick branch above Chris, resting her back on the trunk of the tree. Her white cloak hanging dully over the thick branch. It wavered with every new rush of light wind. Her equipment belt was fastened around her waist, carrying various tools.

"I still don't see why you and I are paired up. What can you do?" Chris asked pompously.

"Things that you can't," Aurora simply said.

"Fine. Let's continue on,"

"No. That's not a good idea." Razor interrupted. "I can't leave you now."

"But you can help Soría and Erianna more," Emma acknowledged.

"There won't be much for me to do," Razor replied. "They don't need me."

"I think it's best if you're with them," she said calmly.

Emma and the others were now far off from the camp, heading to the castle from the south to eliminate any perimeter threats ahead. Emma had second guessed the support of Soría and Erianna because they're powers were far different from the rest, but everyone was different in their own respects. Razor refused Emma because he believed his talents could be utilized if used in battle and not stealth. But it wasn't up to him, but to how Emma wanted him to use his powers. Razor made that agreement when he discovered that the life of his king, his mentor, and his friend would be in their hands. Razor reluctantly followed her orders and followed after Erianna and Soría.

"Are you sure that was a good idea?" asked Daniel.

"I'm sure. He's going to be a big help to the others," Emma said with confidence.

Emma had dispatched the others. Aurora and Chris were to infiltrate the northern part of the castle and provide an archers support to those approaching from the east. Soría, Erianna, and Razor were to approach the castle from the west and sneak inside to release the captured from the dungeon on the bottom half of the massive tower that is the Castle of Sular. Kero, Daniel, Emma, and Alex were to simply approach the castle from the east and part of the north to battle Mytred and most likely their first undead creatures.

"How long do you think this will take?" asked Alex.

"I don't know. Why do you ask?" said Emma.

"Well, from what I see ahead it could take us a bit more than a few days."

They had been walking for quite some time, approaching the castle closer and closer. It had occurred to Alex that the massive amount of Mytred that were lined up in front of the castle were awaiting their arrival. From what Emma observed, they were preparing for a big battle. The Mytred stood there, silent and ready with spears at their sides, awaiting for the new threat that plopped themselves at their feet.

"How are we going to fight so many?" asked Kero.

"Well. We can, it's just that we may not be able to fight all of them off, and if the prisoners aren't released early enough, we're screwed."

"I hope you're right, dying now wouldn't be cool at all," Daniel agreed.

Soría, Erianna and Razor stealthily reached the western part of the castle. They waited for the right moment to head into the north tower where all the prisoners were being held. The three of them were stationed one hundred yards from the tower awaiting the right moment to divert themselves from a small group of Mytred that were patrolling the perimeter.

"I say I block their minds until we can reach the tower," Soría suggested. She was studying the area, watching the movements of the guards.

"I say we knock them out," said Erianna.

"Ladies. There are many possibilities to get over there, but we have to do it quickly. Why don't we do both? Erianna knocks out a few of the guards and Soría blocks their minds?"

"What if more come?" Erianna asked.

"Then I do what I do best," Razor said winking.

The three of them were waiting along the edge of the castle's walls, awaiting the right time to head across to the tower. They waited for a while until something happened. Everyone started to get a bad migraine. Inside their heads a large echo formed, screeching, and then a voice spoke.

"Guys. You can head across now. I have the perfect distraction, wait for my signal," said Emma.

Emma had discovered a way to broadcast her way into their minds. Everyone struggled to shake off the lingering pain from her contact. After a few moments everything was calm once more.

"When did she learn to do that?" asked Razor.

"No idea. But I can tell that she has never done it before today," said Soría. "It was way too sloppy. I owe her a migraine."

"Ok. Let's just wait for this ," Erianna began.

She didn't get to finish her comment because at that moment a giant ball of fire was thrown at one of the Mytred, knocking it flat on its face. More and more balls were thrown and more Mytred were hit. Razor took advantage of the distraction. In the blink of an eye, Razor turned into a very built, dangerous, shaggy wolf. He growled slightly displaying his comfort and dashed off toward the tower.

"Let's go!" Erianna screamed. As she did, several Mytred emerged, ready to stop them. Erianna was ready for them. "*¡Mis enemigos me amenazan! ¡Póngalos para descansar!*" she screamed as she ran, not needing aim. At that moment, a large sphere of puffy yellow smoke encompassed the Mytred, knocking them out, one by one.

"Good one!" said Soría as she ran with Erianna. They were closely behind Razor who was heading toward the tower, legs pumping rapidly as did a wolf's. Fireballs flew past them, hitting other Mytred in the process and creating a cloak for them to enter the tower. More and more Mytred were attempting to attack them, but the oncoming fireballs prevented it, but something unexpected happened. There was no more than thirty yards to the tower when Soría tripped over something, and plummeted to the ground.

"What in the world?" she asked. She looked down at her leg where a very grotesque and dead hand now grasped her foot. **The foot now grew an arm, elbow, and no later had it uprooted from the ground as a full grown zombie.** Before Soría was able to react, an object struck it in the chest and glowed a bright strange light. The creature disintegrated on impact with the strange light. Soría got up, spotting Chris in the distance, with his bow raised, he waved. Soría smiled and caught up with the others.

"That was lucky," said Razor. As Razor said that, other undead creatures uprooted in the distance, at least one hundred of them in several small clusters. They now approached them. The entrance to the tower was not a door, but a pathway.

"How do we stop them from following us?" asked Erianna.

"I got it," said razor. "Go inside. I got this." The others went into the pathway. Razor stepped into the pathway as well and raised his hands. *"Racines! Bloquez Leur Sentier!"* At the saying of his spell, large, thick roots sprang up from the ground and created a wall, blocking the path for the undead to approach. Razor left the sealed off area and followed after the others.

"Ok. They got in. I guess we should start helping the others then?" asked Chris. He was looking down at the battlefield where countless Mytred were being hammered with bombardments of fireballs. He couldn't figure out where they were coming from, but he did know it was none other than Alex, Daniel, Emma, and Kero. They had somehow devised a plan. Chris smiled, thinking of how smart his friends were to him. They got it from him.

"Yep. I guess we should help them whenever they show themselves," Aurora said.

"That was a good plan you guys," said Emma. She was standing in the sphere of invisibility with the others, watching the plan unfurl as Daniel placed fireballs onto the catapult created by Alex's power to alter physical forms. Kero was missing from the scene because he was lucky enough to be volunteered to be the catapult.

"I don't think Kero agrees, he's starting to change back. I don't know how long I can keep him like this, his body wants to change."

"How much time do we have?" asked Daniel loading the fireball onto the catapult. Kero was now becoming a person again, hands forming, head, legs, and then became whole again. Kero now stood where the catapult once was. Kero stretched his arms, waiting for the next orders. The fireball that was once on the catapult fell to the ground and evaporated.

"I guess there is no need to be stealth anymore," said Emma. She waved her hand softly, releasing the energy of the sphere of invisibility she had created. She was very pleased by how long it had lasted. Qatu was a great instructor on telling his mages how to retain energy into a particular spell.

"So what now?" asked Daniel.

"We fight," she answered.

"We need help," the prisoner said. "Please release us."

"Of course, friend," said Razor.

"So they have shown themselves," Chris said. "Let's go."

"Ok. It's time to fight!" said Emma. "Let's go!" They all went running into a battle that was going to be a new experience. Emma and the others were about to face a battle to ensure the fate of the people of Absirthee, king Herbus, and even themselves. They were about to get a taste of what being a mage was all about. It was only a matter of time until they were now adults, powerful, and agile in their arts. Emma, Kero, Daniel, and Alex ran into battle, leading themselves into a fight. Chris and Aurora were close behind, providing support. Soría, Razor, and Erianna were now in the tower, releasing its prisoners, preparing the others for battle. It was time to win back the castle of Sular and to win back the king of Absirthee, Herbus.

CHAPTER SEVENTEEN
The Necromancer

The battle was on. Again the gang was now facing impending danger, but this time there were no powerful adult mages, but weaker, teenage mages who were naïve and inexperienced. The battle would change them forever, alter their minds, bodies and souls as would any dangerous experience. Emma looked onto the army of Mytred lined outside the castle, standing still, awaiting the ones that threaten them. Daniel followed his sister closely, making sure he saw her at all times, ready to be by her side, as he should have done at the Battle for Olgath Castle.

The guards were lined perfectly, in rows of ten and in twelve columns. There were over one hundred and twenty Mytred and one hundred undead creatures. Chris and Aurora joined the others now and were ready for anything. They walked slowly up to the area, a large vast space of land that separated the forest from the castle on the far end. It was larger than Olgath Castle with taller peaks, a larger gate and more rooms. The real difference was that this castle was not made of limestone but a very natural form of bark. The castle still looked formidable despite the material it was made of.

"I guess this is it. Are you guys ready?" asked Emma.

"Hmmm…I'll let you know later," said Chris.

They went unnoticed for a few moments before a large array of spears came hurling towards them.

"Everyone! Move out of the way!" Emma screamed. They were coming in fast and Emma didn't have much time to react. *"Schild der Magie! Schützen Sie uns!"*

As the array of spears converged, Emma's shield caused them to glance off the area where everyone was, protecting them from the onslaught of spears. They all fell to the group like rain drops, hitting the ground softly. Emma stood for a second, focusing on the next movement. She didn't know what she could do with such little planning time. It occurred to her that the Mytred weren't attacking anymore, they seemed to be waiting on something. Her answer came quickly when a dark stream from the sky hit the ground just yards away from them. A young man stepped out.

The man had deep teal eyes with black hair. The clothes he wore were purple with black specks elaborately decorating the cloak. His face was young, he looked to be in his mid twenties. He stepped out solemnly looking around and his eyes stopped when they hit Emma. He crossed his arms strictly, expressing deep regret.

"What a bad girl you have become," he said loudly, addressing Emma in particular.

"What do you mean?" she asked.

"How dare you ask me what I mean?" he objected. "You have come here disobeying your loving uncle to rescue a bunch of defenseless druids. He has treated you so well and you betray him."

"Treated us well?" asked Emma sarcastically. "I don't think so. He tried to kill us to get us out of the way. I don't see how he's helped."

"Oh. The tasks that you will endure may kill you despite Amethyst's efforts. He was doing you a favor. Besides, you'll die right here by the hands of Lucras the necromancer." He lowered his arms from being crossed during the dialogue. He looked down and then back up and raised his hands. *"Oh Necros, kill mine enemies!!!"* At saying of his words, a large black ball appeared and launched itself at the area of the others.

"Anti Necros, stop his attack!"

The ball started to fade, disintegrate as it approached. Emma looked back at Aurora, who had stopped his attack. As being an anti-necrosic cleric, she had the powers to counteract a necromancer's powers. Aurora looked on at Lucras, who wasn't very happy about her spell.

"I guess killing you won't be easy. Oh wait. I sense something." He looked up at the tower where Razor and the others were. His eyes shined from whatever he was sensing. He said in a low tone. "So. You have others. I'll take care of them."

"No you won't!" said Emma. "I will stop you."

"Well. I guess I need a diversion." he said walking away. "Mytred! Attack!"

At this the large group of Mytred standing guard came running towards them quickly. The pulsating ground provided more fear, expressing the large number of Mytred approaching. Emma stood there watching, not able to react. It took her seconds to realize she was in charge. She looked back at the others, realizing they were waiting for her orders. "The strategy is to disarm, knock out and render the Mytred useless. I am going in to help Razor and the others. Daniel is in charge until I return. Go to the castle and rescue Herbus and I'll take care of Lucras. Meet us in the castle!"

Daniel thought he was hearing things until everyone looked at him. He had never been given authority over anything in his life. Why would she leave the group and leave someone like him in charge? Before he could object Emma had already run off towards the tower, psi in hand, legs pumping.

"What do we do? They'll be here any minute," asked Kero

"All right," he said to himself. He was trying to calm himself. "We will fight them. I want Chris and Aurora to provide support while the rest of us fight. We'll need Aurora's blessing ability to provide us with more insight. I will use magic to freeze as many in time as I can. Everyone take advantage and fire away. Use any spell that will knock them out. Alexander. I think I'll leave you to make a distraction."

The distant screams of the Mytred became much more distinct as they appeared. The first group of thirty approached, waiting for something to happen. They arrived at the open area at the beginning of Grotus Forest and saw nothing. The group that they had been ordered to kill wasn't

148

there. The lead Mytred in the formal uniform embellished with small jewels and greenish strips spoke to the group.

"They are hiding and the easiest way to find them would be to sniff them out," he said. He rose his head ready for his spell when a light arrow streaked past his shoulder and hit a guard behind them. "Spread out! There is an archer!" he screamed. But before anyone could move, the ground suddenly grew moist. What appeared to be happening was that the ground turning into a giant pool of mucus. The guards moaned in displeasure, searching for the problem. Then they stopped, not stopped moving, but were stopped in time.

Daniel ran out with Alexander, Kero, and Chris closely behind. "Hurry Kero!" Daniel said. Kero placed his hands together in a ball. *"Kosten!"* he screamed. The process of electrifying his body came quickly, soon he was completely charged, ready for anything. "This may not work too well, I've never done it," he said calmly.

"You can do anything Kero. That's why you're here," said Daniel sincerely.

"Blitz-Verbrennen!" he said loudly, screaming came later as his body went beyond his control. He stood limply as the giant ball of electrical energy increased power by the second. Alex's spell started to wear off, causing the group to reach it's normal state, allowing the Mytred to be safely on the normal surface of the hard ground. As the spell became completely ready, the Mytred started to move, slowly coming out of the spell they had been encompassed in. They frantically looked up at the shiny ball of electricity. Before they had time to move, it came crashing down on them, causing them to fall unconscious. The impact of the fall made the ground quiver. The ball fell apart on impact creating thousands of tiny balls that now caressed the ground near all of the now unconscious Mytred. Kero stood as steady as his could, waiting for his body to catch up with him.

"Are you going to be alright?" asked Daniel.

"Yeah. I just have to take it easier. How did you stop all of them without even getting tired?" he asked Daniel

"I don't know really. I guess it's blood, I mean Amethyst is my uncle," said Daniel laughing. He never thought of the magnitude of the spell he had just completed. "Maybe it was just luck," said Daniel laughing again. It all just seemed so easy. Suddenly Kero just stopped laughing. Kero stood there transfixed by the arrow sticking into his chest. He plummeted to the ground from the pain. "Are you alright? Aurora! I need you!" screamed Daniel. Alex leaned next to him, making sure that he was alright.

"Move away from him," said Aurora as she approached with Chris behind her. She crouched down near Kero and reached in her belt for gloves. "I need you to be still, I'm going to pull the arrow out." Aurora proceeded by putting on her gloves and pulled the arrow straight shot out, blood started to dribble out of the wound uncontrollably. *"Slow the wound!"* she said loudly. The spell stopped the flow of blood long enough to bandage him with a crimson glow coming from his chest.

"Thank you. I am in your debt," said Kero coughing.

"No. It's just what I do best. Now we need to find out where that arrow came from."

"I know where it came from. There, on that northwest tower, there are at least a hundred archers up there, they shot at him when he least expected. They are too high for any of my arrows to reach. But if I can get at least four hundred yards further I could get an easy shot with an explosive arrow, that would destroy them and the tower." said Chris quickly.

Daniel observed the distance. It sounded easy but they would struggle to get there without being shot. There was the other ninety Mytred that placed themselves in various areas, awaiting for them to cross their paths. Daniel surveyed the area closely, looking for an outlet for protection in case things got heavy. He simply decided on using magic to assist him, that and his long staff, perfect for blocking arrows.

"Ok. We're going to knock out those arrows. Use the magic that will help you the most, and try not to get hit." The sun was setting and it began to grow darker. He watched the sky carefully for anymore approaching arrows, they would be hard to see at night, but he had a way of seeing in the dark. He gestured for Chris and Alexander to follow him. They started off in a slow walk and increased into a run, spanning over the area where the Mytred had fallen.

They ran as fast as they could, it was getting too dark to notice any significant features on the ground. Daniel stopped first while the others caught up. "Ok. I'm going to send a flair up into the sky to see if any arrows are coming. It'll stay up there long enough to reach the archers. After that the Mytred and then to help Emma. I hope she's alright," he told them.

"What if any of the arrows start raining on us?" asked Alex.

"Use any magic necessary to avoid them," he told both of them.

They continued on a run and the flair that he sent up was still in the sky. It was slightly like Kero's lightning combustion except it sparkled brilliantly and created a great amount of light to see. They were soon within a hundred yards when the first arrow aimed at Daniel missed him and stuck into the ground. Daniel stopped to look up to see that many more arrows were coming down on them. As the arrows approached them he quickly charged a spell.

"Intimo a parede invisível! Bloqueie ataques do meu inimigo!" The arrows that were converging glanced off an invisible wall created by Daniel's spell. He looked up smiling as each arrow struck the invisible wall he had created. Alex and Chris looked at him disturbingly without Daniel noticing. More and more arrows rained down as they continued on. Chris had conjured a large sword to protect himself while Alex altered his hand into a large metal block. Daniel used his magic to create a large force field to protect him.

In no time they had reached the tower that was built to protect the castle. The castle was further beyond the south tower and the north tower where Emma was. Inside the castle would be Herbus himself most likely in his own dungeon. They stopped in front of the tower. Daniel veered back at his colleagues.

"What's wrong you guys?" asked Daniel. His friends were flustered and their faces were hot with exhaustion. They looked back at him with angry eyes.

"Are you telling me you are not tired of all this magic using and running?" asked Chris. He didn't seem too happy.

"No. I'm not tired at all. I don't think I've ever been tired of using magic," he said casually. Alex and Chris shrugged and looked up at the tower that controlled the northern part of the gate. The two towers had a large gate between them. "Alright Chris, do your thing," he said.

Chris readied his bow without an arrow. Instead he took other precautions such as breathing calmly and closing his eyes. *"Arrow of Explosion!"* he screamed loudly. At the command of his spell, an arrow appeared out of thin air, displaying similar symbols to his other arrows. He strung the bow firmly and launched it into the air. *"Multiply!"* The arrow now became ten arrows. They converged onto the top of the castle and created a chain reaction of explosions, causing the Mytred to fall from above.

"Good job man," Daniel began. "No we can get inside through the large hole in the gate you created. It actually killed the those guards and the archers guarding the gate. Now we just have to go the castle. Hopefully Emma will meet us there like planned."

"You bastard!" screamed Razor. "How dare you come to *my* land and overthrow *my* king. You don't deserve to live not after killing all of the ones you so called prisoners. They were my friends and now I'm going to take your life." Razor had just witnessed the most evil killings in his life. With a blink of his eye, Lucras had killed the prisoners in the tower. Emma had joined them in time to see it. They all stood behind him, allowing him to vent his anger.

"Pish Posh," said Lucras. "Do you obviously think that I can be killed by you, a druid whose powers are only useful for gardening. Don't test me now that *she* is here. The little mage who dare betrayed the great Amethyst. Now if you will, die for me?"

"Lucras. I know that you don't want to do this. I can feel it. You're good inside." said Emma

"No. I don't think that's true. How are you getting into my head girl, your not even a mentalist mage. My mind is not enterable by you."

"Tell that to your sister," said Soría.

"My sister?" asked Lucras, "Stop distracting me! She's dead and now you will be."

"Come. Now it's time! Hurry!" Soría yelled. At that a strange apparition appeared. It was Daniel. He was in the same attire, but now he was in projection formed thanks to his ability to telepathically project himself into people. He turned around and saw Lucras. He dove into his body, making Lucras cry out.

"What are you doing? Get out of my head!"

"Brechen Sie die Barriere auf seiner Meinung. Öffnen Sie es zu unser!" screamed Emma.

"So Lucras. Your sister was killed by Amethyst correct? You only joined him after Vicousir was killed and your sister was killed for rebellion. You were scared weren't you?" asked Soría.

"No," he said quickly. Something inside him refused him the ability to lie, He was talking through someone else now. "Yes. I was scared for my life. I didn't want to end up like my sister so I did everything he asked me."

"Why is he after us? What is he truly looking for?"

"He knows you'll keep him from the power. It'll keep him from making his plan complete, from getting the ultimate power to..." Lucras didn't finish his sentence because he was instantly forced into the wall, killed instantly. A man in a dark hooded cloak appeared from the spot. He kneeled down and replaced the torch on the wall. He then approached the body and spoke quickly, disintegrating the body of Lucras the necromancer. He stood there for a while and then spoke.

"The poor soul. His death will find him happy," he began. "My plan didn't work to get you killed. I hate it when I have to do work myself, but since I already have an idea of how easy it will be I will enjoy this."

"Who are you?" asked Kero. He was in front of the girls, attempting to protect them.

"Why. I'm just an old friend," he said. The man removed his hood. His dark skin shined in the reflection of the torch. His eyes fell upon the group. What was surprising about the man was that he was supposed to be dead. They were looking at Chaos in the flesh.

Chapter Eighteen
The True Evil

Chaos grinned at his guests. He glared at Emma who was now looking at him with questioning eyes. Chaos was presumably dead a few weeks ago and now he stood in front of them, smiling broadly. His face was no longer smooth and unharmed, but with bruises on his eyebrow, cheeks, and a busted lip. Chaos turned around to look at the painting behind him. He didn't talk. He seemed to be waiting for something.

"Chaos?" asked Emma. "You're alive. But my vision showed me that you had died," she said with confusion. She watched as Chaos turned around and walked closer to them. He grinned once more at her, ready to answer her question. His boots clicked as he walked slowly towards them with his hands in his robe pockets. He stared wide eyed at Emma for a few seconds then lowered his gaze.

"You're such a stupid girl," he said softly. "You honestly believed that bogus vision I sent you. You really ought to focus on protecting your mind. I'm not dead girl and I was never near it."

"But how?" Emma asked.

"You see. You have a rare gift called telepathy. This gift lets you link your mind with another mage, knowing what they are wearing, eating, how they feel. This gift is used by a very small percentage of our kind. But the problem with this power is that you cannot close it out if you are trying to be contacted or better yet, you don't know how. You have a weakness my dear girl. This weakness makes you vulnerable in some sense. I sent you the vision, made you think that I was dying and that Derrick and Emily were actually here. You see your father was never spotted here. It was all a ploy to lure you into this deathtrap."

"Where are they?"

"Well. If you must ask they are with the Mytred, being held against their will in a cell with bars, no windows, no comfort at all. They are probably being tortured as we speak, but their role isn't all that important so it makes it for a bit of a wasteful torturing."

"You work for Amethyst? How is that possible?" asked Erianna

"When I first met Emma. I planted an idea in her head, that she could trust me. I knew as a member of the Dale family, she'd naturally be suspicious of me. So I let her believe that as I planted things in her mind. The vision was planted, my death, and other things that she may never be aware of. I've been working for Swiverstheee for quite a while, watching over alliance issues. You see, you are here because Amethyst wants you dead and in the event that Lucras would fail and I would take the job and dispose of you myself." Chaos crossed his arms, waiting for a reaction.

"Hmm…well I guess we'll have to dispose of you before you get the chance," said Emma grinding her teeth in anger. She walked in front of Razor and collected the psis from their ankle holders. She readied herself for an attack.

"Poor girl. I won't waste my time fighting you. I am far superior in battle than you."

"Try me."

"I guess I will," he said. He then threw off his cloak revealing attire he wore underneath. The attire was sleek tight against his body like undergarments, a simple shirt and pants, dark black with symbols written on it. He took his weapon from its hilt off his back. It was a long broadsword that stood six feet tall. He took a stance and charged head first into Emma.

Emma had almost no time to react, in response she performed a front flip over him, but still received damage from it. It sliced her traveling pants and exposed the skin on her legs. Chaos's sword was too tall for her to do that again. She looked at the man before her with his piercing deep brown eyes and his deteriorating youthful visage.

"Why would you turn to such an evil man? Why abandon the side of good?" she asked him this.

"You. You weren't so good yourself. You were a narcissist who believed nothing was more important than herself. Poor girl. I was always evil and it's not by force either. You see, I was born on a small island outside of Swiverstheee known as Syra. As a young man I joined an Arcane Alliance. It's not the alliance you are with, but another. There are more than one alliance and in fact there are hundreds. I joined the Arcane Alliance of Necros and worked in correspondence with the most evil mages of this age, some even deadlier than myself. This world is run by these secret *arcane* alliances."

"How do you know who I *used* to be. I've changed from that young naïve girl who made fun of those people I thought were less than me. How about how I used to hurt my brother to see his sad face or hear him cry out. Now I've learned. Coming here was planned for me and that made me discover myself. I've lost those ways when I came here and I'm happier than I've ever been. It's been six months since leaving Earth Realm. There's one thing I learned that blew everything else out of proportion."

"And what is that my dear girl?" asked Chaos smiling. He held his sword at his side, enjoying their exchange of dialogue.

"Evil is my enemy and I must use all my power to stop it," she said. She watched for a reaction from Chaos, but the surprising thing was his strange emergence of laughter.

"Hah. You're more powerful than me easily, but you don't know why and you won't find out because you'll be dead before you do. Heck I may be the only one that does know, poor Amethyst is unaware. Please. Let's stop this silly chatting and get back to our fight." Chaos lifted his sword and charged directly at her.

Emma had no time to react from this charge either and all she could do was brace herself. He swung his sword vertically down at her, but she veered slightly causing him to miss. She was regaining perspective of her true power. Just as she did with Kero, she would predict his moves before he made them. The problem was when and where would her power falter and cause her to lose concentration. He swung again, this time she jumped into the air and kicked him square in the head, he stumbled back from the impact.

"Foresight. You're a clever girl, but your power can only protect you and not your friends over there," he said. He looked back at the group who watched them battle. He held out his hand and started mumbling under his breath. A large sphere of photonic energy blasted toward the group with great speed. As it approached them, the sphere slowed and stopped in mid-air. Chaos looked puzzled. He turned around and looked at Emma who was just as confused, but a hooded man stood several feet behind her, holding his hand out. He crushed his fist and the photon sphere erupted into tiny shards.

"Who are you?" Chaos asked the hooded figure. The man was wearing a long emerald colored robe with gold trimmings. He was about six feet tall. His beard peeked through the hood. It was an old man who had stopped Chaos's attack. "I am but a friend of these people," the man said quietly. He moved his hand up to his hood and lowered it.

He revealed himself at that moment. He had a haggard looking face that was flustered from extraneous traveling. His eyes sparkled as he looked on. The man walked up to Emma and stood next to her and put a hand on her shoulder. "I am Vyshu, the telekinetic. I think that my service would be appreciated," he said.

Chaos looked at the man as he stealthily took a dagger from his back robe pocket. "Vyshu Axel. I've not seen you since they locked you up months ago. I see that you escaped with that other bastard magus, Kero. Damn you for returning now. I ought to kill you right now. But I won't. You see, there are some things that we need to discuss." At that moment, Chaos threw the dagger directly at Vyshu's head, but it didn't hit him and instead remained hovering three inches from his face. The dagger turned with the movement of Vyshu's eyes and faced its edge toward the thrower.

"I see you didn't know that the eyes are but the window to my power. Would you like to die now or die later? There are lots of ways to die without blood, how about I take an arm or a leg? Would like your heart ripped from your body, or your eyes thrust out of their sockets?"

"Damn you. I'll have to kill you later. I see no reason to be here after all." Chaos stepped back into a dark rainbow that took him out of the tower to only he knew. Chaos had left them now, but the question was not how, but why.

"Why did he leave because you came. Is he afraid of you?" asked Emma. The others were approaching Vyshu as she spoke.

"Power mages are usually evenly matched when it comes to battle. Too bad for him, I senior him in battle and magic quite well. He's afraid to lose and in that case he fled," said Vyshu picking up chaos' cloak from the ground. "I know Chaos well from childhood. He could never beat me in battle because my telekinesis outweighs him and that is why he is fearful of me in total. I'm glad I made it in time to help out, I owe Kero my life and in return I owe his friends their lives as well."

"I'm glad you came Vyshu, I've heard lots about you. I think that we should head towards the castle to meet Herbus who has been captured." said Emma

"Lead the way my dear," said Vyshu smiling.

Emma, along with the others, left the tower and took the short trip into the desolate castle, all that could be heard was the whistling wind. The castle peaked high into the sky as they approached the entrance. The gate had been lowered and the castle walls were damaged to a degree most likely due to magical onslaught. They passed over the drawbridge and into the main hall of the entrance where a large statue of a strange mage stood. *Here we celebrate our ancestor Rian, the greatest Druid in history.* They passed the large statue and to a longer corridor with many doors and entrance ways. Once passed the corridor, they entered the central hall where Herbus sat on his throne, conversing with Daniel, Alex, and Chris.

"Daniel. Chris. Alex. Are all of you alright?" asked Emma as they approached. She had the entire party behind her, waiting to hear Herbus speak.

"Everything went well. Thanks for asking," replied Daniel. "We've been here for a while now and talking to Herbus. He can't talk well so we just told him to wait until you came…"

Emma walked closer to the throne to get a better look at the king. As the man sat, he breathed in and out slowly as if trying to catch air. His gray hair flowed ruggedly down his back and beard caressed a small about of his chest. He looked down at her with brown saddened eyes as he steadied himself in the chair trying to stand.

"Don't. I think you'd better just sit," said Emma consolingly. She walked closer toward the throne, showing that she would move closer to hear him. She reached the bottom step leading to an array of steps to the throne to show respect. She raised from her bow and walked up to the throne. "I am Emma Dale from the Arcane Alliance of Nexus. I am here to help you however we can," she said properly. Now as a considered adult mage, she was a part of an Arcane Alliance. The Arcane Alliance of Nexus was the true name of the organization she represented.

"Many lives lost. Many plants have died, and I still sit here, enduring every minute of it," the king said harshly. "I am very appreciative that you came to help, but you shouldn't have. Now that you have come, I am forced to provide my support for the war. As a payment of respect, my troops are at your disposal."

"Sire. Your troops are all wounded, trapped someone in this castle, or dead. What we need is you. There are problems in Olgath as we speak. Can you come help us?"

"Alas. My body is too weak for travel. If any case it would tear the last few breaths from my lungs. I will send you my only other asset, my son. He will go with you and return here to take the throne as I feel my years leaving me."

"Thank you. May I ask who your son is?" asked Emma.

"Razor. He is around here somewhere. I will send him to assist you in need. I'm sorry to say that only a few of you can go concerning lack of rations and supplies," said the King slowly.

Emma ran her hand through her hair, considering the options. With the new evidence of Razor being the king's son, she was forced to have him go, but it was so many of them. There was no way that all of them would go. She looked at her brother and came up with a solution. "Daniel. You, Chris, Razor, and Vyshu will go to Olgath," she said directly.

"What?" Daniel shrieked. "Are you crazy? What are you going to do?" he asked her.

"I'll remain here with the others to keep things stable until there are supplies for us to meet you in Olgath. Here," she said as she dug into her pocket and handed him the scrying glass. "Take it with you. I'm counting on you Daniel. I need you to help them while we help Absirthee recover. Can I trust you?" she asked.

"Yeah. You can," Daniel replied smiling. He was now given a mission to lead a gang of mages into Everstheee. It laid hundreds of miles away from Absirthee, it's neighbor. As they prepared that night to leave, he recalled that Emma always tried her best to give him credit. Now was his chance to show Salari and the others that he really was useful.

As they left the following morning, he waved goodbye to his sister after just giving her a hug. Behind him, Razor, Chris, and Vyshu followed closely. Daniel was ready for any challenge that he would face. As they left the castle borders he recalled the first time he'd used magic. It had made him so happy and now he felt that again. It was like starting from the beginning once again. Only now, it would be twice as difficult and ten times more thrilling. Olgath was only a small city outside of Olgath Castle. What could be all the hubbub be about?

CHAPTER NINETEEN
The Ballad of Razor

Daniel stood there, perplexed at the spectacle that now stood before him. The white ground reflected the sun from above, as if reflecting the luminescence of it. He looked down at the ground with its soft layer of ice, snow to be exact. He scooped his hand into it, gazing into his hand covered with snow. Absirthee was gone and what stood before them was the oncoming, or already commenced winter. The birds chirped softly from the trees surrounding the frozen pond. Daniel looked into the ice pond and saw his reflection. There he saw who he had become, a daring, dashing, and braver young man. Daniel knew that his existence in Sulex was to bring about a change in himself. He remembered who he once was, someone who couldn't be trusted. Daniel's mission was to simply rid the world of evil, an almost impossible task.

"What are you doing?" asked Razor approaching. The snow crunched under his boots as he approached and sat down next to Daniel, staring out onto the pond. Razor sat quietly, waiting for Daniel to respond.

"I'm just thinking about everything. I mean there are just three more days to travel and we'll be there. I mean what exactly are we going to find there?"

"Chaos. And I don't mean the person. We're going to find something terrible and you know that. The problem is that you know it's bad and yet you still go for it. That's a pretty brave act."

"Hmm. Brave wasn't the word you could describe me with just a few months ago. I not only worry about what'll happen to all of us, but to Emma too. I wish I could talk to her. She knows how to boost my confidence."

"You're an idiot," said Razor defiantly. "Didn't you learn anything from Chaos? Telepathy is mind linking. Don't you know that twins can master telepathy far more superior than any other mages. All you have to do is concentrate on her, and then you'll be able to communicate."

"You're right. I think I will do that, but now isn't a good time. We have to get going soon and I think Vyshu and Chris are taking way too long to collect fire wood."

The dialogue between them ended abruptly as Vyshu and Chris returned flustered from their gatherings. Without any extra talking, they gathered their supplies and headed further south towards Olgath. Chris and Vyshu explained that they were diverted because of a large creature that had attacked them. Neither Chris nor Vyshu was sure of what it was, but it was extraordinarily powerful. As a distraction, they created scapegoats.

Daniel lead the others deeper into the white abyss, fascinated by every minute of it. It was strange that just a few days ago, they were complaining about the heat. The cycle of weather was much faster than he had experienced and it caused him physical discomfort and strange allergic reactions. His skin began to darken as well as his hair. Daniel was perplexed by the rapid change in his body. The weather must have caused it.

He had never found purpose until now, understanding clearly why he had come to the world. He had lost a home and a family only to regain it in a span of days. It was sudden and frightening that he had no idea where his mom was. He was worried about her, for fear of what would happen to her. He recalled telepathy and thought of a plan to finally understand where his mother had gone. The curiosity killed him inside, making him more and more unsteady about his decision.

Over the next few days, Daniel, Chris, Vyshu, and Razor maintained a steady routine. In the morning they would wake up and have a quiet breakfast of sausage and eggs. After preparing their gear, they would walk for hours on end without rest. Absirthee did not believe in domesticating animals and therefore they had no horses for them to travel on. After hours on end of traveling, they would rest, have dinner, and go to sleep. There was only one time that this routine was broken.

Daniel stayed up that night, two more days to Olgath. He looked up into the sky through the translucent tent. The stars were almost complimentary to the moon in brightness. He was overly fascinated with the world he had called home. But there was so much he didn't know. From his knowledge, there was not a shed of early history about Sulex.

As he lay there he thought intensely, one thought finished out the next. He started thinking of Harsie again, the woman he had so called mother without second thoughts. Was it her feelings that he felt, and not his own. Chaos's speech on telepathy made him understand that he was vulnerable as well, unable to close his mind from outside forces.

Questions arose from them, one after another. He had never thought so profoundly of life. At least not since he was in Earth Realm, unable to grasp a true persona and a true reason to exist. Daniel shifted on his back and reached out for his book *Mages of All Kind*, the book Qatu gave him. He looked up telepathy from the index.

Telepathy, in literal terms means "distant feeling", derived from the Latin language. A mage uses it to veer into a mind or communicate with someone far away. Telepathy can be compared to a very active form of scrying, allowing the person scryed for to be communicated with. Mages do this by concentrating on that person and seeing him or her in his or her mind. Telepathy can be used in many ways and many forms. Twin mages are most inherent in the skill because of a mental link formed between them at birth. Twins not only possess a telepathy linking the two, but also with the blood that is closest to them. This fact shows....

Daniel closed the book. That was it. He now knew the most crucial part he had missed. Telepathy allowed him to communicate with his twin, some magical mind linking from birth. But he missed it in lesson, he could communicate with blood. This made Daniel uneasy. Although Emma hadn't learned telepathy before the Alliance, she did use it quite often. Could she have been communicating with Harsie the entire time? Daniel thought on it and came to a conclusion.

He laid flat on his back, closing his eyes tightly. His mind formed the image of a woman with blonde hair, mage robes, and boots. Daniel stood before her, awaiting her response. They were in a large room it seemed, but the surrounding area was completely black, not giving a hint to where they convened or where Harsie was physically.

"What do you need my dear?" she asked quietly. She stood still, as if a statue.

"Why have you left me?" He asked.

"My mission is important and I can't talk about it."

"But you've talked to Emma about it!" Daniel interjected. *"I know you've been talking to her about it. Why can't you tell me?"*

Harsie looked at him broad eyed, transfixed by the events occurring before her. *"It's not your time, son. It will be your time to know when it is necessary, but for now you must leave."*

Daniel reacted negatively to the comment. He grew angry and confused by her words. Harsie walked closely to him, taking slow and steady steps, reaching her hand out. *"Don't hate me for this son, but it's for the safety of your life."* she placed her hand on his head calmly, picking at it as if looking for something. *"It's time for you to go. You're friends are in trouble. Wake up now!"*

Daniel had no time to react. By the time he realized what she was doing, he was already awake. His eyes were now open and he stared straight up through the top of the tent. It had snowed that night, causing the top of the tent to be weighed down by the heavy snow. He sat up, bedazzled by the brightness of the tent. The snow and sun combination made it brighter than he was used to. After giving his eyes time to adjust, he exited the tent into the camp. The area was desolate land, bare even from the snow.

Most of the trees blocked snow from it, so the land was hard dirt and gravel. Daniel searched the area for Vyshu and the others, but no one was in sight. He walked up to the camp fire that had been put out, smoke rose from it. They hadn't left long ago, but the silence was making him edgy, he could feel the tension within. Without warning Vyshu appeared from the bushes and grabbed him. Vyshu tackled him down.

"What are you doing!?" asked Daniel getting up and wiping himself down.

"Oh. It's you," said Vyshu. The old man looked at him with broad eyes. "I'm sorry. I thought you were the beast."

"How did you tackle me down old man?" asked Daniel in frustration. It took him several seconds to take note of Vyshu's comment. "What beast?"

Vyshu sat down on a log by the fire, wiping his sweaty brow with a face towel. "The creature attacked us in the night. We tried to call you, but you never came. It's a big creature with white fangs and white fur. It had talons and big red eyes too."

"White fangs and white fur? It sounds like a yeti to me. But I don't know if they exist in this world or even in Earth Realm."

"Whatever it was, it forced us to split up, the beast is impervious to our uses of magic. Maybe you could make something of it?"

Daniel got up from the log adjacent to Vyshu. "We'll go look for the others. It has to have a weakness," he said. He then led Vyshu through the trees in search of the others, but he stopped suddenly. *"A deusa de Katus do perdido, mostre-nos aos nossos amigos!"* After speaking those words, a small nymph-like creature appeared, flying rapidly around his head. "Find Chris and the others, lead us to them!" The little creature responded to his command instantly, flying to the right rapidly. Daniel and Vyshu ran to keep up with it.

The bug flew fast, possibly thirty miles per hour as Vyshu and Daniel struggled to keep up with it. The snow began to thicken as they were lead further into the direction they had been lead. Their cloaks shook violently as they sped past clusters of trees and shrubs. The creature, Katus, stopped abruptly. "Your friends lie there, in the cave yonder." The creature spun in a circle rapidly, vanishing from thin air.

The cave was down the steep hill, secluded from the rest of the forest. Daniel and Vyshu found themselves quickly at the bottom of the hill, glaring into the dark abyss that was the entrance to the desolate cave. The cave had a small opening with cragged rocks surrounding the interior. As they walked in, it became clearer, absorbing the outside light. Daniel remembered when he traveled to Carl's Bad Cavern and viewed the stalagmites that hung from the cave. But the strange thing about this cave, was that it was a smooth surface, as if it had never suffered from dripping water. The floor was hard and smooth, lacking much room for friction.

There was another weird detail about the cave. There were lights inside. Daniel had mistaken the odd light for light outside. It took him a few minutes of walking to discover the mine cart in front of him. The suspected cave was a mine, but for what? Daniel and Vyshu proceeded forward, dipping down the awkward slope in the mine. The lights above were bright and arranged like any other mine, in a straight line just inches apart. The gravel underneath their feet caused them to slip up on occasion because their shoes did not grip the ground. "Are they even down here?" asked Vyshu. He was rather tired. Being an old man made him a bit more cranky than any other members of the party. "I trust Katus," Daniel replied confidently.

The sudden shuffle of the ground made Daniel uneasy. Something was moving rapidly towards them, but the lights in that part of the mine were out, making it a disadvantage. Before he knew it, he was on the ground. "Stop!" someone yelled. Out of thin air a light appeared above, hovering up and down at a slow speed. Daniel looked into the eyes of his attacker, it was Vyshu. "Oh. I'm sorry," he said embarrassingly. "I thought you were the attacker." Daniel got up and saw the person who had summoned the light, Chris stood before them shaking his head. "You guys don't know how to survive."

Chris then proceeded forward, admiring the embarrassment of his friends. "So where's Razor?" he asked. Daniel looked at him with question. "I though he was with you." No one said anything for a while. "Ok. Tell me what happened and maybe we can find him," said Daniel. Vyshu, Chris, and Daniel all proceeded out of the mine, attempting to piece together a story of razor's absence. "He ran off with us after we tried to fight that beast, I never saw where he went." Daniel scratched his head in confusion.

"Wait," he began. "Katus only brought us here and nowhere else. That means that Razor is definitely in the mine. We should go back in." Chris and Vyshu didn't argue and quickly followed Daniel back into the obscure cave. "Maybe he is somewhere in one of these tunnels?" said Chris. Daniel looked throughout the various tunnels, finding a way to search for Razor efficiently. Chris re-summoned the light that resided in the cave earlier. Their silhouettes danced on the mine wall as they descended.

The ground soon became caressed with smaller pebbles, allowing less chances of slipping down the steep hill. They followed the tunnel walls above, attempting to find a pattern or clue that would lead to Razor himself. The distant humming of a tune resounding from the tunnels as they approached an array of tunnels. As they came closer to one of the intersecting tunnel. The voice sang softly in tandem with the tune.

"Here now I call to thee. My father, blood of blood, death to death. We are the ones at night, calming the ones beyond the blood and tears. Here we hypnotize those dealing with life, the lust of their blood——"

"Psiops! Remove this wall!" screamed Vyshu. The wall that muffled the song collapsed into a large heap of small boulders. Within the small opening sat Razor, on a rock and looking up at Vyshu. Vyshu grasped him, almost as if strangling his coat. "Vampire! How dare you accompany us!?" Daniel and Chris looked on, perplexed by the spectacle.

CHAPTER TWENTY
The Yeti

Vampire. Daniel let the word sink in despite how strange it sounded. Vampires weren't real and never had been. They were fictitious beings that fed off the blood of their victims and turned into bats. A vampire now didn't sound as strange since the world he now stood in brought unimaginable creatures to life. He stared on at Vyshu, violently shaking the collar of Razor's tunic. Chris watched on fearfully, otherwise afraid to interfere.

"Vampire! You have dared to interfere with us!" Vyshu screamed, staring Razor in the eyes, even angrier because of Razor's lack of interest in his anger. "I am a vampire, yes, but it's not what you think," Razor said softly.

"Let him go," said Daniel. "Let him explain himself before you attack him." Vyshu reluctantly obliged to Daniel's command. "Razor. Explain yourself before Vyshu attacks again."

After being released by Vyshu, Razor rose to his feet, unflustered from Vyshu's anger. He walked slowly out of the opening that Vyshu had created and into the tunnel where Daniel and Chris now stood. "I'm not a vampire entirely," he began. "I'm half vampire, half druid." The others stared on questionably. Perplexed at the strange mixture of races that he had so simply explained. As if acknowledging the confusion, Razor continued on.

"My mother birth me from my father, Acula who was a vampire. They loved each other more than any couple could love one another. Vampires were only evil when they wanted to be, and my dad just wasn't that. So when he was murdered by Amethyst, mother couldn't handle it. Months later she died of a mysterious disease and I was left alone as an infant and raised as Herbus's son. Amethyst and his master, Vicousir used the blood of vampires to make their own power for necromancy. As far as I know, vampires are extinct. But with vampiric blood I suffer from not being able to control my powers fully. If it wasn't for Herbus, I wouldn't know where I came from.

"I know it may be hard to understand, but I'm just as good as anyone else here. If you want me to leave I will." He started to walk off after his speech, but stopped abruptly. Daniel stood behind him, grasping his shoulder firmly. "I can't let you leave on account of lineage or heredity. You're a powerful asset and a good friend. I need you here and so does the rest of us." Razor turned around and stood blankly, looking into Daniel's eyes, no longer clutched from Daniel's grasp. From what he saw, he now stood calm. "You have made me most obliged. I will stay at your request, friend."

Razor now lead them back out of the cave, ready for whatever stood next. Although Vyshu didn't reject Daniel's opinion, he did seem uneasy about his decision. Vyshu remained quiet, almost brooding in a way that openly expressed Vyshu's questioning of Daniel's request that Razor remain with them. It wasn't time for that now because of the large creature awaiting them at the mine entrance.

It stood tall in the mine, it's head almost reaching the top of the ceiling. The fur of the beast stood out the most. It was shaggy and very long, making it appear as if it were a big, shaggy dog. The proportion of its body was irregular, the feet were bigger than its hands and the claws were presentable larger than the foot. The beast stood on two feet, as if part of man. Its big red eyes looked down curiously at the group.

"Why is it just standing there?" asked Chris. "Just earlier it wanted to rip us to sheds."

"But there is something different now," said Vyshu walking forward. "The beast has not seen our leader and now it seems to be intrigued by him." Vyshu attempted to walk forward, but Daniel held out his arm, blocking his path.

Daniel walked closer to the Yeti, attempting to discover its true motive. As his boots silently clashed the stone floor, he began to feel strange, almost attracted to the beast. A strange energy emitted from the center of the room, between Daniel and the beast. Strangely enough, this energy projected a person, distinctively a short female in Eskimo-type clothing. She stepped out of the wavering energy circle and walked to Daniel, softly, yet determined. "Daniel. I am the Yeti, the guardian of this land and the one who will give you answers."

Daniel now stood, awaiting for the "Yeti" to get closer. Could this woman actually be a Yeti, or the spirit of one? Her beauty was radiant and attractive to the eyes. She had rosy cheeks, beautiful long black hair, and deep blue eyes. "What answers?" he asked slowly. "I am the Yeti and I have information for you, something that you need to be told. Do you want to obtain this information?" Daniel looked on silently, contemplating the issue. "Yes I do, what do you want?" he asked quickly. "I don't have time for diversions."

"It is you that must defeat me, the Yeti and I will grant you the information you seek," she said. "I am Nora, the spirit of the Yeti and the guardian of the winter, I am winter." Nora turned around from where she stood and walked back to the Yeti that now stood steady, breathing softly and serenely. "Where are you going?" asked Daniel. Nora looked back on him, "A beast cannot fight without its soul." With this she disappeared into the beast, awakening it from its calm serenity.

The beast resumed its position and walked out of the mine. "What is it doing?" asked Vyshu. "It's giving me room to fight. I want you all to stay here and let me handle it. I don't want any interferences." Daniel left the others, jogging outside of the mine and following the Yeti that was leading him to a rather open space, banal and unmarked of trees or any other vegetation. His feet crunched in the snow that was now getting deeper by the second. Daniel found it often strange that the snow was getting deeper on a level elevation, without time to investigate, he continued on.

The Yeti was waiting patiently for him. He arrived short-breathed and red-faced from the cold. "I hope you're ready to be defeated!" Daniel yelled out, attempting to anger it. The beast got angry within seconds and suddenly bolted toward him and waved an arm at Daniel. Before he knew it, he was on the ground ten feet away bruised from the impact. Daniel quickly got up, attempting his first spell. *"Conexão! Fogo de respiração no meu inimigo"* With the formation complete, between his hands formed a streaming inferno headed directly toward the beast.

It looked on at the approaching fire, but simply roared at it, with this coaxing a frozen blizzard from the depths of its mouth. It breathed a blizzard onto the fire, putting it out instantly. Of course, thought Daniel, the beast was the cause of the instantaneous change of seasons from summer to winter. The change had been brought about by the beast itself, the guardian of the winter. Daniel watched as the last speck of his fire exhausted himself. His initial plan had failed. "What am I going to?" he asked himself. The beast crouched low, planning another tackle onto Daniel. This time he was hit harder, knocked twice as hard and far.

Daniel couldn't get up now, his legs were now weak from the second ambush. He tried to rise, but his side, his front, and his back were now aching painfully. He could hear the beast running towards him, ready to kill him with its impact. He attempted to start a spell, but his arms hurt too much to charge one. He only wished that he could stop the beast in its track. "Stop!" he screamed. Although he never would have expected what happened next. The running stopped instantaneously, as he lifted himself up to see the beast frozen in time. Who could have done that?

Now that he had time, he arose as quickly as he could and ran the opposite way of the beast, passing it while he headed toward the opposite direction, limping as he ran. Before he knew it, the beast stood before him, calmly. "You have done well," it said quietly. It was the voice of Nora that now spoke to him. She slowly moved from the body of the Yeti and now existed as a corporeal being. "You have defeated me as you promised," she said softly.

Daniel looked back at her. He couldn't recall defeating the beast, but actually nearly getting killed. "How did I defeat you?" he began. "I would have died if it hadn't been for that ." Nora held up her hand to stop him.

"You see, it was you that stopped me. I was stopped by the secret magic that dwells in you."

"Secret magic?" asked Daniel.

"Your ancestor Olgath was another race of mage, a sorcerer if you must. A sorcerer does not dwell on magics of spells and incantations, but their magic is natural, almost limitless. You have inherited it, become the new knight in shining armor. After using your magic, you freed me from my prison, as promised by the queen of Everstheee."

Following Nora's comment, Daniel stood dumbfounded, almost in a trance of utter confusion. Him? The knight in shining armor? All this time he had been the key. The sudden bursts of magical energy, longer strenuous magic usage without exhaustion, the transformation. It all fit now. He was the destined to follow in the footsteps of his great grandfather. "What do I do now that I know?" he asked her. "Follow your quest and your power will be questioned and there you will meet the summoner who will restore all of the knight's power."

Before Daniel could ask more questions Nora vanished, and with her went the empty shell of the Yeti. He now stood in the green grass without snow, and looked up to the shining sun. He had learned what Harsie was hiding. But did Emma already know or was she only aware of other things? He walked back toward the caves, expecting many questions.

CHAPTER TWENTY-ONE
Olgath, the City of Justice

The wind howled furiously, creating a morbid voice. The wind didn't bother her, nor did it bother the man that stood behind her, gazing silently from behind, touching the inner thoughts surrounding her aura of mental energy. She casually blocked it off, jerking her head in a way that she was showing off. She turned around and stared into the man's deep blue eyes. He smiled at her, and dropped the smile once she recognized him.

"Why do you stalk me brother?" asked Harsie.

"You see, you are hard to find indeed, but this place I knew you'd come. And I've been waiting for some time, hoping that I would get to see you my dear sister." Amethyst said mockingly.

Harsie smirked from his remark, recalling the arrogance of her late brother, not seeing what truly lie beneath. "You won't take the power," she said. "Even if you know where the power lies, it will be impossible to bind."

"Not unless I use dark magic, binding spells of most horror. Besides, the power lies in the bounty and the source is this cave, but to access it puzzles my mind completely." He looked up at the cave scanning with his eyes upon the drastic and hieroglyphically drawn paintings. He then looked back down towards his sister. "I hear your thought and I did do it and without hesitation. They were in the way of the true way of life."

"We're talking an entire people! People who spent the latter of their years protecting us and saving our lives. They were never enemies, but when power became too much for them, they were afraid and so fearfully deserted us, exiled us from what we wanted to stand for. Your plan will not work because I will see to it, life or death!"

Amethyst smiled softly, savoring the brilliant moment that was his sisters stupidity. "Time for you to die! Ball of Death!" With that command a ball of black crimson energy gathered and hurled itself at Harsie. She stood there, not reacting from the spell. It glanced off her chest as it pressed against her. "This cave is in the astral plane, you can't hurt me here."

"Oh fiddlesticks! I don't intend on killing you in the astral plane, it's impossible. But from my knowledge, this is how you will die. It may not be here, but it will be soon and you should prepare for it," he commented. Harsie held her head high, a tear rolling down her cheek. "I've already packed my bags," she said sadly. *The image of the incident grew fuzzy as Daniel slowly returned to reality.*

He had spent the latter of the time thinking and rethinking about the dream that so vividly told him things. There was a plan that Amethyst was trying to make, but it spoke of a people, but who? He also dreadfully learned that his mother would die, or maybe he was saying that to be mean. From what Daniel knew about fate, it had the tendency to backfire or turn out completely opposite of what he thought. But fate did have its ups and downs and turnarounds and in some cases bad became ugly. But this time it had become ugly.

Fire rose from the chimneys as they ascended up the hills, but those fires were not just from the chimneys, but from the house roofs and the burning wagons. Daniel stopped abruptly, shocked from the current state that was the happy city of Olgath. *Olgath, the city of justice fights for what is right and for the people it so loves.* The gate was on the ground, bearing its beautiful inscription and admiring the people that lived there. No people were on the street, just an old man with cloaks over him, hunched back and approaching them. The man stopped and began charging a spell. Daniel did not know who this was but he wasn't going to let him get the better of them. "Stop this man's attack!" he yelled.

The force wave of knight power flung itself into the man, but nothing happened. The spell had been completed and shot itself forward, creating a strange hologram-like vision. What stood in front of them was Harsie, queen of Everstheee. *"It is only I, but in disguise I am, meet me at the local pub, I must talk with you."* The apparition disappeared and the man vanished along with it, he too was a formation of astral energy. They kept walking silently, unable to speak.

His mother. Daniel had not seen her in months and with no goodbye. It seemed odd now that she revealed herself so willingly after being absent for so long. What could have lead her here and what had occurred that they were not aware of? Now that she was here, they would get answers and understand what truly is going on. They walked slowly now, almost lethargically. They weren't tired at all, but the slowness of their movement was from mere stress. When they finally entered the inn, they dropped their jaws.

Standing, several feet from them, were Arsi, Nefarine, Salari, and Yambai. They stood quietly in the empty pub, talking rapidly to each other. It had been so long since Daniel had seen them and now they stood in front of them. The old man who was Harsie in disguise walked to them, he beckoned them closer. "I'm sorry to present myself like this to you," he said calmly. "My magic has been off for a while so I am stuck like this for the moment." The man was hunch-backed, haggard, and walked with a cane. Harsie did quite well of concealing herself. "Salari," he called.

Salari looked toward the door and his eyes beamed up. Daniel had never seen the man so excited to see him. "Daniel," he began. "It has been so long since I've seen you. Where is everyone else?" he asked worryingly.

"They are in Absirthee. They are waiting for Herbus to return to normal conditions and for them to have supplies for the journey here."

"I see. I guess we'll have to wait for them. The knight cannot be summoned until the grand summoner is present," said Salari.

"What? How did you know I was the knight?" he asked with confusion. It was the first time he had heard it in reality. He really was the knight. But how did Salari know and for how long?"

"Daniel. You are the knight and your sister is the grand summoner. Her job is to summon the power you have inside you. Although this is a one time thing, it must be done correctly or you could be harmed. There are abilities that she holds and there are many that you hold. We must do it to rid these people of Amethyst. He has taken over this city and burned the citizens to the ground. Anyone that has survived is no where near here.

"You have to realize that it is time for you to use your full potential. I bet you're wondering how I knew, well Harsie told us and we instantly knew that you had to be here and help us to defeat Amethyst once and for all. He has gone too far. Look out that window. What do you see?"

Daniel did as he was asked. He didn't see any thing odd, but then it struck him that a castle stood in the center of the city. From his experience, the Castle of Olgath collapsed, weakened by the power of Myred and Amethyst. Daniel closed the curtains of the dingy window and returned to Salari's dialogue. The others watched with suspense as Salari continued talking.

The powers were needed to defeat Amethyst. Salari explained the powers of the knight and how they must be used. "Sure will," he said. "Your power comes from will to have it done, such as freezing me in time with a simple thought or single word. A sorcerer's power lies in the will of it be done. There are other things that you must discover on your own."

Salari walked away, slowly making his way back to Yambai and the others. There were no words spoken, but thoughts generated in every head. He could feel it almost. A question here, a prognosis there, it all seemed like a very confusing and thought-provoking time. Salari returned and beckoned him outside to follow him. As they walked toward the edge of town, closest to the castle. He talked rapidly. "A sorcerer does not need the use of long incantations or various spells. They use the elements around them. Air, Fire, Earth, Sound, Nature, Weather, Energy anything that can be used. There are many things you can do now."

"Why are we walking this way?" asked Daniel. He was a little curious as to why they were walking towards the castle. There were miscellaneous fires surrounding them that were finishing their job on nearby houses. The trail they had followed was narrow and earth-stricken. "Is there something you're going to show me?"

Salari never answered him. He apparently heard him because the expression on his face changed. He no longer looked barren, but now somewhat stressed and fatigued. Salari lead him into a large field that separated the town from the castle. The field was the same location in which they landed after the castle collapsed. "I need you to learn immediately," said Salari. "You need the knowledge before we go to the castle and rid the world of Sorus "Amethyst" Dale.

"You want me to kill Amethyst?" asked Daniel. "I'm sure there's something other than killing. I mean killing is wrong right?"

"Whatever way you want to do. We must be rid of him soon before he destroys the world. Look beyond the trees. Do you see that?"

Daniel looked beyond the trees as he was told. At first he saw nothing but trees, but then he recognized the Mytred guards along with what seemed to be very powerful and beefed up guards. They were quite large and in fact looked like giant, bulky Mytred Guards. There were also necro-creatures who had posted themselves along the castle walls. Daniel looked to the top of the castle. It had been rebuilt to duplicate the same fashion as the Castle of Olgath. Inside a plan was unfurling and it was up to them to stop it.

"Now it's time for you to fight me. Defeat me and we will stop Amethyst, if not, you are truly not the knight." Salari did not waste time. He drew his staff out. "*Preobrazujte!*" he screamed. The staff he now held became a sword enshrouded in emerald energy. Daniel backed away, preparing to draw his staff. But before he could, Salari threw a slew of emerald sparks onto him.

"Fight boy! This fight determines the lives of our people!" Salari screamed. Daniel drew his staff quickly. He steadied himself several feet from Salari, ready for anything. Salari shot more sparks from his sword and at this Daniel used his staff to block them. Under the impact the staff broke in half, leaving it useless. He backed away once more. He never knew Salari was this powerful and he didn't know he was so weak. He had to regain confidence. "*Venha à minha ajuda, o escudo do poder! Repila os períodos dos meus adversários!*"

After Daniel recited his spell the barrier of magic repelling surrounded him, protecting him from magic. He now stood perplexed and afraid now of the mage who battled him. He had never faced a power this strong nor anyone who could do extreme damage to him. Before Daniel got his head straight, Salari held out his hand. *"Rasseyajte!!"* The barrier that protected him failed and now he was out of options; Salari had used a spell to dispel his barrier. But out of this came the answer. Maybe he was a Sorcerer and maybe he could use his power.

Daniel looked down at the ground, remembering that a sorcerer could virtually use anything. What about that ground? What if he could use the ground to help him? Daniel looked back up at Salari who stood with impatience. His sword glowed stronger, charging for a final blow. Salari released the energy and it came hurtling toward him. As if on instant, Daniel spoke one word. *"Rise."*

At that moment the square piece of ground he observed rose up, blocking the burst of energy that had ascended upon him. "Now we're talking!" said Salari with enthusiasm. Salari attacked again with his sparks, and this time Daniel had confidence. Instead of raising the ground he put his hands up and caught the energy. From basic knowledge, Daniel drew upon the energy and fueled it. He then hurled the energy towards Salari who successfully evaded it. Salari was tired now. He was now starting to weaken, but from the look on his face he wasn't ready to give up. His sword returned to its original state with the sound of his voice.

Daniel felt the surging energy and it felt as if his blood now pumped faster and he now knew everything. Like a rush of strong wind he felt the knowledge gather inside him, as if it were there the entire time. He smiled to himself, feeling a strong urge to try something. Daniel enclosed his hands tightly, feeding energy into his hands and he began to pull his hands apart. In between a gathering of energy presented itself. It was a dark red ball forming. Daniel then released it. It hit Salari square in the chest and now he fell to the ground, exhausted.

"You've done well," Salari commented. "You will fight Amethyst and when the grand summoner arrives your power will enhance and you will have much more power to feed into." Salari got up off the ground and walked back toward the pub. In the strange field, in a destroyed town, Daniel had proven to himself that he was worthy once and for all. But knowing he had the power made him question whether he truly knew it or just got lucky.

Daniel did not want to return to the pub as quickly as Salari did and from there he walked around. Daniel left the field and returned to the main trail into the city where he saw various stores and houses that had burned down. He felt drawn somehow. Somehow he was being drawn to something or someone who was calling to him. Inside the house he had entered was nothing more than a few furniture pieces and old toys. It had be an orphanage to Daniel's assumptions. Beside him at the entrance was a case of some sort of doll collection. The sign labeled. *Gifts of Royalty.* Daniel looked in and saw a doll labeled, *Given unto us by Harsie, Princess of Everstheee.* The doll was elegant with straight hair, a dress, and strangely pale skin. Daniel opened the case by opening the latch and grabbed the doll.

Inside he felt a connection to it. One that he had never felt for any inanimate thing in his life. Then it spoke to him. The doll said it had something to reveal, something he needed to know. Daniel touched the doll's face and from there he felt energy. The energy he felt was not magical, but precognitive, it was an energy of revelation. "*Reveal the connection,*" said Daniel. At this he blacked out completely, only to wake in a church.

"*I can't believe they're gone,*" said a voice. The girl stood the closest to the coffins, in them laid two deceased adults. They were dressed formally and embellished with precious jewels and fabrics, faces pale as the snow. They had died a terrible death and mauled by a dangerous creature without the slightest realization of its presence. But she knew her parents were not stupid enough to die like that.

"Yes they are, but they are alive in our hearts," said the blue eyed boy. He had lustrous blonde hair and a pudgy nose. The boy reached for the girls shoulder. The girl did not like it and became high exasperated. "Brother!" she said. "You can not be this way for it will make you hard inside, an impassionate zombie who no longer values the life of another."

The boy touched her shoulder, silent despite the brutal and emotional remarks from his sister. He then moved his other arm up to her other shoulder and hugged her gently. "I know sister, but it's best not to breakdown from all this. I loved them as much as I love you now. You have to accept that all lives come to an end and that ours will one day come." The girl resisted his speech by removing her brother's arm and walking closer to the casket, safely concealing the bodies of her parents. The magical glass encasing them glimmered in shiny brilliance. The girl looked down at her dead father, transfixed by the motionless and stillness and peacefulness of the body. Her face began to blur and picture began to fade as Daniel woke up.

Daniel woke to find himself in the pub once more. Everyone in the room paused as he stood up from his sleep. The one person on his mind was Harsie. Daniel proceeded across the room to the old man staring out at the window, speaking to himself in a soft tone. As Daniel approached, he held out his hand firmly. *"Release!"* At this the old man began to reform into the body of Queen Harsie of Everstheee. "I'm sorry," said Daniel. "I didn't know he had done so much evil."

Harsie stood there perplexed. Her head moved slowly down, trying to piece together what evil that Daniel spoke of. "What evil is it that you speak of son?"

Daniel took his time explaining the death of Harsie's parents and how he had tricked her into believing it. In Daniel's dream a figure of a man stood behind them, a black curtain overshadowing the mind of Sorus, or Amethyst. The man had an energy of most evil and he held the sacred symbol on his forehead, he was indeed the former king of Swiverstheee, Vicousir. Her tears shed faster than any he'd ever seen and her heart beat fast against his. He hugged his mother, consoling her for her lost and for her brother who betrayed the family and all it stood for.

CHAPTER TWENTY-TWO
The Grand Summoner

No one saw them coming. It was with a swift and agile motion that they took her from the place she thought was safe. They never had the time to react when it happened because the power that was used was far beyond their comprehension. They looked on at the spot where she disappeared. They had taken her away far unto the depths of that dreadful castle, beyond their reach. The great and power Amethyst took her with a snap of his fingers, instantly summoning his sister Harsie to his side. They stood for seconds afterward, stunned at the severity of the situation. Then one spoke up, calling out the obvious.

"They took her," said Daniel. "What are we going to do?"

Salari stood perplexed, looking onto the spot where Harsie stood only just several seconds before. "What power!" he exclaimed to himself. "What mage in this would could snatch up another in such an instant?" Salari walked forward to spot where Harsie once stood, kneeled down and picked up an item. It was a pendent of some sort, blue in color and attached to a chain. "Why would this object remain?" he asked himself.

"How are we going to get her back?" interrupted Daniel. He was pacing the floor nervously trying to come up with solutions to the mystery.

"I suggest we first find out why that pendent remained," said Yambai gracefully. "There are people here that can answer questions we have no answers to. Perhaps we find the nearest mineralist mage to discover what it is for. Perhaps it may help us get her back."

Salari returned to them with the pendent in his hands. "We will do such things until we further know a way into the castle to retrieve her." Salari placed the locket inside his coat pockets and addressed everyone in the room, Daniel, Yambai, Razor, Vyshu, Arsi, Nefarine, and Chris. "We will follow Yambai's suggestion to discover what this pendent is for," he began, pausing after his first phrase. "I know we don't have much time and it may seem pointless, but this pendent must be extraordinarily powerful to be left behind. It may be of use if we discover its true powers."

Everyone acknowledged his proposal and followed him out of the door. They were going to the local mineralist mage named Ortho, a tall lanky man with deep brown eyes. He had been in Olgath for several decades, absorbing youth from the otherwise lively city where births happened every few years. Ortho lived on the outskirts of town, making himself rather popular with townspeople who found him to be rather strange and isolated. The mage spent his most treasured years studying minerals of the land and allowing the god of craft and minerals, Jémon, to make magical artifacts.

They had arrived to the house within a few minutes considering the size of the town. Before them stood the house of Ortho, rather elegant in design and proper in color. The house stood very still and beautiful in a way that showed he kept his house in good shape. His house was one of few that had not been affected by the fire. The clever mage must have figured that fire safety was important because even the flowers in the flower bed stood with life. All proceeded behind Salari in approaching the door to the house. Salari knocked three times and waited.

Within seconds the man stood before him, dressed elegantly in dress pants, a brilliant purple vest and green shirt. He bowed his head at greeting them. "Greetings neighbors. How may I be of service?" The old man seemed rather jolly to see them. "How do I require your service?" He asked, not apparent to the overwhelming awkwardness of the situation. "We need you to find out the secrets of this," said Salari pulling out the pendent and indicating it. The old man's eyes sparkled at the locket, he was very pleased to see it. "Please come in, it is chilly out. I'll put on a fire and we'll study this beautiful artifact."

Upon entering the house, Daniel noticed the somewhat proper and elegant feel to the house that presented itself before entering. On the walls were very beautiful paintings of dragons and Grotus and other strange creatures unfamiliar to him. As he walked further into the central sitting room, he noticed the strange glowing lights above him, the lights light the entire house. "What are those sparkly things?" asked Daniel. "Upon your request I will answer the question for you. They are Light spheres, small gems that emit eternal light, very good for exploration. I have a store here as well if you wish to purchase anything."

Everyone sat down on the plush couches, watching Ortho place the locket on the table adjacent to them. Ortho sat down behind the long table with several tools and a chamber pot. Several ingredients lie on the table as well. "It is rather simple for me to discover the power of this locket. I will contact the god of craft and minerals to reveal to me its true power. Any questions?"

Ortho placed the locket in the chamber pot and added the ingredients from the table, preparing for a spell to discover the mystery behind the powerful pendent. The chamber pot emitted a puffy blue smoke that climbed through the air and hit the ceiling. *"Jémon, pokazhite mne istinnuyu vlast' etogo nereshennogo!"* At the saying of his spell the puffy blue smoke changed to red, then to blue again, and then to yellow simultaneously. Ortho stood up and spoke in a loud urgent voice. *"I am the power of secret, the power that is held within the locket. Only by the power of the summoner can I be released and revealed as a power source! Only then can I be "changed" and "altered" to my command. I am power!"* Ortho fell to the ground shaking in terror. He soon returned to normal, attempting to get up, but only succeeding with the assistance of Yambai and Salari.

"This pendent holds a power beyond comprehension, beyond Jémon's comprehension. Inside lies the key to an ancient power, a power so old it precedes the creation of this world from the great god Pulvaté. By the gods I warn you of the power within this pendent. It stayed behind for a purpose unknown to my cause. You may shop here and leave soon. I am feeling ill and would like rest as soon as possible."

The old man was unaware of what he had said. He had spoken of the summoner and the power that was held within the pendent. He was right about one thing: the locket had been left behind for a reason. It was for the reason that the summoner should fall upon the pendents's power and release it. The sooner the pendent would find the summoner, the sooner that Daniel could obtain the true power of the knight, save Harsie, his brother and sister, and defeat Amethyst.

Daniel and the others left shortly afterward, buying whatever useful items the old man had to offer. It was curious that Ortho could find out the true origin of an artifact but yet be so unaware of its power. As he walked outside, following the rest of the group, he came to realize that the power he had inside him was far greater than he had imagined. Although the pendant was somehow holding the remains, it scared him how much the power could do to him. Ortho had fallen ill from it, but can Daniel endure the immense amount of power within himself and within the Pendant of The Summoner, a name he had given it. As he walked along in silence, he listened to the others talking.

"The power in that pendant is far greater than I expected," exclaimed Yambai. "There must be a power beyond comprehension within it."

"I believe as well," Salari agreed. "We need to find the summoner soon if we are to unlock its secrets."

At the entrance of the door everyone silently walked in, making heavy sighs of frustration, confusion, and exhaustion. Emma looked on to them, accompanied with the rest of the gang silently, waiting for them to see her well enough. After waiting a few seconds in the pub, in the darkest area of the room, still no one noticed.

"Hey!" she yelled. "I've been standing here forever and none of you notice?"

Everyone looked at Emma with surprise. Her presence was not obvious to them upon arrival. The immediate reaction was shock and then settled down to relief. The darkness in the room no longer remained as an obstacle as Chris summoned his flair. Emma stood in her hooded cloak with Aurora, Alex, Kero, Erianna and Soría, all dressed the same, weathered from travel.

Emma was soon tackled down by her brother in a warm hug. He

hadn't seen her for days and now she stood there before him, relaxed and rather humble with herself.

"I'm glad you made it!" Daniel exclaimed. "What took you so long?"

Emma said nothing, staring at her brother intently. "I wish there was time to talk," she said somberly. "But we have to take out Amethyst now. We think we know what he's up to and it's not good."

"What are you talking about?" asked Daniel.

"We found the ancient texts. We know now what this world is, the time period, the creators, the powers that were hidden. We know everything. Let me tell you now and maybe then you'll understand."

CHAPTER TWENTY-THREE
The Queen of Everstheee

The walls of the castle were grim, corroded by the presence of the horrid and despicable creatures such as the necromonsters, the necro armor, and other beings of degradation. Here now the group of mages, many of them, fourteen of them, a small arsenal of mages preparing to crush an evil power marched swiftly towards the castle, diverging as they got closer, taking their respective positions. The Mytred marched towards as well, hundreds in rows of tens, undead following close behind. The tension rose each second as the array of mages stood there, silent, calm, and in a peace-like manner that hid their worries and regrets; they hid their fears, their apprehensions, their true state of being.

Daniel stood in the center of them all, in front of the formation they had created. Breathing deeply, he took his hands from his cloak pockets and took out what appeared to be a small yellow ball, shining brightly despite the gray skies. "Here goes nothing," he said throwing the ball out in front of him. The army of Mytred and undead marched on, inching closer and closer towards the group of militant mages. The ground rumbled from their steps and the mages stood silent and still. As the Mytred approached the area the ball thrown on the ground started to rumble. At that moment it split in two, three, four parts that scattered themselves about and gathering energy. The wall they made expanded high into the air, like a barrier of some sort. *"The ancient texts were buried in a temple in Absirthee, they reveal all that is true,"* Daniel heard in his mind, recalling the explanation of the ancient texts.

The wall was a brilliant yellow, glimmering from outside stimulants. Daniel knew the device would only hold them off for several minutes but its purpose was to repel evil, as which Ortho explained upon purchase. The other mages walked forward, forming a line now with Daniel its center. Aurora stepped out of the line and walked in front of Daniel, silent and waiting. As the evil approached closer the barrier glowed brighter, charging itself. The leading Mytred, two of them stopped abruptly in front of the barrier.

"What is this contraption?" asked the first Mytred. He looked up, vexed in bewilderment at the height of the barrier.

"I believe it is a *barrier of evil repelling* sir. But this one comes from a device, not nearly as possible. I suppose we can just break it down."

Aurora's hair wavered in the wind uncontrollably as the energy she held in her hands grew stronger. *"Laria, bless us in battle, protect us with your powers of love and devotion!"* she said loudly as the energy from her hand shot up into the air and evaporating into rain drops that were absorbed by the bodies of the mages. It was the blessing of the goddess of love, Laria.

The barrier began to withstand the onslaught of attacks before it now began to dissipate in power. "Get ready," Daniel said to everyone. "It's going to be an interesting battle." Within seconds of his statement, the barrier broke and Mytred began rushing towards the mages. The mages, in response stood calmly, waiting for the attack. "You know what to do!" screamed Daniel over the screaming.

It had happened so fast, Mytred after Mytred attacked with magic and were blocked instantly by the mages. They broke apart without the slightest notice into battle. Daniel stood calmly as the battle began, concentrating intensely. A Mytred began to charge his spell, aiming at Daniel. At that, Daniel lifted his hands to chest level and held his hands out, catching the ball of misty gas, throwing it back and hitting the Mytred with its own spell.

Kero was attacked swiftly by the Mytred. He stood his ground and took out his sword. *"Kosten*!!" he screamed. His sword was now part of him, fueled off of his power. He attacked furiously with it, lightning

187

emmitting from it. In his ignorance his sword was taken from him and he hadn't seen it coming. The Mytred soldier aimed his spell well, but it never hit him because it was blocked. He turned around to see Emma smiling. She had saved him yet again from himself. They fought together.

"Arrow of Fire," Chris said aiming at the Mytred. It struck all five of the Mytred in an instant, rendering them useless. He was fighting a small group of undead, using their weaknesses to fire and light against them. Of course he had only been fighting a while before he realized that he couldn't fight them alone. "Hey. A little help here?" he asked her. Aurora showed up swiftly, banishing the undead creatures back to the earth. "You really should be more careful," she told him.

From flesh to stone it had seemed. Alexander used his powers with confidence, petrifying any that threatened him. He watched Nefarine, Salari, and Arsi fight as well, using powers to knock out the Mytred. He had watched Aurora and Chris fight together and Emma and Razor. Erianna and Soría were fighting well, sword with one and staff with the other. They sliced more than diced. But his eyes carried himself to Daniel who only stood unharmed.

Daniel only watched the battle, standing by in case of an emergency. The harsh array of spells and weapons clashing together made him sick. The man he called his uncle had done this, caused this battle, caused the war that would define the existence of the human race. *"Pulvaté was not a god, but an evil mage who wanted complete control of Sulex, upon its creation,"* Emma had told him. Daniel looked on proud. Despite numbers, they were winning over the Mytred who held no great melee skill for they were a simple police of Myred and were rendered indispensable. Here he stood, watching Emma, Vyshu, Razor, Alex, and the others fight bravely. He was to stay out of the way because he was *important* and his life meant as much as the existence of Sulex.

The clouds suddenly thickened, making it darker in mere seconds. Daniel looked up at the sky as lightning began to strike down on the unsuspecting cluster of battling mages and Mytred. In response each group backed away as the lightning strikes concentrated in one area, striking the same area several times. *"It's him!"* Emma announced telepathically. Amethyst emerged on the fifth strike, dressed in purple ropes with green etching on the sleeves and lower part. His hair was no longer blue, but a snowy white.

"I guess you are here then, I thought it was rather curious that a battle had commenced. Why must you disturb my home?" Without any hesitation Amethyst rose his arm, summoning a cage containing the queen of Everstheee, Harsie. "Why must you disturb my home?" he repeated. He folded his arms as if deserving an explanation.

"They've come to stop you brother," Harsie announced boldly. "It is time for your reign to end and for all natural power to return to the people."

"Ah. So the usual I see? Well the thing is that I am quite happy here in my new castle with my powerful army. *He* started this and I'm going to finish if it's the last thing I do in this world. He was right you know? He was right to not allow those people to threaten our lives and force us to this world that less than 2000 years ago did not even exist." He took a breath, preparing for more words. "I stand here to strike down the knight's power and use it to bring back the almighty, all powerful Pulvaté one of the four who created this world after the human race banished us!"

Amethyst shook his head in shame. "And yet our ancestor, Olgath fought against him, said he was crazy. The human race is filled with ignorant and idiotic humans whose life expands greed, lust, sloth, pride, envy, anger, and gluttony. It was their sin that led to our exile and it will be their downfall. We mages can rise up and control the human world, make them work for us. Enslavement is by far the punishment they must endure for our hardships."

Something in the air stilled. True and very coherent feelings filled the eyes of Amethyst. Sadness filled his eyes, anger fueled his heart, and pride subdued his mind. An evil man with so much emotion toward his own people. Does a true evil deserve such compassion for emotional burdens such as his?

"Amethyst," Harsie called out. "I see your suffering with clear eyes now, your anger, your pain. But the past must remain in the past and not become a part of the present. You are messing with fate and the overall lives of an entire race of people. Forget the mistakes of our ancestors and return this world to its state of normality. Return to your family, your friends. Come back to the side of good."

Amethyst said nothing, hair oscillating uncontrollably in the wind, eyes fierce and cold, body stiff as cement. He rose his arms slowly, waving them through the air. As he did so, his eyes closed and his body became free as it would when reaching a certain sense of a mage's nirvana.

"You ask of me to prevent the past from becoming the present, but my goal today is to make the past as the future. It shall be the future of the human and the magus race alike. We magus will be the superior and all powerful race. They will follow our orders and do our bidding. And I will have all the power and control both worlds."

Muttering uprooted from Amethyst's breath. He began to wave his arms faster as a wave of lavender energy began to encompass him. The sounds coming from the spell were dreadful, as if someone was scratching a nail on a chalk board. From his fingertips the energy coalesced in a way that formed a strong solid ball of magical energies. Harsie, aware of his intensions began to charge a spell.

Before anyone knew it she had shattered the magical shell that was her cage. She hurriedly ran towards the others, fatigued with tired eyes and wild hair. "Sorry I'm late," she said casually. "What did I miss?" Harsie was now beside Emma with the others in back facing the evil that was her brother. "Shall we do this the easy way or the hard way?" she asked her brother, putting her finger to her chin, contemplating the next moves.

Amethyst said nothing, concentrating on a spell that he was charging. The purple energy emitting from Amethyst's hands began to grow rapidly, creating a small, but usable portal. "It would seem that your power is not enough to bring back the dead," said Harsie in a proud tone. "Give up!" Amethyst looked up at his sister with blue eyes, a tear careening down his cheek.

"I am sorry sister. No one will stop me and the power I seek has not yet arrived. There is only one way to allow that to occur." Harsie, afraid of his next move acted hastily. *"Polnomochiya Sv'azi, Zakonchite period moyego brata!"* she screamed. At this a luminescent ball of yellow energy shot out from her palms and placed itself upon Amethyst's wave of energy.

"Goodbye sister," said Amethyst calmly. *"Esfera de morte!"* The onyx sphere struck Harsie hard in the chest causing her to collapse, Emma catching her. Daniel ran to the scene as fast as possible after Emma screamed and shock ran through the group. Yet it was silent, solemn, and calm. What had just happened? Daniel pushed the others out of his way to see her. The sight of her made his heart skip a beat.

The beautiful queen of Everstheee now lie before him, struggling to hang on to a rapidly deteriorating life. Her skin and face were now withered with age and her body began to lose its composition. The hair on her head became as gray as the sky, from the beautiful blonde it had once been.

"Mother!" cried out Emma, bursting into tears. "You *cannot* die on us now, we need you! I need you. We've come so far to find you and now we have to watch you die. It's not fair, I don't want you to die! You have to fight it!"

Harsie remained calm, grasping Emma's hand. "Death comes when life comes to an end. It is my time to leave this world and leave behind my goodness and wisdom to my children. It is your time to make something of this day, of my life, of yours. Find the realm of light, release it into the knight and fulfill your destiny as his Knight's Grand Summoner." Harsie lowered her hand as she began to wither further. In a second's moment she disintegrated into nothingness.

Daniel turned around, unable to bear the death of his so unfamiliar mother. Here Amethyst had taken a mother for whom he had only few months with and now he stood there muttering his spell, not paying attention to them. Daniel moved forward, closer to Amethyst. "Amethyst!" he yelled. Amethyst did not look up nor acknowledge him.

"Quebre a energia, quebra o encantamento," Daniel said. The knight's power flowed slowly into him, but still in its novice stage. Power gathered and formed as energy in the pit of his chest. The bright white light of energy emerged and struck Amethyst's portal, causing it to break.

Amethyst was aware now. Of all the power he had searched for, one still remained a mystery. By mere will his power had been struck down and enfeebled. He watched Daniel, contemplating his next move, absorbing new knowledge.

"Why is he just staring?" Emma whispered to Daniel. She was close behind him, ready for anything. Emma wiped the tears from her eyes as Daniel began to talk again.

"He's figured me out. I don't know what could be going through his mind, but he knows. I think I used up too much power. We need *all* of the knight's power to defeat him and I need you to find it. I hope you do before he gets real serious."

"That is the problem. I don't know how," Emma answered. "I need to find the realm of light, but I have no idea what the first step would be. I need you to distract him while I search through my mind, find some clue about what to do next.

"Here. Take this," said Daniel. He reached from his pocket Harsie's mysterious pendent. Perhaps it had some clues as to obtaining the light of the knight.

"I'll start with this."

CHAPTER TWENTY-FOUR
The Goddess of Light

It was too bright for her to see. It was like looking directly into a lamp, trying to adjust to the impossible immensity of brightness that the eyes could not possibly adhere to. Pulvaté was supposedly their god of creation, but only the creation of their world, not of their people. Where had they come from exactly? What god would create such powerful beings?

Emma felt the walls near her, still blinded by the bright light that existed in the realm. She had made it here by merely concentrating her energies into her mother's mysterious pendent. There were no definite indications to where she was relative to the walls, far, near. All sense of direction was lost with the lack of proper eyesight.

There was an opening now, like a hallway that she felt her way around the corner of the wall, leading down another passageway. Her footsteps echoed softly on the floor, not stone, but what seemed to be clay dirt. She walked faster, attempting to meet that destination.

"Do not move any longer my child," called out a voice. Before Emma stood a woman shrouded in the darkness. The dark tentacles entangled her like a snake, trying to suffocate her. Emma walked closer to the woman who stood before her.

She was beautiful, tall, elegant, stunning. Her thoughts were overcome with these words. This woman that stood before her did not hold the beauty of a normal person such as herself. Her beauty was godly and it slowed Emma's heart to see such a spectral. "Do not walk closer young one," said the woman. "It is far too dangerous for you to be shrouded upon this darkness that binds me."

Emma stopped several feet in front of her and waited for the goddess to respond to her patience. Already she felt the power of the goddess emit from her and she felt the link between her and the god, almost without flaw and definition. The power she felt, felt good and wholehearted. It was strange now that she felt it, at peace instantaneously.

"I am the goddess of light named Luzi and you are Emma Dale age sixteen," she said beautifully.

"But what is this place?" Emma asked. "I can't even see clearly. It's far too bright for my eyes."

"Ah the power of light is easily seen through a god's eyes. Allow me to ease your sight."

The goddess closed her eyes in concentration, whisking away the light-like fog, clearing Emma's vision instantly. Emma's suspicions were correct as she stood in front of the throne of the goddess. The room was wide with various dining tables, large ball room area. The ceiling peaked higher than Emma could see and the floor was made up of a strange clay-like mineral.

"You can see now that our world is rather similar to yours. But you must realize that we gods and goddesses exist only for you. Since the beginning of time we have lived in our world, granting the wishes of our worshippers and feeding them the power that helped to create us. How we exist I do not know. But why you are here I do know. You must take another god's power. The knight of shining armor will be at your side. But be warned, its power is still not defined."

"That's the problem," commented Emma. "I don't know how to get it. I've been given this job that I don't know how to do. It's still a mystery to me." The goddess sat at her throne, wearing the dark snake around her. "The answers you seek exist in the question."

"I'm sorry. I don't understand," said Emma.

"To see the future you must look unto the past. To see the answer you must seek out the question. That is as far as I can tell you."

"He is destined!" said Emma. "My brother was chosen to obtain the power of the knight and I was chosen to deliver it. I can't stay here forever. We are fighting a war at this very moment." Emma was frustrated by the goddess' refusal to be clear with her. She watched idly by as the goddess prepared herself for a response.

"My dear child," she said calmly. "You coming here was never an accident for I chose you and your brother the powers you have obtained. For they come from me, the very person you just lashed out at. Your great grandfather would be ashamed. Olgath was a wonderful mage, a powerful one at that. Granting this power unto his blood was a promise between two lovers.

"It is strange that we fell into a love between goddess and worshipper. He always came to me when trouble brewed, when he believed that his power was a mistake. It was the power I had granted him, the power of the knight. It had come from me that time as well because I had granted it to him to defeat Pulvaté. It banished him and so shall it release him. That is why Amethyst searches.

"Yes I know everything that is going on. I am a goddess and I watch these things. Your great grandfather wanted it taken away and I said only if it could be reborn in another, if evil ever shrouds another mage like Amethyst. Pulvaté and Amethyst are very similar: naïve, impractical, idiotic, prideful. These qualities will be his downfall. Perhaps the love of goddess to worshipper is what caused you to be here."

Emma froze at this. Olgath had been in love with a goddess? The thought scared her. The goddess in front of her held the powers key to saving Sulex from Amethyst. "You must find what you seek on your own. I cannot help for I am trapped by the power of the wicked god of power, Oltent. Find your way out of here, find the cave of revelation and there you will have your question."

"But if our power is tied to you, shouldn't we be weakened too?" asked Emma nervously. "The release of the knight will be the biggest burst of power to hit me. For the knight exists wholly as power vessel. Releasing it will make me stronger and make it harder to control," said the goddess. She got up off her throne and walked out of the room without saying another word.

Emma had been walking quite a while. It seemed almost fruitless that she searched for a cave inside a castle. It was larger than she had expected, corridor after corridor, hallway after hallway. She was utterly confused. Upon her impatience she muttered words in an ancient language. One not known of her tongue, not known of her world.

There it stood, the cave entrance. It was located in Absirthee where the lost records had been. It was the cave where she had visited the past of her mother and her uncle. She saw the walls once more, depicting the journey of the knight dating back to Olgath himself. There she scanned the walls for any clues.

Knight, shining armor, power, destruction. It was all the same to her. But the one thing she searched for was not there on the stone walls of that cave. What the goddess had told her was that she knew the answer. She had known all along. But the question would lead her to the answer. But what was the question?

Perhaps it was when had she gained knowledge of the knight or why she was here. Maybe it was to question her existence or her destiny. Maybe it was about Daniel. Maybe it was about Amethyst. It could be any number of things. Maybe it was why. Or how. How had this all started for her? How had she become a mage and how had she been flung into this tumultuous adventure.

As she looked back she muttered in the ancient language again, unfamiliar of what she drew upon herself. In her head she felt a sharp pain. It was much like the time of her mental fatigue. For before that she was just in the classroom distracted, unaware of what was there before her. There. It stuck out. She kept seeing the same thing, the same picture of that that day. She had written something, something valuable before. *"Offenbaren Sie!"* she said aloud.

It was all clear now, something inside her showed the events she had never seen before. Not since she left Earth and pursued the life that was in Sulex, land of the magical prowess. The poem of power entered her head. The one very that she placed in her pockets oh so many months ago. The one poem that she had written in trance, written under the guidance of fate, of her predetermined destiny. Written under the protection of Scion the abjurer, Harsie the queen, and all those involved in her life. It was all planned.

Emma rubbed the necklace furiously, returning to the battle she had left. For she only hoped that her time in the goddess's realm was only minutes from her. It was only a distraction to keep them busy. She was to go undetected and return as soon as possible. In her mind she was returning, soon came her body, unbalanced and flimsy now from the travel.

No one was on the field. No one except the defeated piles of Mytred that now covered the land. There before her she saw none of her fellow mages. *"Where are you?"* she called out telepathically. She received no answer and in response she made off towards the castle. She ran quickly, entering upon the building that once belonged to Harsie, queen of Everstheee. The gate was open and in she entered, determined to end all this madness.

CHAPTER TWENTY-FIVE
The Knight in Shining Armor

No longer stood the Statue of Olgath. Its rival, Pulvaté stood there in its place, glaring down upon his helpless victims. The corridors stretched farther than she had ever remembered, the walls were tighter, the floor dark as night, doors painted ruby red. It was all different now, scary even to the fact that Emma feared for her safety in the now unfamiliar castle. The darkness pushed down on her heart, crushing her benevolent spirit from the outside. Yet fighting it was only the simplest task, holding back her fear and anxiety that so took her soul. Yet fear itself only presented from her own power.

She continued down the corridors, lost in its darkness and depths. She had run for several minutes only to find herself in her original position. *"What ails you my daughter,"* the voice called out. Emma looked around searching for the being that spoke to her. "Who are you?" Emma called out. For a moment things remained silent and uneventful, but soon a flash of green light surrounded her, ending in the appearance of a strange creature.

She was small, very small in fact, maybe the size of a bumble bee. She was a fairy of sorts, a sprite that stood flapping its wings before her. "I am here to help you," she said. "I am Katus, goddess of the lost." Emma stood still watching the sprite. "Who?" she asked. The beautiful goddess wore a silken gown, beautiful jewelry and moccasins. She was rather pleased with herself.

The sprite made a frown, cute even that she was angry. "My daughter. You only know two hundred of the two thousand gods and goddesses that exist. As the grand summoner, you can call upon any god or goddess to aid you. You may only be aware of them when the time is needed. I am here to help you find your family and friends. Command me to assist and I will do so."

Emma had never seen the beautiful and rather small goddess. She revealed that Daniel only knew of her because he was an evoker, summoning upon the spirits of gods. He had to know of her. "Help me find them Katus, I command you to assist," Emma said. "I will do as you ask, all mighty."

Before Emma knew it, Katus was flying away rapidly through the corridor. Emma raced to catch up with her while attempting to breath. The race was fast and confusing as Katus made arbitrary twists and turns throughout the corridors that Emma could hardly make sense of. "Where are we going?" Emma asked Katus. The little goddess still remained silent as she flew even faster than before. There before them was a dead end. Katus waited for Emma to catch up.

"They are behind this wall," she said calmly. "But I cannot take you there for I have no power to walk through walls." Emma stood staring at the black wall made of strong bricks. "How do you expect to?" asked Emma. Katus did nothing but stare back at her, shaking her head in pity.

"You are the GRAND summoner. That means you have the power to not only summon gods and goddesses, but to use their powers. Call Nexus, ask him for power to walk through that wall. It's simple."

The goddess flew upwards into the air and vanished. Leaving only trails of dust behind. Emma remained dumbfounded. Is that what she was? A summoner of power and gods? She thought on her decision for a moment.

"*Verknüpfung, gewähren Sie mir die Macht, durch Wände spazieren zu gehen. Gewähren Sie mir diese Macht!*" Nothing happened for a moment. It was then that she felt a slip in her body, a slip from solidity, from solid form. There her hands begin to quiver uncontrollably. Before she knew it, her hand was completely pixilated, made up of many tiny dots. Emma refaced the wall and placed her hand upon it. At that moment her hand phased the wall with the slightest of ease. But the rest of Emma's body had not become pixilated.

She concentrated on it for a moment. And then, to here surprise, her entire body became molecularly unstable, not holding its solid form and phasing through the solid brick wall.

"How dare you!!"

Some people were talking when Emma made it through the wall. There stood before her, Amethyst, talking to Daniel who was chained up. The rest of the group was no where to be found. *"Unsichtbarkeit findet mich!"* Emma whispered to herself, cloaking herself with invisibility.

"I can do as I please. Your *people* are so behind us, so below us, there is no need to make them go to waste," said Amethyst to Daniel. "You see this world is known as Sulex or in your world, Exsul. The root for Exile. For that is exactly what they did."

"It's their ancestors' fault because of what they started, what the humans did were only to be cautious. They wanted to be safe," Daniel argued. He was chained tightly to the wall in the main throne room, watching Amethyst as he prepared his spell, placing ingredients into his chamber pot, drawing markings on the wall. "He will return today whether or not I live to see another day!"

Emma listened, hearing Amethyst's plan once again. It was a long story that she had only recently become acquainted with. Amethyst was going to bring Pulvaté back from the dead to help him take over Earth Realm. In 1737 A.D. the world was happy as mages and humans lived in harmony as they had for many years. It was then that many groups or alliances of mages had begun to wage war unto each other. In fear of this, the most powerful world leaders of the age had proclaimed that the magus race of people be exiled from earth. To this day Sulex had only been existent for two hundred and seventy years.

It was then that Pulvaté, Rian, Olgath, and Baroth created Sulex. It was later on that Pulvaté had become angry toward the humans. He vowed to take over the human race, but was stopped by Olgath and sealed within the realm of the dead, a most desolate of places. Pulvaté swore he would return with the coming of a new evil. It was that same evil that caused the rise of the Alliance of Myred.

Emma slowly walked toward Daniel, silently reaching out to his mind without alerting Amethyst of her presence. *"Daniel….,"* she called out silently. *"Emma! Where have you been?"* *"Shhhh!!!"*

It wasn't long before they were conversing mentally between each other. Daniel had told her how the others had disappeared without a trace and how he was captured. Amethyst continued to fiddle with his spell and attempting to find the final ingredient.

"Where is it?" asked Amethyst aloud. He looked toward Daniel, asking him the question.

"Where is what?" asked Daniel. He thought that Amethyst was finally going crazy.

"The grand summoner can call forth the powers of the gods and harness them, control them at their will." he cited. "Where is the grand summoner!?" he asked angrily.

Emma started to tiptoe away from Daniel when her spell wore off, shimmering her back into reality. How it happened she did not know. "I see you…," said Amethyst. "You think you got in here without my knowing. I heard your incredibly loud conversation when you got in here."

Emma stood still now. Not afraid, but confident. "Yes. I am the grand summoner," she began "But there is something that can stop you right now. Something I have inside me and something Daniel has in him. Do you know what that power is?"

"The Knight in Shining Armor. Yes… I know he is the knight and you are the grand summoner. But upon that power, Pulvaté will appear and this world will be all powerful and the humans will kneel before it."

"Not to be mean. But I have something to say." Emma rubbed the necklace around her neck vigorously, reciting something.

> *Auf diesen Grund stehe ich*
> *Für die Mächte, denen ein Mann widerstehen kann*
> *Für die größten von erhaltenen Geschenken ist leicht*
> *Das Bewilligen davon biete ich mich:*
> *Eine Hälfte meine beschränkte Macht*
> *Eine Meinung seine Kraft verband sich*

Eine Stunde widmete Zeit
Zu dem Blut andauern wird
Die größten von allen Übeln," zu vereiteln

"*Lassen Sie es,*" Emma finished. At that moment the necklace disappeared and reappeared upon Daniel, changing from blue to ruby upon his chest. The chains that bound him were gone now and Daniel stood, transfixed by this new coming of power. He was encompassed by light, brilliant and lustrous.

"This is what it feels like. It feels like...," he said. Daniel didn't continue because he noticed that Emma was unconscious, unable to respond to his comment. He ran over to her, attempting to wake her. "Emma, wake up!" He shook her body, but it remained limp and lifeless. Daniel placed his hand over her eyes, attempting to close them. "*Stop!!*".

He heard Emma's voice from inside his head. "*How did you get in there?*" he asked. Emma explained quickly that the spell meant for her to combine with him telepathically. She was there to help him, guide him through the powers of the knight and to serve him. Daniel walked to the center of the room, as did Amethyst, expecting a battle.

"You fight against me? My own blood?" began Amethyst as he began walking down the steps of his alter. "Pulvaté fought for our race, wanted us to be superior and now, you fight to save the human race, those so confused and unaware of the fate that befalls them? Before they discover it, I will have controlled them alongside Pulvaté. Will you stand and fight or step aside!?"

Daniel made no hesitation as he began charging his spell, speaking the incantation, letting its word spill out over the room as the sound blast reached Amethyst he caught it in his hand, throwing it back at incredible speed. "*Skill number one, deflection of magical energies,*" Emma said from within. Daniel held his right hand up as if blocking the power. It glowed just as the white light that created it, and returned the blast to sender.

Amethyst was struck hard in the chest and with more force into the wall, rock shards came tumbling down on top of him. He hastily got back up sending a stream of crimson energy towards the knight who stood without fear and without any reasons to have fear. "*Skill number two, molecular disconfiguration,"* Emma said from within. Daniel close his eyes, allowing the strange energy to phase right through him. Daniel watched Amethyst break mentally from frustration.

"How dare you! I will take thy power and use it to bring him. I know of this power. I know that if I harness it correctly Pulvaté will return through my portal!" Amethyst said. "Fight me!" Amethyst took his sword from its sheath, charging quickly. *"Skill three telekinesis. Skill four shining blade. Skill five shining armor,"* Emma said ever so calmly. Amethyst lost his blade with a wave of Daniel's hand.

Daniel held his hand up summoning the blade that belonged to the knight. Amethyst was stuck without a weapon, facing Daniel with the Blade of Shining Light. It pierced his eyes and distorted his perception, but he attacked anyway. *"Ball of Death!"* he screamed. Daniel had no time to react. He stood his ground focusing energy, as the ball struck the invisible wall that was his armor. Daniel stumbled back in response.

"Yes. I have weakened you. It is now time," said Amethyst smiling. He walked back to his alter, holding his hands high above himself, speaking in the ancient language. *"Vis religui et! Coniungi mecum!"* Daniel felt a strong tug on him now, pulling the power from him. *"He's taking your power!"* screamed Emma. Daniel attempted to fight the incantation but found himself faltering in power. He had used so much from the last blast. He could not pull from it. Within moments the power stood before him in a gigantic heap of light.

It ascended into the air, following the call of Amethyst, the call of evil. Emma reawakened inside her body, running towards Daniel. "We have to get it back," she said. "He can't have it now!" Daniel stood still unable to move or think about what to do. He was in shock. The power felt good and he almost felt guilty for it.

The ceiling began to fall in response to the release of the knight's power. Amethyst looked up curiously. He had not been the cause of this. Soon light from outside became visible and single lightning bolt struck down hard onto the floor. A man remained staring up at Amethyst. His eyes were glowing a powerful emerald color and his hair was gray. He was older, wore royal robes, and spoke one word upon entering the room.

"Hello," said Herbus joyfully. "Sorry I'm late. The weather was terrible."

Herbus had come into the battle, standing and erect as if his current fatigue and weakness had not existed. He looked on the three of them, Daniel, Emma, and Amethyst. He saw the knight's power floating in the air, waiting to be called forth.

"I'm here to stop you, Amethyst. It's time that you stop this charade."

Amethyst stood pompously, unthreatened by Herbus' presence. He was an old druid who hadn't left his castle in almost one hundred years. His power would more likely be useless against him. He pondered his next move. "Come to me my undead! Do as I command!" They appeared in black clouds from no where. The clouds held them in and released them like baby spiders hatching from their eggs.

Amethyst had summoned his army of undead. Herbus was not struck with fear upon the appearance of Amethyst's undead army. He stood still unimpressed by Amethyst's party. He then spoke only two words. *"Zabastovka Molnii!"*

To everyone's amazement multiple lightning bolts struck down into the room, hitting every undead one by one like a powerful force of the gods. He had killed all of them with two words. Herbus looked on once more. "I see you are still naïve as you were when you were a child. I am still powerful despite my age and I am still leader of the druids. Such as these."

The ceiling was ripped apart by a powerful gust of wind and many clouds came tumbling down like cotton balls. Upon them were druidic warriors from Absirthee. It was the army that Herbus himself controlled. They had arrived by cloud per Herbus's power. The druids hopped off, arming themselves in weaponry.

Emma and Daniel watched as the large army of druids descended into the room, all preparing for a battle. Emma then ran up to Herbus.

"I thought you weren't allowed to interfere," Emma said. She watched him as he lowered his gaze upon her. "My dear girl, when the ancient teachings of Rian are subject to heresy I am at liberty to interfere.

Amethyst stood still wondering what next to do. "So you've brought an entire army to stop me? I shall have the knight's power. Come to me!"

The power of the knight began to move towards him. Amethyst braced himself for it. Upon his surprise he was struck by a force. The knight's power paused once more.

Nefarine stood now with the others behind him. "Amethyst stop! This has gone on long too far." Amethyst got up angry now charging a spell. *"Sterben Sie!"* he said as Nefarine was thrust back into the wall, crushed by the shards of wall that fell onto him. He was dead.

Amethyst was furious. He charged a spell once more but couldn't complete because he was struck by a lightning bolt, an arrow of light, a ball of confusion, a spear of servitude, mind break, a psi. Everyone had struck him at once. "I see my naiveté has been my downfall but I shall learn. I shall gain my true strategy. I will kill you once and for all." The portal behind him began to fade and dissipate. Amethyst began charging a spell to depart.

"Now!" Daniel announced. Upon that the entire room of mages began reciting something, a spell to banish the powerful Amethyst. *"Com este período mágico ele pode ser banido. Ele será empurrado no portal e ido para sempre!"*

Upon this Amethyst was thrust into the portal, banished to the place where Pulvaté had been two hundred and seventy years before. It was the combined power of Herbus, the Arcane Alliance of Nexus, and the druids who banished the powerful Amethyst. It was his pride that had destroyed him and allowed for his plan to fail. He would never be seen again. It was a powerful day for Sulex now that the king of Swiverstheee and the leader of Myred was banished from the known world.

They had won the battle for Sulex, but the war was just beginning. Daniel turned around to see the light of the knight that had been separated from him before. It hovered uncontrollably now as it had no vessel to return to. As the portal closed the knight's power began to disappear into nothingness, Daniel tried to receive it but was not in time. It was gone. And with Amethyst it had become nonexistent in the world. Daniel now stood silent as the rest celebrated unaware of what had truly happened. The knight's power was gone and now there was no hope to defeat Myred once and for all.

CHAPTER TWENTY-SIX
The Final Decision

Everything was not still the same when the castle returned to its original status. For the queen was dead and the Mytred had so disgraced the castle. But it wasn't over for they belonged to Myred who still had its power. The battle was over, but the war was just getting started. They stood in the throne room, remembering those lost, recalling the events that took their lives. Yet there was an uneasiness from everyone. Someone in the crowd held secrets perhaps important or perhaps something held within.

"Here we pray to the gods to watch their souls, to protect them in death," said Aurora peacefully. "May the powers that be protect those leaving for another world. Those who have been sent away for their own well being. Let it be done that they leave only to return stronger, healthier, and more aware of your powers."

There were many things that happened. Many of which that Daniel had only just become aware of upon their victory. One: Yambai had been missing the last few days, not being seen by anyone. Two: The power of the knight was gone and he didn't know how he'd get it back nor who could. Three: There was in need of a leader for the Arcane Alliance of Nexus.

It was strange now that he sat at the dinner table inside the castle with all his friends. They had grown along with him. Some into courage, some into love, some into a variety of things. He himself had grown into a man who takes responsibility and actions that reflect the lives of a people. He was announced as a council member for Everstheee as well as his sister. They would take part in the reconstruction of the country and the rehabilitation of those retrieved from the Castle of Oltent.

Emma was now as happy as she had been before Reater and Malitus began to keep secrets. She was in love, happy to be with Kero. They had connected on their journey towards Olgath and in ways grew together. Daniel was proud and happy to have Kero has a friend and as his sister's boyfriend. Arsi, Rayziel, and Wyter were announced as the premier guards of the Castle of Olgath and given metals of honor for their work to fight against Amethyst.

Herbus, the power druid with powers over the weather was inaugurated as the head of the Arcane Alliance of Nexus for his loyal service and dedication to the defeat of Amethyst. To his surrogate son he announced him the king of Absirthee because of his loyalty to his people, his king, and to the well being of the druidic race.

It all seemed like everything was well. But Daniel only saw it as a gilded victory as he had lost the power that could defeat Myred and that could hold Amethyst in his prison. He was in his room, now alone and in deep thought over this victory. No one seemed to worry about the knight's power as much because they said it would return to him. But what if it didn't? What if he never got it back and Amethyst or some other evil would threaten them again?

He got up off the bed and sat up, watching the slow fire that he had made earlier. The winter had come now and he watched the snow fall swiftly to the ground. It was the most beautiful thing he had ever seen. It was then that he realized that Yambai sat in a chair opposite him, hurt, exhausted and blood running down his face. He breath heavily. "Daniel," he called.

Daniel ran to him as soon as he noticed him. Yambai was dressed in his usual clothing and he was bruised and beat up. He was having trouble getting his words out. "Beware…of the….power….that has hurt me. The knight's power can….be….found by finding *him*. Only he can return it. He can call it forth once more. *He*….can….bring…it…back…to…you.

They don't want you to. But you have to find him soon. Before they kill him. Hurry." As his last breaths emptied from his mouth Daniel began to tear up. He hadn't cried since Reater and Malitus died. He had tried to be strong for everyone, but now he lost one in his arms. He was crying now for Harsie, for Nefarine, for Yambai, for the killed druids, the lost of a potentially good man, his uncle Amethyst.

As they entered his room they picked him up and carried the body to the alter. There he was buried with the others. He was distraught now, unable to acknowledge the death of Yambai the prophet. He had been so calm and so affluent in his power and so wise. The man who had never doubted him, his mentor, a man who was as loyal to him as he was to his mother.

"This *they* is a threat now. They've killed Yambai coldly," said Salari. "I don't know what to do now that we know that the knight's power must be summoned by *him*. We'll have to find this person. We have to discover what's going on. But I can't risk your life. I can't risk hers either."

Salari had proposed that Emma and Daniel go back to Earth Realm now that this threat was supposedly after them. It was announced that they should go and live their under the supervision of Emily and Derrick, separately to ensure safety. It was to be that Arsi and the others investigate this *him* and find the threat that had murdered Yambai. No one wanted it to be that way but it had to be that way. They were leaving Sulex.

Emma stood in the tower alone that night. They were leaving tomorrow and it was almost nostalgic. In a way if felt like they had left in such a hurry to see another world that they had not a chance to see the world they had held for granted. It was the world that Amethyst wanted desperately. For so many reasons they had left and so many reasons they had stayed. It was heartbreaking now. It was horrible, ugly, saddening. It was that now she had to leave all of them. She had to leave her friends, her first love, and her "uncle" Salari.

Daniel came up from behind her, seeing the thoughts about her face. "I know you don't want to leave. But they're right. We can't risk anything now that there's a new threat."

Emma said nothing and continued to look about the night sky. Her eyes filled with tears. "I wish we didn't have to leave. I love it here, but I love it there too. Why can't we stay here with them, our friends, Salari, Arsi. It's like everything something good happens it all goes to crap."

"I know what you mean, but you know it's for the best. We can see them when things calm down. We still have Emily and Derrick and they are our only family. I think that that is the best thing for us as family to do. I think that this threat may have something to do with my power disappearing. Without it both of us are vulnerable. We don't have as much power without it. We're as normal as any other mage. If we're attacked we might not make it."

"Screw weakness. Screw this whole thing. I want to stay," said Emma. She wiped her tears furiously.

"I know you. You'll go because it's the right thing to do. Come on now. Come down to dinner. We have to say goodbye tonight. Tell me that you'll say goodbye to them."

Emma didn't answer as she stepped off the top step of the balcony and walked further down now. They walked down the narrow stairway back into the top parts of the castle. Emma and Daniel slowly walked down to the dining room where everyone sat: Derrick, Emily, Kero, Rayziel, Erianna, Soría, Alexander, Salari, and Arsi sat. The dinner table was aligned with various foods and drinks.

An artist had given them a painting of Queen Harsie to share his condolences for her death. The entire nation of Absirthee had sent things to remember their great queen. That painting now caressed the wall over the dining room table. Emma gazed at it. She was such a beautiful woman. Perhaps she had gotten her beauty from her. Her father would love to see her. Perhaps he would return to them one day.

"We're here to say goodbye," Arsi began. "We want to wish Emma, Daniel, Derrick, and Emily a safe journey back to Earth Realm." Arsi lifted his glass, indicating the toast. They all drank from their glasses in recognition. There was an awkward silence following. In all the journeys and adventures they had succumbed to, this one was the most dangerous.

They were going to lose Emma and Daniel. In a tragic death they would lose the two that had warmed the hearts of everyone around them. Emma's intellect, passion, and commitment had led them through Absirthee and a battle with Lucras. Daniel's courage, wit, and power had made him a useful asset for leading his party to Olgath and into the Battle for Sulex. They were losing warriors, planners, political leaders, and friends.

The next morning came faster than they had imagined. They coalesced in the study, full of books and texts that would help to find out who *he* was. Emma and Daniel had prepared their belongings and their hearts to leave Sulex, but not forever. Maybe there would be a time when they could return, but now it was too dangerous. Emily and Derrick began to say their goodbyes when Emma and Daniel began theirs.

Daniel approached Alexander first. "I'm going to miss you man, it's been really fun knowing you." Alexander smiled at him, he had grown several inches and they now stood face to face. "I know it's going to be pretty boring without out. But here." Alexander handed him a book and told him to keep his cool, he should write in it to record everything that would happen so that he could read it one day. "Thanks man."

"Oh. I have one too, so you can write in yours, I'll get the message and write mine back so you'll know what's going on here. It's called a messenger book."

Emma had said goodbye to everyone except Kero who waited silently to be approached. She slowly walked to him for fear of leaving without saying goodbye. "I'm sorry you're the last one, but I was just so scared to say goodbye to you," she started.

"It's not goodbye. It's *see you later.* You won't be gone forever. I think of it as a short trip. I did get you something," Kero said handing her a necklace. It was a chain with a ruby attached to it. "It's a *ruby of fire.* Ortho sold it to me for half price. If you get in trouble throw it on the ground and it'll make a ring of fire around your enemy."

"Thanks. That's really sweet. Umm…I'll miss you," she said hugging him tightly. Sheran her hand through his hair wishing she wouldn't have to leave. "Too bad The Pendent of The Knight was useless or I'd use it."

Everyone had been said goodbye too. Arsi and Salari had chipped in to get them both scrying glasses to talk to each other. Daniel was to go back to the house Reater and Malitus died in and Emma was to be sent over two thousands miles to the west in California. Derrick and Daniel were to live with each other, Derrick working as an accountant at a local firm and claiming to be his father's brother. Emma and Emily would live in California where Emily would work as a doctor at a free clinic. Magic had made all this possible. Emma would lose her identity and Daniel would keep his.

There were so many changes that were going to occur. Daniel would go back to his school with Bert and all the other people he hated, say his sister died with his parents in a car crash and claim his brother to be his uncle. Emma would be renamed Sarah and go to an entirely new place where Emily would be declared as her single mom. It was all for safety. The world of Nexus was not blind to Earth Realm. If they would be searched for there was no possibility that they would not be found.

Emily and Emma were first to go through the portal, hugging Derrick and Daniel as they went. The jell-o like portal sucked them into oblivion, waiting on Derrick and Daniel to enter. It was a revelation now that Emma and Daniel had gone from living the same life, to living separate lives. It was ironic now that the one thing that brought the closer had inevitably separated them. It was altogether strange.

Daniel stepped up first, then Derrick, walking through the portal which signaled they were now at a point of no return....

CPSIA information can be obtained at www.ICGtesting.com
Printed in the USA
LVOW050750191212

312289LV00003B/143/P